isabelle
of the Moon & Stars

About the Author

S. A. Jones was born in England and raised on a remote island in the Buccaneer Archipelago off the Kimberley Coast, Western Australia. She gained a PhD in history and now works as a novelist, regulatory analyst and commentator. Her work has been widely published, including in *The Age*, *Crikey*, *The Guardian*, *The Drum*, *Overland*, *Page Seventeen* and *Kill Your Darlings*. She has been shortlisted for the Fish International Short Story Prize and Memoir Prize, and was named one of Australia's 100 Women of Influence by the *Australian Financial Review* and Westpac in 2013. Jones's first novel, *Red Dress Walking*, was published in 2008 to considerable critical acclaim. She currently lives in Melbourne with her husband and daughter.

isabelle

of the Moon & Stars

S.A. Jones

UWA PUBLISHING

First published in 2014 by
UWA Publishing
Crawley, Western Australia 6009
www.uwap.uwa.edu.au

UWAP is an imprint of UWA Publishing,
a division of The University of Western Australia.

 THE UNIVERSITY OF
WESTERN AUSTRALIA

National Library of Australia
Cataloguing-in-Publication entry:

Jones, S. A. (Sarah A.)
Isabelle of the moon and stars / S. A. (Sarah) Jones
ISBN: 9781742586038 (paperback)
Man–woman relationships–Fiction; Mental illness–Fiction
A823.4

Cover photograph by Paige Westberg
Typeset in Bembo by Lasertype
Printed by Griffin Press

For Jason, who makes all things possible

I
Perth

Sire, the night is darker now
And the wind blows stronger
Fails my heart, I know not how,
I can go no longer.

– 'Good King Wenceslas',
traditional Christmas carol

ONE

It is a Monday morning and the train is thick with lassitude. Wherever you look heads loll onto shoulders and eyes are glazed. Only a young woman in the middle carriage named Isabelle seems immune to the warm treacle atmosphere. She sits, straight-backed, intent on the scene scrolling by. It is high summer. The sky is candy-hard and cloudless with the roofs of the houses cut stark against it. The lines are so sharp you might slice your finger if you traced them on the window. She breathes in the lavender and fresh laundry scent of her home town in January and smiles.

The train stops at Mount Lawley and as the doors open heat rolls onto the carriage. The commuters move slowly, damp patches already spreading on their clothes. Without disentangling their sweaty palms a couple squeezes through the corridor to claim a small square of space. The man presses his back to the wall and folds the woman in his arms to keep her still against the jolt of the departure. As the train picks up speed he bends his head to whisper something in her ear and she smiles – a delighted, knowing smile.

Something has been said that is uniquely and intimately theirs, a filthy recollection or a silly endearment. The man's fingers strafe her dark hair, gently undoing the morning's work with the straightening iron. The woman rests her head on his chest, her lip gloss perilously close to his white shirt. Their senses are locked on one another so although the woman's gaze is on Isabelle she doesn't see her sitting there. He whispers something else and she closes her eyes as if to trap her delight.

Isabelle wonders what could have been said to create such bliss.

I love you.

You're beautiful.

You are the moon to me.

Isabelle has a fleeting memory of being the recipient of such words but she evicts Karl from her thoughts almost the instant he appears. She watches as the man's long, balletic fingers step delicately from his lover's mussed hair down her spine. He glances around the train and then slips his fingers beneath her waistband. Isabelle imagines the woman's marrow-tingle. She knows she should look away but the glow of their tenderness seems to include her somehow. Perhaps, she thinks, this is a sign.

The train lurches as it rounds a bend and the woman opens her eyes, sighted now, to find herself observed. Isabelle is too deep under the couple's spell to realise she has been caught.

'What are *you* looking at?' the woman demands.

The man snatches his hand from his girlfriend's underwear and rests it innocently on the railing. Conflict thrills the carriage. The gentleman sitting next to

Isabelle stops playing with his phone and holds it still in his lap, waiting. *Nothing* runs at Isabelle's throat but is beaten by what she really thinks.

'Love, I think. Is it love?'

The woman's cherry-frosted mouth falls open. Isabelle, too, is surprised at her words. The train wheels chug a chorus beneath them.

whatwillhappennextwhatwillhappennextwhatwillhappen nextwhatwillhappennext

The man bends to his girlfriend's ear and whispers urgently, not a private endearment as before but an exhortation. She seems oblivious, continuing to stare at Isabelle.

'I hope it's love,' Isabelle says. *My God*, she thinks, *just shut up, Isabelle*. It is as if the boom gate between her mind and her mouth has seized and refuses to close.

'It's none of your goddamn business is what it is. What is wrong with you?'

I don't know.

The woman has transferred all her intensity to Isabelle. The exclusion riles her boyfriend.

'She's just a nutter. Leave it, come on.'

He pushes from the wall and grabs her hand. The other passengers bunch together to clear a path for them, but the woman hesitates. She is dying to say something unanswerable but cannot settle on the words. Finally, her boyfriend takes hold of her shoulders and steers her through the gap. The commuters close around them and they are gone. The man sitting next to Isabelle pockets his phone and moves to the space they vacated, careful that he and Isabelle have no eye contact.

When the carriage empties at East Perth there is an exclusion zone around Isabelle. She pauses on the platform, searching for her phone in her handbag while the crowd rushes over the drawbridge to the ugly government building opposite. Seagulls straying from the river circle overhead as Isabelle takes deep breaths of the scented air. She brings up Evan's number to tell him what just happened, then thinks better of it. She avoids telling him things that make him worry and these days, where she is concerned, that covers just about everything.

Feeling rattled after the confrontation, she sits down on one of the metal benches to collect herself. Overhead the gulls are gathering in a tight spiral. Round and round they fly without breaking formation. In their symmetry and precision they seem to intend something, some portent.

Great, she thinks, *now I'm bird divining. What next?*

She waits until the shakiness passes then walks over the bridge to the building where Jack will be.

Isabelle and Jack fuss about with pens and forms and cups of coffee until neither is able to delay the purpose of their meeting any longer. Jack's eyes stray to the management texts he keeps within reach. Reassured, he opens the folder in front of him and takes a deep, resolute breath.

'So, Isabelle. Resident data analyst and all-round stats whiz, let's start your appraisal with a general overview. P3 has been operational now for what, four months? How have you found the new strategy has changed your work life?'

'To be honest, I haven't found it's made that much difference to what I do.'

'To the actual task no, probably not, but to the general work environment, the culture. Your vision of what work is and could be.' Jack sweeps the air as if to reveal the abundant corporate glory before him. He has hands so large that if he splayed them from the thumbs they would almost circle Isabelle's waist.

'Well, I think the strategy is...sound.'

'It should be. It's completely best practice and we workshopped it for months before we rolled it out.'

Isabelle thinks furiously for something positive she can volunteer. She cannot afford to lose this job. 'Focusing on people, performance and planning...the whole P3 strategy. I think it's...those principles seem...appropriate.'

Jack smiles and ticks the first of the boxes on the form.

'Now, can you read out to me the goals you set last year and your KPIs?'

Isabelle reads from the paper in front of her, careful to keep her voice upbeat and even. 'Continue to develop statistical analysis skills through targeted training and development.' She looks up. 'I did an online tutorial on the new version of the database.'

'Good, good,' Jack says as he takes notes. 'What else?'

She reads, 'Add value through extending networks and advocating for the department.'

'Still completely relevant for P3. How did you reach that target?'

'I went to the alumni sundowner at UWA.' As always happens when she lies, red gridlines map the sharp curve from her temples to her cheeks. *But it's not entirely untrue*, she thinks. *I only pulled out when I heard Karl was going.*

'That's great, Isabelle. You can't underestimate the power of those connections. Got to work at maintaining them. Anything else?'

'Pursue further stretch and development through short-term acting opportunities at higher levels.'

'And how did you go there?'

'Applied for two roles. Unsuccessful in both of them.' *As you know*, she thinks. *You were my referee.*

Jack scribbles a note and turns the page. He runs his index finger down a column and Isabelle's stomach plummets. She has come to think of it as the column of shame.

'Your sick leave and personal leave have ratcheted up, Isabelle.'

'I know.'

'Does this have anything to do with, you know...' He drops his voice to a whisper, '...*the incident?*'

Isabelle nods, pushing back against the memory. The tick of the clock becomes suddenly, insistently audible. Jack considers the heading on the form. *Health and Wellbeing.* He taps his pen lid on the desk, his habit when he is nervous. Three short taps to one circle. He is clearly afraid they are about to stray into murky uterine territory, something bloody and womanish. Isabelle wouldn't tell him anyway. She hates the words 'depression' and 'anxiety.' They are blank, nothing words that pretend 'the incident' can be corralled into neat and comprehensible English. Those words convey nothing of the horror of it, nothing of her heroism in standing up to it. To her it is The Black Place. Jack writes 'n/a' on the form.

'Moving on to how you've been living the values. I know it's hard, but if you had to pick just one value that you think you really embody, which would it be?'

Isabelle, unable to resist, says, 'Work–life balance.' *I'm definitely telling Evan that*, she thinks. *He'll piss himself.*

Jack gives his peculiar half-smile, the one where the right part of his mouth curves into his cheek revealing his dimple but the left slopes downwards as if he cannot quite commit to the one expression. 'Is that a joke, Isabelle?'

'Look, Jack, I know you don't like to be the bad guy so I'll save you the trouble. I'm not a star performer. I wish I was for your sake as well as my own. You put yourself out there to give me an opportunity and I let you down. I'm sorrier about that than you will ever know.'

He taps his pen again. On impulse Isabelle reaches across Jack's desk and picks up his photograph frame. All the staff were given one of these frames by a former minister at Christmas. Isabelle's contains a photo of the Charles Bridge in Prague, the snow collecting in the outstretched hands of the statues. Jack's photo is of him and his wife Kate. Jack stands under the shade of a tree, a cricket bat in one hand, his other arm around Kate. She is a slender, dainty woman reaching easily to Jack's shoulder. Their smiling faces are dappled in the shadow print of the leaves. Isabelle pictures the scene: a mild spring day, a family cricket match, an esky somewhere out of the frame, and a bunch of cousins and friends taking their turn at fielding and turning the sausages on the barbecue.

'How long have you been married?'

'Twenty-two years.'

'She's lovely, your wife.'

'Yes, she is.'

Jack bends forward and takes the frame from Isabelle's hand. She catches the distinctive watermelon and cinnamon scent he wears.

'Let's talk about how your work contributes to the strategic vision.'

Isabelle begins to feel slightly panicked as nothing plausible comes to her.

'I'll pose the question another way. If you weren't here doing your job, how would it limit everyone else's capacity to do their work?'

'I give my reports to you.'

'Yes. So what do you think they do for me? How do they help me to do my work?'

'I would think you could answer that better than me.'

'Take a guess.'

'My reports track volumes for various government services. Calls in, calls out, number of customers coming into the centres for different services, that sort of thing. So I would say that helps you, um, plan.'

'Exactly!' Jack ticks a box on the form with a mighty flourish. 'Your data helps me predict required resources and where to target them for alignment with our results profile. *Planning* and *performance*. Two of the elements of

10

P3. You see, you've hit on exactly how you contribute to the strategic vision.'

For an instant Isabelle feels contemptuous of him. He really believes this stuff. But who is she to begrudge other people their certainties? She would take them, and gladly, if she could.

'Now, what are your goals for the next twelve months?'

'To stare down fear and to live.' The boom gate between her mind and her mouth has failed her again. The words sound hopelessly jejune.

'To stare down fear?' Jack repeats the words carefully, patting them down for signs of sarcasm. 'Well that's... ambitious. I have to say no one's ever offered that in their performance appraisal before.' Tap, tap, tap, circle. 'If you're going to be courageous, perhaps we should make you the new ministerial aide.'

'Perhaps you should.'

Jack laughs, confident now that Isabelle is making a joke. That position is reserved for *performers*. 'Can we say something like "Improve strategic value through more sophisticated use of data"?'

'If you like.'

'It's not if *I* like, Isabelle. You really need to own this plan.' He balls his fingers into fists to emphasise the point.

Isabelle sighs. 'How about "Contributes to the vision through fearless appraisal of realities"?'

'Could we say "Supports the vision through evidence-based decision-making"? It's basically the same thing, just more —'

'Corporate.'

'More aligned to language the rest of the organisation will understand.'

'Whatever. I mean, yes. Absolutely. Sounds good.'

Jack summarises Isabelle's performance in a couple of inane sentences, signs the form and hands it to Isabelle, who signs it too, both of them relieved to have that unpleasant task behind them for another year.

'Thanks, Isabelle.'

Jack extends his hand across the desk and Isabelle takes it. His hand encloses hers completely, warm and sure. She thinks of the couple on the train. The way the man had held his girlfriend still against the rollick and jolt of the carriage. How long is it since she was sheltered like that? A sudden yearning constricts her throat and pricks at the back of her eyeballs. Unconsciously, she tightens her grip on Jack's hand. He gives her his half-smile, running his thumb along her soft, white skin. The consciousness of prolonged physical contact explodes in both at the same moment. They drop their hands as if from a great height and step backwards from one another. There is a brief pause before they dive for their pens, folders and coffee mugs and go bustling about their day.

TWO

Evan leaps into the water, sinks to the bottom in a net of bubbles then star-jumps to the surface. He looks like a keen but graceless substitute for a synchronised swimming troupe. Isabelle's entry is less dramatic. She drops in neatly from a sitting position so the pool swallows her with barely a ripple. She sits, frog-like, under the surface while her anticipation builds. Evan pushes off from the wall first. Isabelle gives him a lead of several metres then sets off after him. Where Evan is a furious windmill of splash and churn, Isabelle's stroke is clean and precise. As they approach the far end, Isabelle decelerates to stay clear of Evan's thrashing limbs as he throws himself into reverse. Isabelle tucks into a neat tumble, shoots through the confused vortex of swirling water and dancing sunlight, and pursues him.

After a few laps they stop and stretch, splaying their palms on the tiles and turning at right angles to the wall to lengthen their muscles. Isabelle watches the droplets cut through the sharp indents of Evan's bare, coffee-coloured torso. The cross tattooed on his shoulder contracts and expands with the stretch. It doesn't occur to her to wonder if Evan scrutinises her when they repeat the stretch in the opposite direction. *Evan*, she thinks, *isn't like that*. They duck under the lane rope into the sprint lane.

'How much of a start do you want?'

Evan ponders, pressing his goggles until the rubber sucks at his eye sockets. 'Two metres.'

'Two metres? You're feeling awfully confident today.'

'Damn straight. I've been working out. Getting stronger.' He flexes his biceps in proof, oblivious to the admiring glances of the women in the adjoining lanes. 'Your days of aquatic dominion are over.'

'Ooh, them's fightin' words.'

Isabelle disciplines herself to give him precisely two metres then dives in after him. Midway up the lap Evan's toes are centimetres from her fingers. He senses her at his heels and kicks even more ferociously. The white water bounces off her forehead. Fearing a boot to the face she slows at the turn, gulps air, then zeroes in. She scoops the water behind her with every stroke, making it look effortless. She loves this, loves racing. To feel her heart thrashing from exertion, not fear. Loves the way she can command her limbs, heart and lungs to get her to the wall first. With fifteen metres to go Isabelle ducks to the side of the lane and keeps her head down. She touches just ahead of Evan. He doesn't pretend otherwise when they stop, both breathing hard.

'Did you give me two metres?' he asks, gasping.

'Of course I did.'

'Damn it.' He playfully hits the wall with his palm, chest heaving as he vacuums air. 'You're so fast. I

14

thought I could,' gasp, 'hold you off today. Have to work,' breath, 'more on my kick. Get some more power behind it.' He rinses his goggles then straps them back to his head. 'The swim club here has a special training session on kick style. I might go.'

Isabelle shakes the water from her ear. 'You really need to get a puppy. Or a girlfriend. If anyone would have you.'

'I'll have you know there's a huge demand for Christian male virgins.'

'As altar boys the world over will testify.'

He smiles. 'Good one.'

Isabelle had wondered, long ago, if Evan's self-imposed chastity was a result of childhood trauma at the hands of a priest. 'No,' he had assured her, 'just garden-variety biblical literalness.'

They sprint several times more, Evan losing each time, before changing lanes and cruising into a leisurely breaststroke. Soon, the endorphins and the black-line hypnosis produce their strange alchemy, parting the water into an Isabelle-shaped space. This is the transformation she has been waiting for. She slips and turns through the bubbles without effort, almost without the consciousness that she is doing it. Her mind empties, but it is not a panicked emptiness. It is a serene, open-vista emptiness that only the water can bring her.

When Isabelle permits herself the indulgence of nostalgia, this is what she most often returns to: that heady day when she spearheaded the high-school relay team to victory at the all-schools carnival. Her team–mates hoisted her onto their shoulders and carried her around the platform. Never mind that she slipped and fell hard on her ankle, making it sprout like an eggplant the next day. There was great conviviality between the team for weeks after that. Passing each other in the corridors at school they would spontaneously erupt into high fives and rousing victory chants, Isabelle wincing as she came down on her sprained ankle. She had felt part of some vital energy. Connected. The way she had felt with Karl, but that is something she never voluntarily recalls.

After an hour Evan signals that he's had enough. Reluctantly, Isabelle follows him to the stairs. With each step into air she feels less adapted, less suited. It is six thirty but there is no sign of the approaching evening. The aquatic centre is thriving. In one of the shallower pools an instructor corrects technique as children half-bellyflop, half-dive into the water. A whistle calls time on a game of water polo in the deep pool. Bare–chested dads with towels around their waists turn sausages on the hot plates in the picnic area.

'Smells good,' says Evan. 'Smells like summer.'

'Mmmm,' says Isabelle, but she turns her head away. She cannot stand the smell of smoke.

Isabelle and Evan thread through the crowd and clamber into the spa. Warm, frothy water erupts around them. Isabelle sits hard against one of the jets so it pounds the muscles in her shoulders and neck.

'I can't believe you beat me. I thought I had you today.'

'Why this sudden burst of confidence?'

Evan plays a drum roll on the surface of the water. 'I was promoted today. Da da da da da da da!'

'What? You haven't applied for a new job. Or did I vague out somewhere?'

'Nope. Didn't apply. Wasn't looking. Got tapped on the shoulder.'

'Wow,' she says limply. 'Well done.'

'Please, you know I hate it when you gush.'

She shakes herself. 'Hey, I'm sorry. That came out all wrong. Sorry, I'm just – I had my performance appraisal today and I'm not exactly employee of the year so I'm just feeling a bit, um, inadequate, I guess.'

'Oh, Belle,' Evan's face crinkles with concern.

'Hey, it's fine. It's not about me. I'm just being selfish.' Isabelle plays her own imaginary drum on the water and forces down her dejection. 'C'mon, I want to hear all about it. What's the job?'

'You sure you want to talk about this now? It's really no drama if we left it for another time.'

'No. I must have details. What are you going to be doing?'

'From Monday you'll be looking at the new manager, strategy. Level seven.'

'God, that's great. Sorry.' But this time she is apologising for taking the Lord's name in vain.

'That's all right.'

'Are you excited?'

'A bit nervous, actually.'

'How did all of this come about?'

Evan shrugs. 'All I can think of is that at last my brown-nosing has paid dividends.'

17

'You're being modest. I've worked with you, remember? I know how smart you are. What are you going to do with all that extra cash?'

'Cocaine. Hookers. Papal absolution.'

'Hah!'

'Seriously, though, I'd like to do something special. To celebrate.'

'Absolutely. We must.'

'How about dinner on Saturday night? Can you come?'

'Oh, let me check my calendar,' she pretends to consult a diary. 'If I just move that and postpone that... Of *course* I can come. I'll be there with bells on.' This time Isabelle manages to inject some real enthusiasm into her voice. She loves Evan and knows that when her feelings of failure stop biting so hard she will feel triumphant for him. She is so determined to make up for her desultory congratulations that when Saturday comes she splurges on a bottle of expensive champagne and wraps up the gift she has been saving for his birthday, a DVD called *Soccer's Greatest Kicks*. She dresses with care, putting on her blue 'special occasion' dress and high heels. She is applying mascara when she is interrupted by a knock at the door.

'Hi, Mrs Graham. What's up?'

Isabelle unlocks her flywire door and ushers her elderly neighbour into her flat.

'Hello, dear. I'm so sorry to bother you but I've got a bit of a problem.'

'You're not bothering me at all. What can I do for you? Would you like to sit down?'

'Thank you, no. I can't stay. It's just…well…I've managed to knock over some of my pots. You know those large blue ones? They've landed on the reticulation and I think I might have blocked the circuit.' Mrs Graham runs her liver-spotted hands over each other as if she is washing them. 'I tried to right them, but with my arthritis…' She holds up her tree-root hands in evidence.

'Oh look, no dramas at all. Just let me change my shoes and I'll be right there.'

'So sorry, dear. You're obviously getting ready to go out. You look lovely, by the way.'

'Oh, thank you. But I've got plenty of time.'

Isabelle changes out of her heels and into thongs, and together the two women make slow, careful progress down the stairwell, Isabelle supporting Mrs Graham by her papery elbow. Mrs Graham's small square of garden is delightful. Isabelle often pauses there after swimming to chat to her and marvel afresh at how beautiful she has made her unpromising few metres of courtyard. Hanging baskets fringe the awning around her flat, spilling over with white and purple flowers. In the spring they hum with the low drone of bee life. Her concrete slabs are scrubbed clean and run through with dark-green moss, putting Isabelle in mind of a giant game of noughts-and-crosses. In place of a fence Mrs Graham has installed a row of hefty azure pots frothing with flowers, four of which are now upturned. One has shattered. Isabelle wonders how a woman as frail as Mrs Graham managed to push them over.

'My poor plants. They're quite ruined.'

19

Isabelle bends down to take a closer look. The heavy pots are crushing the spongy green network of hose that feeds the ground-floor gardens. Isabelle hitches up her dress then pulls the pot into a standing position. Its white rose springs upwards, seemingly unhurt.

'I think this plant's going to be all right.'

Mrs Graham pushes her spectacles to the bridge of her nose and peers at the rose. Her gnarled fingers tenderly brush the leaves. Isabelle hauls the three undamaged pots upright. Mrs Graham hovers behind her, her worry crackling through the still, dry air.

'Is the reticulation all right? Does it look damaged?'

Isabelle bends lower and pokes at the hose. That is when she notices the running-shoe imprints in the flowerbed. A quick, fiery rage takes hold of her. If the offender were within reach she would earth her knee in their kidneys for their casual vandalism.

'Can you turn this on manually, Mrs Graham? That's probably the only way we'll know if it's leaking.'

'No. The system is automatic. The body corporate sends someone out to program the watering time twice a year. It won't be on now until five tomorrow morning.'

Isabelle hears the bird-wing flutter of anxiety in Mrs Graham's voice and fears she will spend the evening in a tight, fretful ball counting down to the daylight. 'I tell you what,' she says, standing upright and brushing the dirt from her hands, 'I'll pop round tomorrow morning and see how the land's lying. If it's damaged I'll get Jim to have a look at it. It's probably just a matter of replacing a small piece of piping. The strata company won't need to know a thing.' Jim is Isabelle's neighbour but one.

'Do you think he'd mind? Only, you see I can't really, I don't have the means…for a tradesman.'

'Don't worry about that. He's a nice guy. He's always helping me get back in when I lock myself out of my bathroom. He'd be happy to help. He might appreciate a cutting from one of your plants, though.'

'Oh, well if you think so.' Mrs Graham pauses for a moment. 'Isabelle, perhaps you might like to take a seat and I could bring you a ginger beer. I make my own.' Her voice is carefully uninflected, all vestige of question snuffed out so as not to suffer a refusal. Isabelle would like to stay and make what amends she can for the trespasser's cruelty but time is starting to run short.

'Could I take a raincheck on that, Mrs Graham? I'd love to try your ginger beer. Perhaps I could drop round one afternoon this week after work. Would that be all right?'

'Of course, Isabelle. I'll look forward to it. I forgot it's Saturday night. It must be a whirl for you.'

Isabelle laughs. 'Oh yes, the gentlemen callers are beating a path to my door, as you can see.' She sweeps her hand before the vacant stairwell.

'So who is he, dear? Butcher, baker, candlestick maker?'

'He's a humble servant of the public, like me.'

'And is he coming to pick you up?'

'He is, actually.'

She nods approvingly. 'Good. He sounds like a gentleman.'

'You know, that's the perfect word to describe Evan.'

'Is this the young chap I see around here from time to time?'

'If you mean the tall, dark-haired guy with the ridiculous cheekbones, then yes.'

'That's him. Quite the dish. Well done, Isabelle.'

Isabelle laughs. 'No, it's not like that. We're friends. Very good friends.'

'He hasn't declared himself yet?'

'Evan doesn't...declare.'

'He's gay?'

Isabelle is rather surprised that Mrs Graham should be au fait with such a term. 'No. Just Catholic.'

Mrs Graham's eyes open wide. 'He's a *priest*?'

Isabelle laughs again. 'No, no, nothing like that. He just doesn't...You know...'

'Enjoy earthly delights?'

'Precisely.'

'Foolish boy.' Mrs Graham shakes her head. 'He'll regret it when he's my age. Could you wait one moment?'

Mrs Graham goes into her flat and returns holding a pair of bronze secateurs and a plastic cup half-filled with water. She cuts a red flower trailing from a hanging basket and places it in the cup.

'Put this behind your ear when you go out tonight. The colour will be lovely on you.'

'Thank you. And we're on for ginger beer later in the week, yeah?'

'Absolutely.'

Back in her flat Isabelle puts the red flower to her nose and inhales. It smells of watermelon and cinnamon and there, suddenly, is that heat in her underwear again. She returns the flower to the cup and retreats, deliberating. She circles the flower warily. From the expression on her face you might suspect it of pumping noxious gas into her flat.

Over the past year she has welded the shattered fragments of her life back together with routine, force of will and punishing physical exercise. It's an ordered place from which to withstand the incursions of The Black Place.

But sometimes…

Isabelle thinks of the couple on the train, their tenderness. The way the gulls had circled overhead.

She picks the flower up again, gently wipes the water away from the stem and tucks it behind her ear.

THREE

The couple are on the train again, sitting a few rows ahead of Isabelle. He saw her when they boarded, turned white, and is now intent on looking everywhere but in Isabelle's direction. His girlfriend, however, can look nowhere else. The sticky fibres of her attention collect around Isabelle's seat, making her feel heavy. The man absently strokes his girlfriend's arm, seemingly as an afterthought. Even on the tiny seats they have contrived space between them. When Isabelle gets out at her stop the woman presses her face against the glass, watching. 'Love, I think,' Isabelle had said when asked what she was looking at. 'I hope it's love.' The woman's face tells Isabelle her hope was misplaced.

Isabelle wonders what has happened to fray the connection between them. Sour morning breath, perhaps, or toe-picking on the couch in front of the television. A compulsion to repeat the same anecdotes, as if the mind's needle cannot retract from the grooves it has worn. Those little frictions that erode affection. Or maybe it is something more cataclysmic. A third party? Isabelle has a stark, vicious sense-memory of what it is to be the expendable point in a love triangle.

It occurs to Isabelle that there is a finite amount of love in the world and it merely transfers itself between the hungry multitudes, a fleeting visitant. You never know when you will be at the front of the queue or shunted to the back. She turns towards her building. It would seem an unlikely place for love to stop. It is a high, blank, pebble-dash rectangle ringed by a cheap concrete forecourt. Stainless-steel ashtrays are bolted to the ground. Grey smoke rises from one of them. Concrete shutters, heavy now with three decades of pigeon crust, filter out the light. Yet, incongruously, this is where Jack is. At the thought of him Isabelle conjures his watermelon and cinnamon scent. The gulls squawk above her.

Overnight the office has been festooned with new corporate regalia. *P3 – I Believe!* blares a poster with a photograph of a wildly smiling Carol Anne giving the thumbs-up. P3 paraphernalia litters Isabelle's desk – a sticker (*P3, PYou, PMe*), a box of pencils emblazoned with *Performance* with a star for the 'a' and a new name tag (*I am Isabelle and I am P3*). When Isabelle turns on her computer a message bleeps at her encouraging her to 'like' P3 on Facebook.

She opens her daily stats file and stares at the neat columns of numbers. Each number has a back story, a myriad of reasons for the citizenry's interaction with their government. A dispute over car ownership. A change of name after marriage. A challenge to a planning decision. Isabelle's job is to take these disparate transactions and turn them into trends. Under her fingertips linear projections and graphs emerge from the chrysalis of raw data to reveal *how things are*. Isabelle finds a dumb comfort in creating the illusion of certainty from all the randomness.

'Thanks, Isabelle,' Jack says as Isabelle drops the folder on his desk. 'How are you today?'

'Wonderful,' she says.

'Wonderful?' he gives his lopsided smile. 'And why's that?'

'No reason.'

'Hmmm. Perhaps there's romance in the air? A new suitor in the wings?'

Isabelle laughs and shakes her head.

'Oh, come on,' he says, leaning back in his chair and resting his fingertips together in a steeple. 'Give me the goss. It's about time you moved on from, what was his name, Karl?' Isabelle winces but Jack seems not to notice. 'We old married people have to live vicariously, you know.'

'If you were to pick a life to live vicariously through, Jack, believe me, it wouldn't be mine.'

'No?' he looks disappointed. 'Surely we need to do something about that.'

'Is that a formal directive from my boss?'

'Ha ha. Yes. Let's revise your performance plan to include romance as a goal.'

Isabelle hesitates before answering, testing the heft and dimension of this new banter between them. 'Passion is one of our values, isn't it?'

'At last. Isabelle embraces the corporate philosophy. My work here is done.'

Isabelle edges closer to Jack's desk. 'If I'm going to really pursue this new direction, Jack, you'll need to approve my study leave.'

Jack roots through his second drawer, withdraws a departmental study-leave form and signs it with a flourish. 'Here.' He passes the form across the desk then withdraws it just as Isabelle moves to take it. 'But —' he holds her eyes, 'only on the condition that I get a full and frank report of the outcomes.'

Isabelle closes her fingers on the paper. 'Just how full and frank are we talking?'

'I want,' he lowers his tone, 'everything.'

'Jack?' Isabelle turns toward the voice that has spoken from the doorway. She recognises Kate from the photograph on Jack's desk.

'Hello,' says Jack, flustered. 'What are you doing here?'

'Nice to see you, too,' comes the droll response. 'Security let me through. I was in the area and I thought I'd drop by. Maybe we could grab a coffee?'

'Yes, for sure. Absolutely, yes. Just let me finish up here.' He makes a pretence of flicking through some files while Kate looks expectantly at Isabelle.

'Kate, this is Isabelle. Isabelle, Kate.'

The two women shake hands. Kate sizes Isabelle up in the way pretty women do when confronted with other pretty women. Kate moves some stationery from Jack's desk and rests her pert bottom on the cleared space.

'So. Are you a member of Jack's team, Isabelle?'

'Yes.'

'And what is it you do?'

'I'm the data analyst.'

'Oh, statistics and what-have-you.' Kate gives an airy wave of her hand. 'I never could see the point myself.

27

I mean sin, cos and tan, what function do they serve in everyday life? Though I'm sure what you do is very important. Do you enjoy it?'

Isabelle fans herself with the study-leave form, resisting the urge to point out that sin, cos and tan are trigonometric, not statistical, functions. 'I like the certainty of mathematics, the symmetry. To know that the sum of the squares of the two shorter sides of a right-angled triangle will always equal the square of the third. It's comforting in a way.'

'I suppose so. But don't you find it a little dull after a while? I mean, if two plus two is always four, where's the element of surprise?' Kate preens a little. Isabelle suspects that if she peered down her throat she would find half-digested bird feathers.

'Are you ready, Kate?' Jack asks.

'Yes, after you.'

'Nice to meet you, Isabelle. Bye.'

'We'll finish this up later, Isabelle.'

'Okay.'

Kate takes Jack's hand and Isabelle watches the two of them disappear along the corridor in the dissipating cloud of scent.

Isabelle is leafing through the dictionary for synonyms for 'incompetent' to soften the messages from a stake-holder survey when the book falls open at the definition of 'goodness'. It reads:

> The state or quality of being good.
> Moral excellence; virtue.

Kindly feeling; kindness; generosity.
Excellence of quality: *goodness of workmanship*.
The best part of anything; essence; strength.
A euphemism for God: *thank goodness!*

It is the last one that keeps belting around her frontal lobe as she manipulates the data. Goodness and God are interchangeable. Goodness would speak for her on the other side if the worst should happen. (*Not that it will. This is just hypothetical.*) Isabelle tries to picture what goodness might look like but the things that occur to her – reading to sick children in hospital or ladling out soup in a shelter – seem self-aggrandising and impersonal. She may as well march the streets waving a placard that says 'Goodness'.

Thanks to her underwhelming career trajectory and the cost of her treatment, Isabelle has lived close to her means for most of her adult life. She knows what it is to agonise over a purchase. She has never been dirt-poor, but she did once walk the length of a department store deliberating over whether to buy the cut-price underwear clutched in her hand. It occurred to her then that the worst thing about a tight budget is not actually the going without; after all, she could keep wearing her sorry excuse for knickers that had long since lost their shape. No, the worst thing was how the inability to be spontaneous leached the elasticity from your bones. It made you stiff and brittle, like wearing a corset of no.

Isabelle thinks that real goodness would loosen those straps for someone, give them room to stretch and fill their lungs. She pictures herself taking kids to the park for an afternoon to give their parents their first real date in years. Or springing for a raucous meal with wine at the local Chinese. Something that makes romance and joy rear up from the laundry and the commute and the dirty dishes. Something that resists endings. But where to find someone who could take up the slack she can provide? Her only really close friend, Evan, is provokingly functional despite his quirks, and her network of casual acquaintances seems to be doing just fine.

Isabelle looks up from her keyboard. Carole Anne is on the phone, using those extravagant gestures she reserves for communication with the minister's office. Jack's blinds are closed, which means he is meeting with The Important People. The rest of her colleagues are either intent on their screens or explaining procedure through their headsets to customers. It is a picture of competence and completion that has no need of her. Isabelle sighs, but she knows that if she were confronted with real need she would be frightened by the smelly, violent reality of it. She lives in a suburb of trimmed lawns and mended fences but there is a public-housing building plonked in the middle of it. On still nights the bass music jolts through Isabelle's complex but she can still hear the yelling above it. A couple of times a year the police helicopter floods the place in light, hovering and inquisitive. The inhabitants seem volatile and unpredictable, like the couple who live between Isabelle and Jim. When Isabelle walks past the building she unconsciously speeds up.

Isabelle shakes herself and tries to focus on the column of numbers in front of her. She doesn't need to stash goodness away like some karmic saving. She reminds herself that the drugs are gone. She will live. Only live. Isabelle runs her deft fingers over the keyboard and the columns and rows invert. She sets her functions and is about to press enter when a speech bubble bursts open on her screen declaring *PYou! PMe! P3!* It makes her jump.

'Jesus Christ,' she mutters, then apologises automatically, even though Evan is not there.

After a few flashing, garish seconds the bubble dissolves, taking with it the tables and formulas that Isabelle has spent most of the morning preparing. A groan rises like a dust cloud in the office. *PissUoff! PissMeoff!* she thinks. Jack emerges from his office into the grumbling chorus. Carol Anne bustles over to tell him what has happened. He rubs his hand over his chin and nods. Isabelle watches his enormous hands flare in their gestures of sympathy and exhortation. He looks uncomfortable in his expensive suit, as if constrained by it. She thinks he should be upturning soil or tethering a vine to a stake. Under a broiling sun. Stripped to the waist. Jack begins to walk between the desks, commiserating and encouraging. She looks back at her empty spreadsheet, trying to summon the energy to start again. *Fuck it.* The graph that lands on Jack's desk at three pm shows a rush on boat registrations in landlocked Narrogin and an unprecedented spike in people taking their driving test in Aramaic.

That afternoon Isabelle pauses on her way through the courtyard to her flat. She had intended to run upstairs, change into her bathers and expend the afternoon on laps. Instead, she turns towards Mrs Graham's flat for ginger beer and chitchat. Isabelle pauses to check on the reticulation, which all still seems to be working fine. Mrs Graham is not outside but she cannot be far away because her precious gardening implements are on the outdoor table, along with a pot of tea and reading glasses.

'Hello,' Isabelle hollers through the locked screen door. 'Any one there?'

There is no answer. Isabelle presses her finger against the teapot on the table. It is cold.

'Mrs Graham, are you there?'

Still there is no answer. Isabelle feels slightly panicked. She tries the screen door but it is locked. A hunched shadow emerges on the hallway wall, followed a second later by its original. Mrs Graham doesn't raise her foot from the ground when she walks but pushes it out in front of her, pauses for a moment, then hauls the rest of her body after it. The dragging foot leaves a deep furrow on the carpet. She braces herself then repeats the process. Isabelle wants to yell at Mrs Graham to stay where she is, that she will fetch Jim and they can prise the door open. But what if Jim isn't home? Isabelle senses that if she invites Mrs Graham to stillness then it will be near impossible to coax her to movement again. So she watches, anxious and impotent, as Mrs Graham conquers the space between them step by agonising step.

'Nearly there, Mrs Graham, just a little way to go.'

Isabelle is close enough now to see the sweat beading on Mrs Graham's lip and the way her face looks to be streaked with powdered ash. Her right hand is gnarled to a claw. The two women pause on either side of the screen. Isabelle can feel Mrs Graham dredging up every ounce of her will to raise her hands to the key in the lock and turn it.

'Take a moment,' Isabelle says softly. 'Breathe in, two, three, four and out, two, three, four.'

Mrs Graham's frozen fingers refuse to assume the shape required to turn the key. She supports her wrist with one hand and lines her fingers up against the latch. Isabelle holds her breath. If Mrs Graham miscalculates she might knock the key from the hole to the floor. Isabelle is about to try hacking through the flywire with the secateurs when Mrs Graham somehow manages to turn the lock. Isabelle draws the door along its runner and steps into Mrs Graham's flat. She grabs the nearest chair and places it behind Mrs Graham, then gently but firmly takes her by the elbows and lowers her into it.

'Can I get you something? Is there someone I should call?'

Mrs Graham answers with a slight twist of her head.

'Is it the arthritis? Do you have something you can take?'

Mrs Graham doesn't answer. Her eyes are vacant, as if pain has colonised her entire consciousness. Isabelle crouches in front of Mrs Graham's chair, trying to decide what to do. There is a strange smell in the air. Old tea, sweat, lavender and something else Isabelle cannot place. Something fetid and dank that lodges in the back of her throat like a hair she cannot reach. Isabelle thinks of all those lovely, lulling candies she threw away a year ago. She wishes she had them back so she could give Mrs Graham some relief. She could buy something from her dodgy neighbours but it might be cut, impure. Besides, they're a bit scary, always yelling and carrying on. Isabelle stands up and walks to Mrs Graham's pantry. She riffles through the tins until she finds a bottle of olive oil, pours some of the liquid into a bowl and carries it back to the table. She takes a cushion from a chair and throws it on the ground in front of Mrs Graham then kneels.

'Mrs Graham, listen to me, okay? I'm going to massage some of this oil onto your hands and wrists to try and give you some relief. Is that all right?'

Mrs Graham inclines her head in a slow, juddering motion. Isabelle can almost hear the crunch of bone on bone. She runs the oil over her hands then starts with the thumb of Mrs Graham's right hand. She exerts a gentle pressure as she massages the oil into the joints. She can feel the resistance in Mrs Graham's digit, as if her thumb has frozen and might snap clean off if she is not careful. Isabelle keeps up a steady prattle as she moves from thumb to index finger, telling Mrs Graham about her day at work, the foul-up with the corporate slogan and her subversive data analysis. Isabelle squeezes Mrs Graham's finger between her finger and thumb, working from the knuckle to the tip and then back down. With each press she imagines she is transmitting a jolt of electricity across the boundary of their skins and into Mrs Graham's creaking network of axons and dendrites.

Once she has finished with the fingers, Isabelle presses her thumbs into the other woman's forearms and runs them from her wrist bone to her elbow, feeling how friable the chicken-bone limbs are. Isabelle pours more oil and keeps running her hands over the brown and red patchwork of skin until the oil parts in Mrs Graham's iris and a timorous light beams out.

'That's it,' Isabelle croons, 'just relax. Imagine that your ankles are filling with warm orange light. The light moves across your feet, fills up your toes and starts to light up your calves.' She goes on like this, repeating the familiar meditation and all the while rubbing oil into Mrs Graham's forearms. Mrs Graham flexes her fingers and Isabelle senses something vital pulse under her hands. She redoubles her efforts, feeling as if she is blowing on hot coals, trying to make them flare. Mrs Graham sighs and sinks deeper into the chair. When Isabelle has finished both arms she washes her hands and prepares fresh tea. Mrs Graham's fingers are now pliable enough to hold the cup to her lips.

'Thank you, Isabelle,' she croaks.

'It's my pleasure. Now, what can I get you? Some food, some drugs?'

Mrs Graham directs her to a packet of tablets in the bathroom cabinet that she swallows with her tea. Isabelle heats up some baked beans and butters toast for the two of them to share. As she eats, Mrs Graham straightens and smooths before her eyes, like an airbed being inflated.

'How long has it been like this, Mrs Graham?'

'Since last night.'

'You've been like this since last night? Why didn't you call me?'

'How?' Mrs Graham says simply.

Isabelle scribbles her phone number on the back of an automatic teller receipt and sticks it on Mrs Graham's fridge.

'Next time you call me, all right? Promise me you will.'

Mrs Graham nods but Isabelle doesn't believe her.

'Can I move you somewhere more comfortable? Is that the lounge room through there?'

Isabelle points to the hallway. Their movement is slow but Mrs Graham is walking much more fluidly. The lounge room is dark and smells fusty. Again, Isabelle is conscious of something rank and organic growing like fur on her tongue. She plumps up the cushions then helps Mrs Graham to a seated position. Isabelle pulls the cord on the curtains to reveal twirling columns of dust motes suspended in the air. Old sandwich crusts, teacups and encrusted forks litter the corners of the room. Isabelle bustles around collecting them, each woman pretending not to notice the other's embarrassment. She runs the kitchen sink with soapy water and leaves the dishes to soak.

Returning to the lounge room she finds Mrs Graham absorbed in the photographs on the wall in front of her. There are so many that the cream-coloured walls are barely visible behind them. Isabelle drifts along the gallery, taking in gap-toothed children in school uniform, a strikingly handsome man in military dress, a blue heeler leaping to catch a frisbee. Isabelle pauses in front of a black-and-white wedding photograph. A beaming young couple stare back at her. Isabelle looks closer.

'Is this you, Mrs Graham?'

The woman reflected back at Isabelle is dazzling. Her blonde hair falls in wide, bouncing curls to her shoulders. Her dark eyes gleam and it is in the cheekiness of the expression that this young woman reveals herself to be Mrs Graham. She carries a single, long-stemmed rose in one hand and clutches her man's hand in the other. It is so unlike the carefully stage-managed photos of the time with which Isabelle is familiar. She imagines Mrs Graham reaching down just before the flash went off, unable to resist contact with this man who had just become hers in the sight of God. The poignancy of the gesture constricts Isabelle's throat.

'Your dress is gorgeous. Very daring with that neckline.'

'I know. It was thought a bit scandalous at the time. My sister made it. There was nothing she couldn't do with a needle and thread.'

'Does she live nearby?'

'No. She's passed away. All my siblings have passed away.'

'Tell me about Mr Graham.'

'He was very handsome, as you can see. A very physical man. He was into every kind of sport. Cricket. Football. Boxing. There was a sort of...vibrancy to him. If we went to a barbecue it was never long before he'd organised the kids into teams and was refereeing a soccer game.'

'Yes.' Isabelle studies the man staring at her from the past. 'Yes, I can easily believe that. He radiates health even from his photograph. Was he in the army?'

'The navy. He loved the sea. Loved boats. When he was on leave we used to go down to Fremantle. Of course it wasn't posh then. We'd buy fish and chips and sit on the pier, watching all the Italians and the Slavs coming in with their catch.'

Suddenly, Isabelle is there on that pier, her mouth redolent with oily batter, licking the salt from her fingers. The seagulls coast overhead, diving for the chips she throws, some falling through the slats to the green water. The fishermen call to one another in languages she doesn't understand. She turns her face to the sun and leans against the man beside her, at once familiar and foreign.

'He bought me long-stemmed roses for every anniversary, always from the same place. Six months after he passed away they filled the order, assuming he'd just forgotten.'

Isabelle feels that she has entered a mausoleum. This is how Mrs Graham spends her days: among relics. A passing cloud leaves the room in shadow so the dust motes disappear. Mrs Graham has shrunk back into the cushions. The oil is pooling in her eyes again, her bones drying as the pain sucks the vital juices from her body. Panicked, Isabelle casts around for a lure to the present. Impulsively, she drops onto the sofa next to Mrs Graham, making her gestures as large as she can.

'That reminds me. I wasn't just making a random call. I came over to ask you something.'

'Hmmm?' Mrs Graham's voice is thin and reedy, a fragile thread recalled from her memories.

'I wanted to invite you to a party. An Australia Day party I'm hosting up on the roof of our building.' Improvisation makes Isabelle talk fast. 'Nothing fancy. Just finger food and a few drinks, but there's a great view up there. We should have a clear shot at the fireworks. I'm inviting all our neighbours, starting with you, of course. What do you think?'

Mrs Graham doesn't move but a smile – no, so much more than a smile: a physical manifestation of utter delight – spreads across her face. The connection between the young bride of the photo and this Mrs Graham in front of her crystallises.

'So, can you come?'

Mrs Graham is silent for a moment, leaving Isabelle to wonder if she has comprehended the question. She is about to repeat it when Mrs Graham speaks.

'I would be delighted, utterly delighted, to attend your party.'

'Marvellous. So, what shall we do this afternoon?'

'I'm not up for much, I'm afraid.'

'What are you reading?' Isabelle reaches for the book splayed on the carpet. She reads the spine. '*And Love Shall Conquer All*. Sounds racy.'

'It is. They keep trying to foist Jane Austen on me at the Seniors' Centre. "No, thank you," I say. I like corsets well enough, but only if they're ripped off at some point.'

Isabelle laughs. 'Would you like me to read to you?'

Mrs Graham nods her acquiescence.

Isabelle reads in a low, calm voice till Mrs Graham falls into a doze. Isabelle stands up and quietly returns to the dishes, a little shell-shocked at how she has committed herself and only dimly aware of how wonderful is the gift of something to look forward to.

FOUR

Isabelle is stunned by what she has promised Mrs Graham. She is glad to have made her neighbour happy with the prospect of a party, but the practical reality is another matter. For one thing she will be expected at her mother's. For some reason, Australia Day is the holiday that awakens her mother's sense of family obligation. ('No presents?' Evan had once suggested. 'It's the low-cost festive option.') Always a good sport, Evan ditches his soccer barbecue to accompany her, making determined small talk with the ragtag of aunts, uncles and cousins her mother has been able to collect. It is an awkward affair, made worse by too much alcohol, too little food and too long a wait for the traffic to unsnarl so they can all return to the polite reserve that usually characterises their family relationship.

And for another thing Isabelle doesn't like cooking for herself, let alone for groups, and goes to quite ingenious lengths to avoid it.

But the real reason the party is pushing up sweat beads of anxiety at her hairline is the location. *Why*, she thinks, *why would I say we'd have it on the rooftop?*

She was completely sober when she had made the suggestion and not suffering the unwelcome presence of

The Black Place, so she cannot blame it on not being in her right mind. Isabelle presses her hands to her stomach, feeling it grind and shudder as it chews over the rooftop idea. She considers changing the venue to her lounge room, but her flat faces away from the river and the fireworks. She could drop the idea altogether, say she has changed her mind. Or that something has come up. Her brother could be in hospital. She nods vigorously as the thought occurs to her. No one would argue with that. But she is a terrible liar, always has been. And then Mrs Graham's disappointment would be painful to endure, the more so because she would pretend she wasn't disappointed at all.

Isabelle checks her watch. Five forty-five. Still another two hours before it starts to get dark. It occurs to her that although she has spent hours up there on the rooftop she has never once seen it in daylight. Her unwilling visits are always made in the blue-ink small hours when The Black Place is at full strength. She pulls the kitchen curtains aside and looks out, as if reassuring herself that the sun is still there in the sky.

She exits her flat and walks to the stairwell and up a single flight of stairs then pauses at the heavy door at the top. The door is old and unwieldy, not quite filling the spaces around it so chinks of sunlight break through into the stairwell. Someone has painted a warning on the door: *Do Not Enter.* Each letter drips purple, pooling in a teardrop halfway down the door. Isabelle muscles the door open, takes the few steps skyward and walks onto the flat, white-painted concrete expanse.

The glare is so intense that she has to cover her face with her hands, hesitantly peeking out through the slits between her fingers. There are the bollards around the edge, twelve in all, that support the fragile railings. She has spent grim hours up here, her hands gripped around these very railings, but until now she didn't know they were green, or flaking so badly.

Isabelle touches the nearest railing then retracts her fingers. It is blindingly hot. She walks the perimeter, shielding her eyes with her hand. She skirts grey milk cartons and abandoned wine bottles thick with the chalky residue of cigarette butts. All up, the rooftop is about a hundred metres square. It is perfectly flat other than an iron flue on a concrete box placed roughly in the middle. Isabelle peers into the incinerator, wondering what it was for.

Someone has drawn obscene cartoons around the base. She scrapes at them with her sandal. A pile of condom wrappers, neatly stacked and held down with a stone, sits beneath the crude erotica. Isabelle has never noticed these curious trophies in the dark, nor run into the lovers during her flights. She wonders whose they might be. The arrangement is too orderly for her speed-freak neighbours and she has never seen Jim with a girlfriend. Mrs Graham is out of the question. Before she can kill it in embryo, the thought is born that the condoms might be Karl's. Preposterous, of course. Karl doesn't know where she lives now. Isabelle screws the image of Karl and Cindy up into a tight ball and casts it out the hatch of her mind, a survivalist's trick she has forced herself to learn.

Other than a wedge of shadow thrown by the flue there is no shade. Isabelle drags a milk crate into the shadow and sits down, resting her elbows on her knees. Her eyes stray to the north-eastern corner where the railing drops away to the letterboxes about fifty metres beneath. When The Black Place is at its most savage it propels her here. Only her fraying will keeps her fingers tight around the railings when the rest of her wants to slip through the air to nothingness against the hard concrete beneath.

That same will rears up now, recognising an irresistible symmetry in the party idea.

This is a bad place. A place where she has been at her worst. But she will oversee its rebirth as something else. Something convivial and light. Something Good. On impulse she stands and does an absurd little dance, waving her arms above her head and hula-hooping her hips. It is her homage to her own courage. When the sun starts to drop she walks briskly back to her flat. She has been brave, but she will need to be braver still to stare down the rooftop at night-time.

At work the next day, Isabelle sets about planning the party. If Jack or Carole Anne were to peer a little more closely at the object of Isabelle's industry they would see that her project chart lists the following milestones:

- Scrub the rooftop clean.
- Paint over the obscene drawings on the flue.
- Shade cloth – requires further investigation. Perhaps consult Jim.
- Organise tables and chairs.
- Design an invitation.

- Find out neighbours' names. Recon at the mailboxes?
- Deliver invitations.
- Buy ingredients for food and practise cooking – sausage rolls, sandwiches, salads, quiche, fruit salad, etc. Ask Evan?
- Figure out how to power a CD player on the rooftop.
- Buy wine, beer and soft drink.
- Prepare food.

She draws up a budget then divides it into food, furnishings and decorations and turns it into a pie chart in the colours of the Czech flag. Isabelle prints the plan on A3 paper and tacks it to her bedroom door between pictures of Kafka and of the metronome in Letná Park, Prague. She peels off her work clothes and pulls on paint-splattered shorts and one of Evan's old soccer shirts. She slaps on sunscreen and a hat and draws a line of green zinc on the bridge of her nose. Clattering through her cupboards she collects a stiff-bristled broom, buckets, gloves, scrubbing brushes, plastic bags and detergents, and lugs them to the roof.

Defiantly, she starts in the north-eastern corner, methodically sweeping up dirt, cigarette butts, bottles, pie wrappers and corks. She works slowly but purposefully in the viscid, syrupy air, pausing every few minutes to gulp water from her bottle. She fills bag after bag with litter and stacks them against the incinerator flue. By the time the shadows start to lengthen she has swept the entire rooftop clean. Sunsets here, like seasons, are certain and swift, with barely a linger between opposites. Soon the rooftop will be in darkness. She collects her implements and returns to her apartment.

Shit. Lighting.

Lying in bed, Isabelle tries to visualise the rooftop as she has seen it at night but cannot get a picture. She has never struggled to find her way, but then she is driven by forces outside herself. At work the next day Isabelle adds another task to her project plan: lighting. The problem occupies her for most of the morning, far more pressing than the file that sits – unzipped – from finance. She ponders various possibilities. The easiest thing would be to sling a long cord from Jim's window up onto the roof to power a light and a CD player. Alternatively, dozens of tea lights might work if the night is still.

On her way home from work, the data file still untouched, Isabelle stops at a hardware store and buys a pot of neutral-coloured paint and a large brush. She hauls her cleaning equipment onto the roof and sets to scrubbing the flue with soapy water and a brush. The water dries almost the instant it hits the concrete. Rivulets of sweat rush down her arm and drip from her elbows. But she won't be deterred. Bending low to efface the primitive porn Isabelle looks closer. The drawings are crude stick figures in various modes of copulation. One stick figure has an absurdly outsized member that appears to be knocking things over. In another a female stick figure is whacking the member with a truncheon, the speech bubble from her mouth unreadable. There is such a cheeky verve to the pictures that for a moment Isabelle considers sparing them. But no, some of the people in the complex have small children and she doesn't want any awkwardness. She dips the brush into the paint and carefully covers the figures. It takes her three coats to make them disappear. The pot is still three-quarters full so she paints the entire flue.

Exhausted, she pulls up the milk crate to survey her handiwork. The rooftop seems suddenly more wholesome. More welcoming. Isabelle feels as if she is prising territory from The Black Place, inch by inch.

At work, Isabelle brings up stock photos and graphics on her computer and scrolls through them for images for the party invitations. She doesn't have much in the way of artistic flair but resists the idea of buying invitations as too cool and impersonal. Having committed herself, she will be as in for a pound as a penny. She rejects image after image as too vulgar (the boxing kangaroo), too obvious (a bottle of champagne) or too jingoistic (the Southern Cross). Eventually she settles on a jpeg of a fireworks display and embeds it in a word document. She superimposes the text in large, bold white lettering.

Dear Neighbour,

I would be utterly delighted if you joined me on the rooftop of our building to enjoy the Australia Day fireworks. Catering provided. Please BYO drinks and good cheer. From 5 pm.

Your neighbour and friend-in-waiting,

Isabelle Northwell at number 7

(Entrance to the rooftop is through the stairwell on the third floor. Parents – please be extra careful as the railings on the rooftop are not secure)

On second thought she removes the word 'catering' and replaces it with 'food.' Catering implies a gastronomic flair of which she is likely to fall short. Her fingers hover over the keyboard, pondering whether to request an RSVP. She decides against it. She has been so brave that the universe could not possibly refuse her, could it?

Isabelle is about to press the print button when she senses Jack behind her. It is the cinnamon and watermelon scent that gives him away. She freezes, waiting. He leans low over her chair and whispers, so close that she can feel the warmth of his breath on her neck.

'Isabelle. Would you come into my office, please?'

She presses 'save' and locks her workstation.

'Could you close the door, please, Isabelle?'

She shuts the door and sits down. Jack leans forward, his elbows on the desk.

'Isabelle, are you currently working on a task related to this department?'

'No.'

'Do you mind if I ask how much time you have devoted to tasks of a personal nature today?'

She checks her watch. 'About three hours.'

He sighs heavily. 'Look, I'm not a micro-manager as you know. I don't like looking over the shoulders of my staff to make sure they're on task. And I don't mind a reasonable amount of time being spent on personal projects. But that's the clincher, Isabelle: *reasonable*. Our policy is very clear on that.'

He waits, presumably for Isabelle to say something, but she doesn't. 'Would you describe the amount of time you've devoted to personal business today as *reasonable*, Isabelle?'

'No.'

He sets his face to *understanding boss*. It is the expression he gives Isabelle when her sick leave has escalated beyond the acceptable level.

'Is there something wrong, Isabelle? Something I should know about? I'm not trying to pry, but if there's something in your life that's making it difficult for you to concentrate at work, then I'm here to listen. I know that in the past you've had, ahem, health issues. You know...' he waves his hand, *'the incident.'*

A surge of fury takes hold of Isabelle. If Jack lost a leg in a car accident or developed glaucoma and went blind, how would he feel if she reduced his trauma to 'the incident'? Sometimes she wishes The Black Place came with a cast or a splint, something visible and explanatory. Anger makes her honest.

'My work is meaningless.'

Jack's features ripple like a flag in a light breeze before settling into place again. This is not what he was expecting. 'What do you mean, Isabelle?'

'Who looks at the stats I prepare?'

'Well, me for one.'

'And what do you do with them?'

'I table them at the leadership and performance meetings. You know that.'

'Could I have the file? The one you table?'

Jacks swivels in his chair to the shelving behind him. He thumbs through folders, disks and reports until he finds the green folder in which he stores Isabelle's charts. He hands it to her. Isabelle opens the file and leafs through the first few pages.

'This is what you table?'

'Yes.'

'Every week?'

'Every week.'

Isabelle peels the first report from the file and places it on the desk between her and Jack. She adjusts it slightly to make it completely level. As Jack studies her graph on the unprecedented demand for driving tests in Aramaic she places the report on skyrocketing boat registrations in landlocked rural towns next to it. Then the equally fanciful reports she created when these two went unnoticed. 'Sucking up to management: good or bad for building ventilation?' 'Gonorrhoea and P3: a comparative analysis.' She can almost hear the whirring mechanics of his mind as he computes her nonsense diagrams. Tap, tap, tap, circle.

All at once he sighs again and leans back in his chair. The last vestiges of *understanding boss* face dissolve and he looks at Isabelle with a frankness she has never seen before. She realises that his office face is a patina applied at the door. Not a lie so much as a version of self, an amplification of elements most likely to thrive in the environment. This naked face is shrewder, more animal.

'Okay,' he says. 'You got me. I don't look at your reports.'

'Why do you keep getting me to do them?'

'For show, mainly.'

'I don't understand. What about "evidence-based decision-making" and "policy from planning" and all the other guff P3 bangs on about?'

'I know and you know that we do what the minister asks us to do. And she does what the paper tells her to do. So the evidence is largely —'

'Pointless?'

'No, not pointless.' He thinks carefully for the word. 'Serendipitous. Sometimes it aligns. Sometimes not.'

'You don't have something more meaningful I could do? Something useful?'

'Excuse me for being blunt, but "*the incident*",' he draws quotation marks in the air, 'isn't exactly a state secret, Isabelle. Your performance with the board did you no favours. How can I justify taking more interesting work from someone else to give it to you?'

'You probably can't.'

'Well, then. Where does that leave us?'

Isabelle thinks for a moment. 'Why do you keep me on if I'm not delivering anything? Why haven't you transferred me or even, God forbid, performance-managed me?'

'I may yet,' he says deliberately, 'find a use for you.'

And I for you.

They stare at each other over the table. Suddenly Jack laughs. 'Look. Just make a show of doing the stats, all right? Do a half-arsed job. And whatever else it is you're doing, do it discreetly. I don't need a mutiny. If anyone asks we never had this conversation.'

'Understood.'

He reaches across the desk to shake her hand. On contact a shatter of sparks descends from her head to her groin.

FIVE

On most afternoons you will find Isabelle on the roof.
Evan has accused her of desertion.

'What can be so important it keeps you from caning
my arse in the pool?'

'I do so love these Catholic-schoolboy metaphors
of yours, but there's something I have to do. Just keep
Australia Day free like I asked. All will be revealed.'

She carts buckets and buckets of warm soapy water
and sloshes them around. She attacks the cracked and
grimy concrete, scraping away the carapace of neglect. It
is very hard going, like wading through treacle, and she
is developing a rough callous on the inside of her right
thumb. Long afternoons spent in the heat are turning
her already honey-coloured limbs a deep suede. She
rubs down the bollards with steel wool, prising off the
worst of the flaking paint. She polishes the railings till
they gleam. One of the bolts holding the railing onto its
bollard has come loose. Isabelle tests the railing, shaking
it. A running child might easily barrel right through the
railing to the concrete below.

'Hi, Isabelle,' says Jim as he opens his door. 'Locked
yourself out of the bathroom again?'

'No, surprisingly. I was just wondering if I could have a rummage through your toolkit. I need a um, a um…' She mimes tightening a bolt, gripping her index finger with the thumb and index finger of her other hand and turning it.

'A root? A spanner?'

'A spanner. And maybe a bolt thingy.'

'A bolt thingy. Right. That's a bit technical for me,' he says laughing.

Jim waves Isabelle into his deliciously air-conditioned flat. 'Oh, it's so lovely and cool in here.'

'I don't know how you stand your place in the summer. Mine was a sweatbox until I put the unit in.'

'Air conditioning, like feature walls,' she points, 'and terrariums,' she points again, 'are for owners, not renters, Jim.'

'You should buy, Isabelle. Just to get a foothold in the property market. It's not getting any cheaper, you know. Plus you might be eligible for the first home buyer's grant.'

Jim hauls one of his toolboxes from the kitchen cupboard. 'Will this do?' he asks, handing her a large spanner. 'It's adjustable, see. Look.' He shows Isabelle how to manipulate the tension so the clench expands and contracts. He picks four bolts and nuts from his large collection. 'Do you want some help?'

'No, thanks. I'm good. Feeling very manly today.'

He chuckles, evidently doubting Isabelle's ability to accomplish this simple task (as, in fact, does she). 'Any dramas, give me a shout, all right?'

'Will do. Thanks.'

Jim jerks his thumb towards the adjoining flat. 'Did you hear them at it again last night?'

'Yes. How do they generate so much noise?'

'God knows. I wish they'd just overdose and be done with it.'

'Ouch, Jim. That's harsh.'

'Yeah, well, they're so useless I don't see that they contribute much to the greater good. There should be a law that forces the government to tell you when the property you're buying is next to public-housing fucktards. If you bought your place we'd stand half a chance of squeezing them out.'

Isabelle thinks about her tenuous hold on her job. She's probably not that far from being a public-housing fucktard herself. 'Thanks for the spanner, Jim. I'll bring it back in a couple of hours.'

'No worries.'

The bolt crumbles against the pressure of the spanner like a rotten hazelnut. With some difficulty Isabelle prises the railing out of the hole in the bollard and leans it on the floor. She flushes the hole out and replaces railing, nut and bolt. With the last turn of the spanner she feels the acute satisfaction of the do-it-yourselfer. The railing is much more secure.

Every square foot of the rooftop made habitable by Isabelle's endeavours is a victory against The Black Place. The rooftop looks clean, pristine even, but it needs something to break up the glare and give it colour and life. As she does every Saturday, Mrs Graham sits in her lovely courtyard enjoying the morning. She is drinking tea from one of those gold-edged floral tea sets that Isabelle associates with old people. She is browsing through a cookbook.

'Good morning, Mrs Graham.'

'Morning, my dear. You're up and about early.' She peers behind Isabelle expectantly. 'Where is that nice young man of yours?'

'You mean Evan? He's certainly a nice young man but I've told you before, we're besties without benefits.'

'You haven't won him over to the pleasures of the flesh yet?'

'You're incorrigible.'

Mrs Graham chuckles. 'Can I offer you tea, Isabelle?'

'Thank you, no. But I will take some of your ginger beer if that's all right.'

'Of course.' Mrs Graham pushes back her chair and stands awkwardly, grimacing a little.

'How's the arthritis today?'

'I'm thinking of giving it a name. Hitler maybe. Or Pol Pot.'

'That good, huh?'

She shuffles into her flat and returns with a beaded glass of ginger beer.

'Oh God, that's delicious.' Isabelle smacks her lips. 'All pepper and bubbles. Here's your invitation to the party.'

Isabelle hands Mrs Graham her painstakingly pre-pared invitation, printed out at work right under Jack's nose on the expensive glossy paper she is supposed to ask Carol Anne for permission to use.

'Oh, thank you, my dear.' Mrs Graham reads the invitation aloud. If it had come from the Queen of

England it is hard to imagine she could be any more pleased. 'I'm so looking forward to this I can't tell you. I've been going through my cookbooks to see what I could make.'

'Don't go to any trouble.'

'It's no trouble,' Mrs Graham says quickly, as if afraid Isabelle might snatch the activity away, leaving her day yawning ahead of her.

'Oh well, if you're sure. Look, I wonder if I might pick your brains about something. I'm off to buy some pot plants this morning but I've no idea what would be appropriate. I need something colourful and hardy. Something that can withstand full sun and get by without much water.'

Isabelle has sparked Mrs Graham's life-wire. Immediately she is up and out of her chair, tea forgotten. She takes Isabelle by the arm and leads her slowly around her courtyard, pointing out various plants and making numerous recommendations. She hurries away for pen and paper, untroubled by her joints. She writes Isabelle a list in elegant, old-fashioned script.

'Thank you so much, Mrs Graham. I appreciate this.'

'Any time, my dear.' She beams. 'I'd love to have a look at your handiwork when you're done.'

'Of course. Let's see how long I can keep the little critters alive.'

Isabelle arrives at the nursery just before nine expecting to have it to herself, but the place is bustling. Parents with small children, elderly couples, girlfriends in groups of twos and threes, all busily pressing their noses to flowers and reading instructions on the plant labels. She finds a sales assistant and faithfully dictates Mrs Graham's list. She lingers around some brightly glazed pots in deep reds and blues, thinking how lovely they would look dotted around the rooftop. Reluctantly she has to concede that her budget won't run to them. She will have to settle for the earthy brown of the cheaper pots.

By the time she leaves the nursery, her boot and back seat are thriving with plant life. It is a quarter past ten and already prickly and sapping. Getting the plants to the roof is going to be hot work. She takes two bags of peat to the roof, collects one of the milk crates and jogs back down. As she rounds the bend to the second floor she very nearly collides with Evan making his way up.

'Hello, darling.' She drops the crate and blows him a kiss. 'I'd kiss you properly but I'm horribly sweaty.'

'I need to talk to you, Belle. Can we go to your flat?'

'Of course. But can you give me a hand with something first? I've got a small fortune's worth of plants in the car and if I don't get them out they'll wilt to nothing.'

'I need to talk to you *now*, Belle. It's important.'

There is a flint in Evan's voice that unnerves her. He looks queasy. A flurry of worst-case scenarios crowds her mind. Evan with cancer. Evan joining the priesthood. Evan leaving the country for good. 'Oh God, Evan, what is it?'

'Can we go to your flat?'

She walks fast, her thoughts wild and terrifying. They enter her flat and stand facing one another.

'Tell me,' she says.

He looks at the ground, shoring up his courage, then speaks.

'It's Karl. He's getting married. To Cindy.' Evan keeps his eyes on the ground so that the news enters Isabelle unseen. He bores into a dark, wine-coloured stain on the rug, forcing himself not to look at her. 'I didn't want you to hear it from anyone else.'

'When did you find out?'

'This morning. He phoned me.'

'Is it…Is it going to be a church wedding? Or something more informal?'

He looks up. 'I don't know.'

'Big wedding or small?'

'I didn't ask.'

'Men,' she says breezily, 'always scrimp on the details.'

'Belle, honey.'

There is such sympathy in his voice, such kindness, that Isabelle wobbles. He takes a step towards her, then another. He pulls her to him, not urgently, but tentatively, giving her room to wriggle away without causing either of them too much embarrassment. She submits to the embrace, feeling like an over-full jar. *Don't you cry, Isabelle. Don't you dare bloody well cry.* But her body is not listening to her, or has not heard the injunction above the sound of her heart re-shearing along the Karl fault line. The tears run from her eyes, dampening Evan's shirt.

'Ergggh.' She makes an inarticulate sound of frustration, wiping the tears with her index fingers. 'I don't know why I'm crying, really. It's not like it's unexpected. Or like I still miss him.'

'Good,' spits Evan, 'because he's a prick. And another —'

But Isabelle holds up a hand to stop him. She doesn't want to know more. She takes a few deep breaths, determined to bring herself to order.

'Do you want a drink?' he asks. 'Scotch? Wine? Have you got anything? I can go get something.'

'It's not even midday.'

'Yeah. And?'

'No, I'm fine, really. I just need a minute.'

'Do you want to go for a swim? Do some sprints?'

'Something like that. I need to move. Can you help me with these plants?'

'Yep. Let's do it. But afterwards we're having a drink.'

'Deal.'

Together they shoulder plants, pots, fertiliser and mulch from the car to the roof. Isabelle loads her crate to the very top, heaving under it, submitting to the exertion. At the rooftop she drops her crate, arches her straining back and walks to the edge to check how far below Jim's window is if she needs to throw an extension cord to the roof. She senses, rather than sees, Evan throw out his hand to pull her back.

She turns. His face is stricken, his arm outstretched. They remain frozen like that for a second or two until Isabelle whispers, 'I gave you my word, remember? You can stop worrying.'

In every relationship of long standing there is at least one ravine. An ugly, treacherous place that you learn to skirt around, pretending deafness to the occasional rock-fall. Isabelle and Evan are dangerously close to

58

theirs. Evan looks down, making a show of checking the contents of the crate. 'There's no watering can. We'll need water straight away. I'll go get some.' He disappears down the stairwell. Isabelle plants her face in her hands. She imagines him leaning against her sink, forcing his panic back down. She wants to relieve him of this constant worry but doesn't know how.

'You have a new picture,' he says when he returns, dropping a crate full of water-filled orange juice bottles and milk cartons.

'What's that?'

'On your fridge. There's a new picture. The lady. The one reclining on the cushions with the ample bosom.'

'I didn't think you Catholic boys were supposed to notice bosom,' she says, seizing on the levity.

'Oh, we notice. We just suppress it. It's why we're such models of psychological health. So who is she, my lady of the mammaries?'

'That's Libussa, the founder of Prague.'

'A woman? Really?'

'So the myth goes. She was a bit mad but a seer, a visionary. She fell into a trance in the hills in Hradčany, which is just outside of where Prague now stands, and saw a beautiful city. Spires. Squares. Castles. And when she came to, her people went about building it for her.'

Evan grins. 'Interesting approach to town planning. What happened to her?'

'The old men, the old leaders, were scared of her. Jealous of her visions, I suppose. So they cut her a deal. In order to remain their leader she had to marry. They were trying to domesticate her. If they were hoping for a dynastic alliance they were disappointed. She chose a farmer.'

'And then?'

'And then she had truckloads of kids and kept on prophesying.'

Evan pushes his hair back from his face, streaking dirt along his forehead. 'Why are you so fascinated by Prague?'

'Why are any of us drawn to the things we're drawn to?' Isabelle thinks of Jack. 'Chance. Alignment of the stars. Chemistry. No reason at all.'

'But what kicked it off?'

Isabelle sits back on her heels, a trowel still in her hands, trying to locate the root of her affinity. 'I think I fell in love with the word first. Say it out loud. *Prague.* It's like a close cousin to an English word, but ultimately exotic. Unknowable.' *Somewhere between prayer and plague, a fitting place for me,* she thinks.

Evan tries the word out, lingering on the long 'a'. 'Yeah, you're right. It's an unusual word. What do the locals call it?'

'Praha.'

'When I was little I had a thing for Ancient Rome. I made myself a toga out of some bed sheets and used to parade through the house colonising rooms and declaiming new laws.'

'How very pagan of you. I hope you've sought penance for worshipping idols.'

'Hah.'

'It's strange when you think about it, though, isn't it? The way your childhood imagination comes up with these things and why they stick? I remember singing the Christmas carol about the Czech King Wenceslas at a school concert. We must have rehearsed it dozens of times but suddenly as I was singing, that part about the footsteps really hit me.'

'What part?'

'You know.' Isabelle sings in a tremulous, low voice. '*In his master's steps he trod, where the snow lay dinted. Heat was in the very sod, which the saint had printed.* The King and the page braving the storm to take food and firewood to a poor man. The servant freezing to death as the night draws in. Then stepping in the King's footsteps and miraculously the tracks are warm and he can keep going. I remember getting it and thinking, "Oh. Oh, that's so beautiful. So hopeful."' She doesn't tell Evan that when Karl left she had the image on constant rotation in her head. That she comforts herself with it when The Black Place has laid waste to her once again.

The two of them work in companionable silence, massaging the plants from their tubs and into the new pots. They fertilise and water them, then place them at the base of the incinerator so that they have the benefit of at least some shade. According to Mrs Graham's instructions Isabelle has pelargoniums, agave, bromeliads, petunias, echeveria and ixora. The dirt in the pots is sodden from the drenchings that have cost Evan and Isabelle a dozen trips up and down the stairwell. The plants are a bright cluster bomb of optimism. The rooftop suddenly looks cared for and inviting.

Yes, Isabelle thinks, pressing her full weight on the folds of her mind where Karl hides, *this will do very well indeed.*

'Come on,' she tells Evan. 'You've earned that drink.'

Isabelle and Evan lie propped up on pillows, top to toe on Isabelle's bed. Evan is wearing the soccer shorts he keeps at Isabelle's for just such occasions and the oversized Wiggles shirt that belongs to no-one-knows-who. Isabelle wears a loose green cotton dress. Both of them nurse ice-filled glasses and lie as still as possible under the whirring fan.

'It's so farkin hot,' Evan mumbles. He reaches beside the bed for the vodka bottle sweating in a bucket of ice and fills first Isabelle's glass then his own. Isabelle holds the glass up to her temple.

'In Prague they'll be complaining about the cold.'

'Your point being?'

'No point, really. Only that somewhere someone wants what we don't. And vice versa.'

Evan gives a mock grimace. 'Don't get philosophical on me. I'm too drunk. Hurts my head.'

'Want me to get you some water? Some coffee?'

He grips his glass tighter with both hands, as if Isabelle has threatened to take it from him. 'My wodka. Mine. Mine. Mine.'

'Lush.'

He laughs. The Powderfinger CD they are playing comes to an end. 'What next?' Evan flips over to remove the CD from the stereo. He picks up one of the dozen or so discs piled up, turns it over, considers then puts it back. 'I'll never understand your thing for musicals.'

'*The Magic Flute* is more of an opera than a musical.'

'Same thing.'

'Not the same thing.'

'Just as painful.'

'Which doesn't make them the same thing. You're misapplying your Euclid. Shame on you.'

'Arrrggggh. Again with the thinking and the philosophy and the hurting of my tiny brain.'

Isabelle throws a cushion at him.

'No violence, please. I'm prepared to tolerate your terrible taste in music because you bought the vodka.' Evan slips a CD into the system. 'Smetana. *My Country*. Let's see if something Czech makes me feel cooler.' Evan sinks back into the pillows and listens to the music. 'No. Just as hot. But feeling strange patriotic stirrings…surge of nationalism…urge to invade something…preferably something small and puny.'

'Would you go to war? If you had to?'

'Yes. No. I don't know. It would depend on the war, what was at stake. For oil? Nup. Something like the Nazis? I guess. If there was no other way.' He takes a sip of his drink. 'You're making me think and I don't like it. I just want to lie here and feel pleasantly drunk.'

'Can't you be pleasantly drunk and think at the same time?'

'I'm a man,' he mumbles through a mouthful of ice. 'Can't multitask.' He closes his eyes and sinks further back into the pillows.

Isabelle doesn't want him to go to sleep. His presence reassures her and helps salve the reopened Karl wound. 'Does drinking make you more or less horny than usual?'

Evan splutters. 'Sorry to break it to you, but your come-ons need work.'

'Hah. I was just seeing if you were awake.' Isabelle sips her vodka. 'Seriously, though. We're old friends. You can tell me. How *do* you keep it in your pants?'

'Horse-hair jocks. Aversion therapy. Cold showers.'

'I'm being serious. You're a good-looking guy and you have girlfriends. Intermittently. Surely it's come up.' She raises her eyebrow. 'Pardon the pun.'

'You really want to know?'

She sits up straighter against the pillows, attentive. 'Yes. I really want to know.'

'It was a bargain I made.'

'A bargain? With who?'

Evan hesitates, then drains the rest of his glass. He reaches for the bottle and re-pours with an unsteady hand. He lifts the bottle towards Isabelle, who shakes her head.

'It's hard to explain.'

'Try. I'd like to know.'

'Do you remember when we were at Civics and Arts we funded that inter-faith exhibition? We hadn't known each other very long but we went along together and you asked me about my faith in God. About where it came from?'

Isabelle nods. 'You said you inherited it along with your devastating good looks.'

'That's part of the story. Both my parents believed and we went to church, so it was just part of who we were. But I don't remember having strong feelings about it either way until my dad died. Maybe if he'd survived the heart attack my scientific bent would have seen off my belief.' He falls silent. Isabelle knows that his dad's death still affects him and that his mum has never really recovered. She is on the point of changing the subject when he continues. 'When you were a kid, were you ever frustrated that you *were* a kid?'

'Not that I remember, no. Why?'

'It was tough after Dad passed away. Mum and Dad had what I realise now was a really traditional relationship. He went to work, Mum stayed home. They didn't even have a joint bank account. Can you believe that? So suddenly Mum has to engage with the world and she's just not equipped. Dealing with bureaucracy sucks at the best of times, but try it when you're incoherent with grief and the most sophisticated organisational thing you've ever done is write a cheque. I just wanted to leap over the next ten years straight into adulthood and get a job and take charge and have money to pay for the electricity to get reconnected.'

'They cut off your electricity?'

Evan nods. 'Again, everything in Dad's name. It took a while for settlement of his will and the transfer of money.' His voice shakes a little. 'It was fucked.'

Impulsively, she throws herself from her end of the bed to his and puts her arm around him, burrowing her face into his chest. Evan is visibly surprised. It's not like Isabelle to be this physically demonstrative. 'I hate to think of you going through that. My poor Evan.'

He wraps her up in his arms, bends and kisses the top of her head. 'It's all right. It's all right.' She lies against him for a while, then props herself up on her elbow beside him.

'You said there was a bargain. What bargain?'

'I'm going to tell you something but I want you to promise me you won't laugh.'

'Oh God, you're not a flagellant, are you?'

He lobs the cushion back at her. 'I'm being serious.'

'I won't laugh,' she says solemnly.

'I was in the church, this was maybe two months after Dad died and the money and organisational stuff was at its worst. I was praying, asking God if he could grow me up faster so I could take care of things.'

'Oh, Evan.'

'And that's when I felt it.'

'What?'

'Something bigger than me. The way I remember it I heard someone say my name, but I think I've created that memory as a way of making sense of what happened. Because I'm not sure that I exactly heard a voice. I felt a voice. It was in me. Or it was a particle in everything around me and at that moment all of those particles shifted to tell me they were there. The feeling, Belle, I've never forgotten it. It was peaceful. But it wasn't an inert, insensate peace like being drunk or going under anaesthetic. This was a ringing, joyful peace. Everything around me was white-fringed, zinging. All of these particles fizzing around to let me know that I was a part of something bigger. That feeling that there was a pattern, a plan – a link between me and everything else was so…I can only say joyful. Over the years I've…I've reworked it in my memory so it became an aural experience. But I'm pretty sure it wasn't. It was no sense I've ever known before. Or, it was like all my senses merged so that I tasted and saw and heard the same thing. What's that word for when your senses get mixed up so you can taste blue and smell red?'

'Synaesthesia.'

'Yeah. That word. It was like that.'

Isabelle struggles to think of something in her experience to compare it with. 'How do you know that it objectively happened?' She chooses her words carefully. 'I mean, couldn't it have been something your child self created as a kind of palliative?'

'I've thought about that. Does it make sense that my ten-year-old self would conjure an almighty benevolent presence to make me feel safe again? Of course it does. But I know, Belle, I am absolutely certain that I didn't create this. I don't have that kind of imagination. This thing, this experience, was an external presence making itself known to me. Am I making any sense?'

'I don't know. I don't know how to conceptualise it.'

'You've never felt something, can I use the word, *otherworldly*?'

Isabelle waves away some of the happy fog of her tipsiness. She considers telling Evan about The Black Place. He is her best friend, after all, and the person she loves most in this world. She opens her mouth to speak then thinks better of it. Karl had known. And in knowing he had ceased to love her.

'I still don't understand where the bargaining comes in.'

'The relief that came over me after that experience in the church, it was so intense. You know that feeling where you've got a cracking headache and everything is so bright that it hurts your eyes and then the painkillers kick in and you just want to cry with relief?'

She nods.

'It was like that. I wanted God to know how grateful I was. I knew I'd experienced something rare. Something special. It didn't seem right to offer up a prayer of thanks and just be done with it. It had to cost me something. For years I didn't know what that something might be. Then in my teens it became obvious. Virginity.'

'Kind of like giving up the things you like for Lent?'

'Kind of. Look, I'm not going to bullshit you, I know I'm an all right–looking guy and I don't seem to have any problems attracting women. You'd be surprised how many approach me like I'm a challenge they can win over. And to answer your question, sometimes I get so horny I think I'm going to explode. But this was the thing. The thing I could offer God in thanks.'

'Your goodness,' she says quietly.

'Yes.'

'So it's not a "I'm a virgin till I marry" type of thing? A fixed moral code?'

'Not really, no.'

She props herself up higher on her elbow to be at eye-height with him. 'So when do you know you're done? When God's satisfied?'

He brushes a loose strand of hair from her face. His fingers linger at the side of her cheek. 'I'll know.'

'Well.' She scoots back to her side of the bed and pours another vodka. 'Whoever she is, she'd better be fabulous, 'cos she's gonna have me to contend with.'

'And what about you, Belle? Do you think you're ready to re-enter the romantic fray?'

She picks at knobbles of fluff on the bedclothes and thinks of Jack. 'I think so. Yeah. I think I am.'

Evan smiles, then sips his drink.

SIX

The attraction between Isabelle and Jack is stirring like a bear waking from a long, hard winter. Since the day when Isabelle confronted him with her fanciful charts they have the intimacy of collusion. On the surface, things look much as normal. He darts in and out of his office with his set jaw and ministerial folders. He has a peculiar gait. He walks fast, but his head juts out from his shoulders and chest, as if his mind is already in attendance on the next problem but his body (dreaming, she thinks, of boat races and vineyards at harvest) is reluctant to catch up. Managers and executives cluster in his office, closing the door and pulling down the blinds to emphasise their importance. Sometimes the ministerial chief of staff descends on the floor with her entourage and even the pot plants stand straighter.

While all this bustle goes on around him, Isabelle sits at her desk tinkering with her party plan and wandering through virtual Prague streetscapes. She has inputted increasingly fanciful data for her reports: the recommended watering levels for her plants, the results of football games in Evan's soccer league, the dates on which non-communists were liquidated from the Czech parliament. Jack looks at her work and then quietly shreds it. When he catches her eye the left corner of his mouth turns up in involuntary amusement. Occasionally, he slightly shakes his head in conflicting disbelief and admiration. Sometimes he gives her a sly wink.

At the sound of her voice his ears twitch slightly. Isabelle watches for the gesture: it reminds her of an animal approaching a watering hole at dusk. Alert. Alive. Aflutter. She notices too how, when they pass each other in the corridors, there is a slight tic in his hand, an involuntary spasm of the fist.

Isabelle is not anxious to shrug off her romantic hibernation. Instead she savours the crackling frisson between them. The exquisite sense of being primed to see him (even though a whole day can pass when she doesn't) is delicious. Her cells whirr with life and anticipation. The feelings, so unlike Black Place feelings, enthral her.

At one thirty Isabelle and Jack are due to meet. The entry sits there, irreproachably official, in her electronic calendar under 'Subject: New opportunities'. For the location Jack has typed 'off-site'. A shiver ran through her arm as she clicked her acceptance. Just before twelve, as her cells taper towards some exquisite pinnacle, Isabelle's phone rings. It is Kate. Could Isabelle meet her in the lunch room?

'Oh, Isabelle,' she says in a sprightly tone as if surprised to see her, despite the summons.

'Hello, Kate. What can I do for you?'

'I was hoping you could magic my husband here.'

'Excuse me?'

'He was supposed to meet me for lunch but he's nowhere to be found.'

'Oh.' Isabelle checks her watch. 'The leadership team meeting finished up about half an hour ago. He's usually in his office by now. I can check with Carol Anne if you like.'

'No, no that's okay. He's probably hosing down some crisis or another. I'll just wait. Does he have a busy afternoon, do you know?'

'He's meeting with me at one thirty, but other than that I don't know.'

'I see.' Kate runs her index finger along the side of her mouth as if to corral her lipstick within the confines of her perfectly pink mouth. Isabelle is reminded of a cat lunching on a budgie.

'Help yourself to tea and coffee while you wait. Mugs are kept here,' Isabelle opens the cupboard door. 'Hot water here. We even have chocolate biscuits, remaindered largesse from the Christmas wind-ups.' She pushes the packet towards Kate who recoils affectedly.

'No, thank you. I'm watching my weight after the festive excess.' She pats her flat stomach and turns side on to Isabelle, jutting her chin out a little and dropping her shoulders to emphasise her slim, elegant lines.

'Suit yourself.' Isabelle takes a biscuit.

'So. Are you still playing with your numbers, Isabelle?'

'Yes.'

'I imagine you must have been a bit of a rarity, doing maths at university. All those boys to yourself. Is your boyfriend scientifically minded too?'

'I didn't do maths. I did psychology.'

'Oh.' Kate's nostrils flare with frustration, quickly tamped down, at failing to secure the information she wants: whether Isabelle has a boyfriend or not. She steps backwards and turns absently to a pile of magazines on the table between them, then ambles towards the cupboard. She doesn't pause to remove a glass as Isabelle expects but skirts the table towards her, high heels tapping on the tiled floor. Isabelle retreats and soon the two women are circling the table, slowly, watching one another.

Kate raises her hand to brush a strand of hair from her face. The gesture sets her bracelets ringing against each other. Isabelle feels Kate's super-accurate tape measure snaking around her. Kate's nostrils quiver again as she digests the data: Isabelle's smoky beauty against Kate's china-doll daintiness. The clack of Kate's stilettos and swish of Isabelle's skirt play rhythmically as the two women perform their strange ceremony around the table.

Isabelle imagines that Cindy paces the table with them too. Her memory, habituated to the ruthless censorship of the past, cranks out disjointed pictures. Cindy's apple cheeks rising and falling in the swift flow of her conversation. Her ample bottom undulating in a maroon swing skirt. A glass of wine held against the deep plunge of her cleavage. Slowly, the fragments cohere and Cindy's hologram joins the other two women in their wary patrol. Isabelle appraises the ghost before her: a tankard-wielding, salty wench to Isabelle's tight-wired Amazon.

'How is it you became a data analyst, Isabelle?' Kate's voice startles Isabelle. 'Why aren't you practising psychology somewhere?'

Cindy pixelates and shimmers. 'A series of accidents, I suppose,' says Isabelle, barely aware of what she is saying. 'Spending my days with the unbalanced and distressed didn't appeal overly much.' Cindy is gone, leaving only the echo of her fruity laugh and jasmine perfume. 'I like the statistical side, though. The problem-solving. What did you study?'

Kate pauses for a moment, the click–clack of her heels stilled, and reads the headline in one of the magazines on the table. ' "Lose ten kilos in ten weeks with our amazing grapefruit diet!" Honestly, how many times can they recycle these miracle weight-loss cures? And people are gullible enough to buy these rags.'

'What did you study, Kate?'

'Oh, bits and pieces. Here and there.'

But Isabelle, high on libido and competitive adrenalin, won't let it go. 'What's your degree in?'

The tendons of Kate's hand arch upwards as her painted nails scratch at the glossy magazine paper. 'I've done a few short courses. Fundamentals of business. Massage. Life writing.'

'TAFE courses.'

For an instant Kate's guard drops. In the sudden candour of her expression Isabelle sees the frustration – the choking frustration – of a woman whose place changed too late for her to capitalise on it. Isabelle, born nearly a quarter of a century later, was raised on the expectation of a university education. A career. Something that is hers. She is ashamed of herself for pressing the point.

'TAFE has some great courses,' Isabelle says limply, trying to make amends.

Her condescension revives Kate's pluck. 'Education doesn't necessarily buy wisdom'.

The candour is gone, replaced by a shrewd strategist. Kate's not the sort to hurl accusations and seek weepy solace with her girlfriends because her man has a wandering eye. No. Kate will manufacture her own abstraction. She will send herself anonymous flowers, shrugging quizzically when Jack inquires as to their origin. Her odd absences will be half-explained, even though she has done nothing more than read a fashion magazine in a cafe while sipping a low-fat latte. Jack will notice her sudden penchant for sexy clothing and the new scent she is trailing, a men's cologne she has buried behind her tampons and sanitary pads in the bathroom cupboard. Kate will squirt just enough foreign piss through their home to trip Jack's caveman instinct and set him prowling his territory for the interloper. Isabelle recognises the danger that he will drop his own prey – Isabelle – as he sees off his rival.

'Isabelle.' Jack's voice booms from the entrance to the tearoom. 'Have you met any of your new outcomes yet? I'm impatient for progress.'

'Nothing to report as yet. But you'll be the first to know.'

'Excellent,' he chuckles. He spies his wife and stops laughing. 'Hello, Kate. This is a surprise.'

'It shouldn't be. We're having lunch today.' Kate gives him an icy smile then turns to Isabelle. 'New outcomes? Have you found a way to make a and b unequal to c?'

'Nearly.'

'Lunch,' says Jack. 'Sorry, Kate. It's been one thing after another today and I clean forgot. I hope you haven't been waiting long.'

'A little while.'

'Sorry, love.'

'That's all right. Shall we eat?'

Kate steps towards him and draws his arm around her waist. She reaches up, tilts Jack's head towards her and gives him a soft kiss on the mouth before turning to give Isabelle a perfunctory wave.

'Bye, Isabelle,' says Jack as his wife steers him down the corridor.

Isabelle straightens the magazines and winds an elastic band around the open packet of biscuits. Her stomach is a writhing mess of shame and desire. She needs Kate to be abstract. Unreal. She doesn't want to know that Kate has pressed herself into the outline of 'Jack's wife', first out of conviction, then out of necessity. We are a human *race*, Isabelle reminds herself. The very coinage of our species puts competition front and centre. It's inevitable. She thinks of Cindy.

There will always be winners and losers.

Jack returns to the office late, the start time for their meeting long past.

'Isabelle, I'm so sorry. I was waylaid.' The buttons on his shirt are askew, and a fusty, yeasty stench trails after him. Isabelle has an urge to vomit. Cindy, once conjured, has proven difficult to banish. All afternoon, needles of grief and rejection have been injecting their slow poison into her blood.

'Shall we meet now?' Jack says it with the certainty that Isabelle will be available.

'What?'

'Um, I said shall we meet now?'

Isabelle stares at her screen, as if engrossed by its contents. 'No,' she says without looking up. 'It'll have to wait.'

'Oh,' he stands there awkwardly. 'What are you working on?'

'A regression analysis of the road safety data.' The lie sends the blood rushing to her face, infuriating her even more. She is, in fact, comparing hotel prices in Prague.

'Will it take long?'

'It takes as long as it takes.'

'Well, can we reschedule for tomorrow morning? It's actually pretty important that we meet.'

'Not that important, obviously.'

He looks sheepish. 'I'm sorry about today. Really. Are you free tomorrow?'

'I'll have to see. Check in with me then.'

Isabelle clicks off her computer and leaves without another word. She takes the train home, half-hoping for someone on the carriage to pick a fight with her. She wants to spill blood. To feel bone splinter underneath her straining knuckles. But the commuters are quiet newspaper-reading types. From the station Isabelle slips off her shoes and, heedless of the burning pavement, runs to her apartment. She peels off her damp clothes, changes into her bathers and runs, goggles in hand, back down the stairwell. Mrs Graham is sitting in her courtyard and hollers to Isabelle as she runs out again, but Isabelle can do no more than wave. If she stops, lets stillness assume control, the acid will burn through her. The only hope of draining it is through motion.

The next day Jack proposes that they get out of the office for a while. 'I thought it might make a nice change. We could go get a decent coffee somewhere while we go over the reports.'

Jack speaks louder than usual, taking out his social insurance against innuendo. He and Isabelle walk through the automatic doors to the gated enclosure reserved for the government vehicles. Jack flicks a button and the car bleeps a polite electronic acknowledgement.

'It's open.'

They drive in silence, the radio playing classical music. Despite her sunglasses the world looks to Isabelle as if it is reflective. Light bounces from every surface. The asphalt shimmers, doorknobs gleam. The very hood of the car seems to have trapped sunbeams under the polish. Students from the nearby vocational college walk drowsily by, their shoulders bare. She is frolicking in Jack's scent, rejoicing to have him clean again. It makes it easier to push Kate from her consciousness. The air conditioning freezes the portions of her face and limbs that catch the blast. The rest of her burns. She shifts slightly in her seat, unconscious that her skirt rides up as she does so. Jack forces his eyes to the white lines on the road.

'Well. Here we are.'

Isabelle opens the car door and steps into the heat.

'What would you like, Isabelle?'

'A peppermint tea, please. With honey.'

'Nothing else? They do excellent muffins here. Or biscuits? Florentines?'

'Just tea, please.'

He places their order at the counter while Isabelle chooses a table near the window. When he returns he makes a show of opening his folder and removing a fountain pen from his pocket. He clicks off the lid and presses the nib onto a blank page, carefully writing his name and Isabelle's. Jack and Isabelle. Isabelle and Jack.

'Isabelle. I've been thinking about our meeting the other day. About the work that you do. It's not really fair on you to do all this analysis that, for political reasons, we don't use. It's not what P3 is about. And it's definitely not living the values. Between us I'm sure we can come up with something more meaningful for you to do.'

'I'd like that.'

Their drinks arrive. Isabelle pushes the plunger on her canister of tea and watches the little flakes swirl around before compressing them into green mush. She tears the corner off her sachet of honey and spoons it carefully into her mug. The tinkle of the spoon against the mug is melodious and extraordinarily loud. Jack lifts the coffee to his lips. His hand trembles. He seeks the support of his other hand to bring the cup to his lips. He takes a sip then carefully, slowly places the mug back onto the saucer. A rivulet of milky coffee runs down the side. Isabelle watches it tear down and dribble into nothing on the saucer.

'I was thinking,' his voice fails him. 'I was thinking you might like a change. Sometimes it does you good to get out of your comfort zone.'

Isabelle waits for him to continue but he seems to be having difficulty shifting his verbal boom gate. The opposite of her problem, she thinks. He rubs his thumb up and down the cup, scrabbling at the drip of coffee.

'So I thought you might like a transfer.'

'Where to?'

He coughs slightly. 'With your stats background, I thought, maybe, Finance.'

'Finance.' She repeats dully. 'With Magnus?'

He nods. Magnus Miller is the famously delusional head of the Finance Department. He got his job claiming an MBA only to be outed as a liar at a networking event with his supposed alumni. He still has the degree on his business card, though. Isabelle feels chilled at the idea of being cut off from her supply of intoxication.

'I spoke with him earlier about you and your qualifications and he has some very interesting work you could get involved in.'

'Like what?'

'They're revising all the KPIs for the whole department. Completely gutting all the outputs-based stuff and bringing in outcomes-based management.'

'Sounds fascinating.'

'It is,' he says, then realises she is being sarcastic. 'I think it's a good opportunity for you,' he says quietly.

Isabelle circles her tea around her cup with the spoon, as if she can divine something from the swirling leaves that escaped the strainer.

'Magnus is a member of the board. He was there in the boardroom that day I did my presentation. Or tried to.'

'Was he? I'd forgotten.'

'No, you haven't. He was there and he saw me. And he would've been there when "the incident", as you like to call it, was discussed. There's no way on God's green earth he would think I was an asset to his team. Magnus is crazy, but he's not that crazy.' Isabelle looks up from her tea, suddenly understanding the truth of it. 'You asked him to take me. As a favour.'

'Isabelle.' Jack says it again: 'Isabelle.' There is a pleading note in his voice, a cry for clemency. He looks to her to extricate him from this thing for which they don't have a name. He wants her to collect the fizzing atoms between them and squash them back into a manageable shape. A collegial shape. The evolutionary moment Isabelle has been sitting astride is tapering to its apex.

'I don't want to be transferred.'

'Granted Magnus isn't perfect, but it would get you out of a rut.'

'You mean it would get me away. From you.'

'Yes,' he says, dropping his eyes.

The atoms effervesce, sensing their moment is near.

Isabelle has a curious feeling, as if she doesn't need her skin any more, as if she has run into everything else that is. She is indistinct from sky and sea and rock. Jack runs his trembling hand across his forehead.

'It's all right.'

'In what possible way is it all right?' he speaks low and soft. 'I'm your boss. I'm a married man. I'm not perfect, but I do love my wife.'

Isabelle does not want to think about Kate. She lifts her arm and places her fingers lightly on Jack's wrist. She grazes his forearm with her fingernails. His skin

81

is hot. Isabelle can feel his high-velocity pulse through his brown skin and wiry hair. He watches the spiralling motion of her nails on his arm. His phone rings. He keeps his wrist, the one she is stroking, resolutely still and picks up the phone with his other hand.

'Jack Willoughby.'

Immediately Isabelle can tell that it is Kate on the line. Jack twists in his chair, away from her. He slides his wrist – the one she has been caressing – across the table and secretes his arm in his lap. He looks at his big hand, flexing and unflexing it. Can he still feel her there? Does Karl retain a cellular memory of her that Cindy has not erased?

'How are you?' Jack's voice is conscious, strained.

Isabelle watches him intently, feeling a strange mixture of emotions, at once pitying and territorial, aroused and ashamed.

Jack keeps his eyes resolutely on the ground. A pink flush spreads across his cheeks and ears. 'Oh, just meeting with a colleague…No…No one you know… Sure, we can do that. What time? Uh-huh…Do you need me to pick anything up on the way home…Wine? Okay, then. I love you too, honey. Bye.'

He taps his phone and bores his eyes into the ground. 'I can't do this.'

But you will. You must. I need this.

'We should go,' Jack says. His hand continues to spasm and the spot on the floor retains its fascination for him. Isabelle looks down at it too, wondering if Jack sees a portent in the square reddish tiles. 'We should go,' he says again but still he sits there, unmoving.

Finally, Isabelle gathers up his notepad, his pen, his phone and his files and makes for the door. Outside, everything is preternaturally loud. Much louder than usual. The slam of a car door. A crying baby. Isabelle's heels on the asphalt. She feels white-fringed in the glare. After a moment Jack emerges from the cafe. He shakes himself, as if sloughing off the last ten minutes, and opens the car.

'So,' he says brightly once they're underway, 'do you have plans for tonight, Isabelle?'

'No.'

'We're having some friends from Melbourne over. He's in IT. She's a lawyer with a mining company. A ferociously bright woman. You'd like her. We've been friends since uni. Kate's cooking. It should be fun. I haven't seen them for about five years.'

'What are you doing?'

'Hmmm?' He slightly inclines his head towards her, keeping his eyes on the road. His torso is rigid.

'I said what are you doing?'

'Ummm. Just chatting.'

'We're beyond that now, don't you think?'

'I don't know what you mean.'

Isabelle feels herself diminishing under Jack's denial, feels him trying to force down her desire, leaving all those airy spaces for The Black Place to furnish.

'You've uncorked the bottle and no matter what you do the genie cannot be stuffed back inside.' *You can say 'I didn't mean it' or 'I'm sorry' but the words are a historical fact, part of the temporal fabric that cannot be unpicked. I won't let you.*

'What do you want me to do?' There is a plaintive, helpless tone in his voice that panics her. This is not the Jack she needs. The Jack she has created.

'Be real. Or be silent.'

They pull into the executive parking lot at their work. Neither one of them moves. The gulls gyre overhead.

'This is very difficult for me,' he says softly.

Isabelle tries to imagine Karl having offered Cindy this kind of platitude, but it's too diffuse, too hesitant for Karl.

'I don't know what to do,' Jack continues. 'Everything I want to do, everything my body is screaming out to do compromises every single other thing in my life. I'm not going to sit here and bullshit you about my wife not understanding me. She does. She's a lovely woman. I just…I can't explain this. I'm at a complete loss. Help me.' For the first time since his phone rang he looks into Isabelle's eyes.

For answer she dives towards him, seemingly elevated out of her seat, and circles his head with her palm. The taste of him, his saliva, hollows Isabelle out and refills her instantaneously. She is reconstituted. They pull away with difficulty, like magnets prised from a fridge door.

'Christ,' he says, glancing in the rear-view mirror.

'What is it?'

Isabelle turns to see the receding backs of two of their colleagues. 'Did they see us?'

'I don't know. Jesus Christ.'

Isabelle's newly calibrated organs taste the hot salt of him and want, want, want more. She kisses him again, slow and light.

'Isabelle. Isabelle. I really have to go.'

'Board meeting?'

'Yes.'

'Do you have my reports ready?'

He laughs, darkly. 'Come on. Let's go.'

'Wait,' Isabelle says.

'No, I really have to go.' She leans towards him and wipes her thumb along his lips.

'Lipstick.'

He rubs at his lips vigorously with the back of his hand. 'Gone?'

'Yes.'

He flicks the mirror on the visor and inspects his mouth. 'God, that's a quality pash rash.'

'Pash rash?'

'I know. It's like I'm regressing back to high school.' He surveys his chastened mouth and chin. 'I'll just say I was eating mango.' He repositions the mirror and looks at her. 'I love mangoes but they make my lips swell.'

And so they come at familiarity with the quirks of each other's bodies. A sudden, tight intimacy. They exit the car, Isabelle practically floating on air, and walk towards the building entrance. They keep a closely monitored physical distance. There is enough space between them for the entity they have conjured, that amalgam of buzzing and fizzing atoms that knows Jack's mouth swells and reddens if he eats mangoes. That knows Isabelle involuntarily sighs when someone lightly runs their tongue over the underside of her lip – a secret her body has kept from her until now.

The presence divides when they separate and becomes two identical molecules of memory and anticipation. It glides into Jack's next meeting and throws itself into the chair next to Isabelle. A tissue of fibres around her cheeks is aching from a smile she is trying to suppress. She can barely breathe for the darkening canyon between her legs. At such a moment, she can almost believe that The Black Place does not exist.

SEVEN

The humidity, unusual for Perth, is so intense you feel you need to part the air with your hands to walk through it. It is the sort of heat that plugs into your organs, draining vitality from the body. Isabelle has wound down all of her car windows in a hopeful attempt to collect the breeze. What she wants to be doing is lolling on Evan's couch watching DVDs in the chill of his air-conditioned lounge room. Instead she is forcing herself to movement and goodness. She trundles through the tip, which is not the rat's nest of steaming filth she had been expecting but a well-organised hamlet. She drives past the utes queuing for the woodchipper and around the paint-disposal unit, looking for household goods. She finds the shed – a low, squat building – and parks.

Inside the shed the air is so dense it might liquefy into rain. Isabelle's flimsy summer dress has moulded to her body. Pyramids of refuse are piled almost to the ceiling. She stands before the closest pyramid, awed by the ramshackle of discard. She reaches for the back of a chair and works it gingerly from the jumble. A girl of about eleven or twelve circles the heap. Keeping a wary eye on Isabelle, she starts pulling placard boards, window frames and wooden struts from the pile. Isabelle surveys her find: a solid mahogany chair without legs.

'What are you looking for?' the child asks her.

'I'm not entirely sure. Chairs mainly.'

'Dining or recliner?'

'Both. Either.'

The girl sighs at Isabelle's amateurism. 'Do you want the chairs for inside or outside?'

'Outside.'

'I saw some all-weather plastic ones in that pile there.' She points. 'Anything else?'

'Perhaps a table.'

'There's lots of tables. Not in the piles, though. They keep them up the back there, resting on the wall. They just don't have legs. Most of 'em, anyways.'

'Oh. Thanks'

'Anything else?'

'No, no, I think that's all.'

'Okay.'

Another child appears, evidently her younger brother. Then another. And another. They are all lank-haired, long-limbed and brown-eyed.

'What are you looking for?' Isabelle asks.

The girl mumbles something Isabelle cannot make out. 'We're getting Becca a bed,' her brother exclaims. 'A foot-on.'

'Shut up, Jai. And it's a futon.'

'I GOT ONE!'

The boys whoop and run to where a man stands holding a smooth, wooden floorboard above his head. He is grinning ecstatically, as if ascending the Tour de France podium. Becca follows slowly, her thin arms folded against her chest.

'Well done, Dave.' His wife hugs him around the waist. 'Look, kids. Halfway there.' The boys clamber over the base of a futon Dave is assembling on a patch of ground between the piles. The original slats are gone, replaced with odd assortments of boards and runners plundered from the junk heaps. Some are too long and will have to be cut back. Without a word, Becca returns to Isabelle's pile and resumes desultorily picking through it.

'Looks like your dad nearly has a full base.'

'He's not my dad,' she says crisply.

'Oh. Sorry. Very funky of you to have decided on a futon.'

Becca's expression is one of guarded curiosity, ready at a moment to harden into indifference.

'I love the Japanese aesthetic, don't you?'

'What's that when it's at home?'

'Aesthetic. It means perspective on beauty.'

'I have no idea what you're talking about,' Becca says breezily, but she doesn't move away.

'Have you seen pictures of Japanese gardens? Beautiful cherry blossoms and those small trees, bonsais I think they're called. Lovely tumbling streams and mossy rocks. Order. Simplicity. Serenity. It's a very specific style.'

'Anaesthetic?'

'Aesthetic.'

'Aesthetic.' Becca tries the word out. 'Aesthetic,' she says again, more confidently. 'What does the futon have to do with it?'

'Well, it's the Japanese version of the bed. Lower than ours with much cleaner lines. Less fuss.'

'And they're…cool?'

'Oh, very much so.'

The child looks over to where her family is hoarding boards. 'Even when the boards don't match?'

'Yes, even when the boards don't match.'

'Do you have a futon?'

'Yes,' Isabelle lies. 'It's quite similar to yours but it's a double. In jarrah. With an engraving of a dragon on the bedhead.' The vein grid on Isabelle's face grows redder with each embellishment.

'I'll show you where I saw the chairs. Come on.' Becca leads Isabelle towards a pyramid at the far end of the shed and matter-of-factly pulls three perfectly serviceable blue plastic chairs from the heap.

'Wow. Thank you.'

'That's okay.' Becca crosses her arms and considers the pile intently, scrutinising it through narrowed lids. She moves aside a bathroom mirror and the remains of a fireplace mantle, revealing the green plastic underside of a recliner. 'I'll need your help to get this out.' Together they prise the recliner from the chaos. The canvas lining is frayed at the joins and what was once a cream colour is now a rusty yellow. Becca lowers herself gingerly into the recliner then, when it holds her weight wriggles from side to side as if she might upturn it.

'Yep. This is fine. Just needs a wash.'

'It's better than fine. It's perfect.' Isabelle does a quick mental calculation. Between her haphazard collection of chairs at home and what she has found at the tip there should be enough seating. 'You're a miracle worker.'

Becca beams a frank, childish smile that shows how designed her earlier expressions were.

It saddens Isabelle to think they are necessary. 'You have an amazing eye. Have you thought about being a designer when you grow up?'

'What's one of those?'

Isabelle, not entirely certain herself, improvises. 'The people who design furniture and ornaments and decide which colours go together. They sketch out the plans and then other people build what they've designed.'

'That sounds pretty good. Making things and all that. I'd like that.'

'With your attention to detail you'd be a natural.' On impulse Isabelle bends towards the child and whispers into her ear, 'I think you're a very special little person.'

'Really?' Becca whispers back.

'Cross my heart, hope to die.'

So here it is: Isabelle's offering.

A clean expanse of concrete ringed with shining green bollards. In the centre an incinerator flue, freshly painted and soot-scoured. From the flue blooms a candy-striped umbrella dragged from the tip, the sort that sun-shy Victorian ladies perched under at the beach. It is so large it is very nearly a marquee. In the arc of its shade crowd the flowers that she thinks of as her babies. They are little troopers, these plants, standing up to the heat and waving their flowery heads at her. Some have even grown new shoots and buds since

Isabelle transplanted them here, a confidence that moves her. She talks to the plants during their twice-daily drenching before and after work, encouraging them along and praising their beauty.

She has trimmed the recliner of its frayed ends, bleached out the rust stains and sprinkled it with rose water. The milk crates now serve as table legs for a seventies-issue vinyl table. Around the setting are four tall bamboo torches bought from the hardware store. When their kerosene wicks are lit they throw a cheerful, festive light across the roof. At first, Isabelle had experimented with tea lights in paper bags. They looked beautiful ringing the rooftop, but then the flames kindled the bags and the smoke was too much. Isabelle cannot bear the smell of smoke after…

It doesn't matter. Look how lovely this is. This garden. This sanctuary. She knows it is foolish: what has she done after all but clear away cigarette ends, bottles and crude drawings for a ragtag collection of other people's cast-offs? Yet she feels buoyant and masterly because she has refused to bow to The Black Place and its wastrel energy. Because she has brought some happiness to Mrs Graham. Because she feels lusty and ripe for the first time in a long while. Isabelle does her rooftop dance, waving her arms above her head as she pivots in a circle.

EIGHT

Oh no.

Oh, please God, no.

Isabelle puts her spoon down. Slowly, silently. She stands very still, planting her weight in her feet as if she might earth herself. She splays her hands on the benchtop where she has been experimenting with a sausage roll recipe for the party. She feels the hard, tangible fact of the vinyl under her fingers. Perhaps if she is very still, very sure, The Black Place will fail to sniff her out and will sweep past. Isabelle imagines that she has locked her ribcage and must breathe without even the gentlest rise and fall of the chest. Her every follicle, every pore becomes a watchtower.

All the world's darkness is being called home, pooling in her hallway.

A faint charge of static licks the hairs at the base of her neck.

The temperature drops.

Everything quiets – the children skipping on the ground floor, the barking dogs, her neighbours' argument.

It all recedes.

There is just her, Isabelle, and The Black Place.

The effort of holding herself rigid folds in on itself, like a tremor at maximum velocity. Pins and needles prick her hands and feet. Pain radiates from her blue-turning heart. Involuntarily, her grasping lungs buckle and suck at the air.

The Black Place glides under Isabelle's skin and displaces her. Isabelle is no longer Isabelle. She is a container of despair, a repository of every free-floating grief seeking a home. The panic is as foul as it is inexplicable. It is the panic of the diver breaking the surface and turning, turning, turning to find water at every horizon, the boat gone. Of the woman who wakes in the dark to the shadow of the intruder on the bedroom wall. Isabelle's mind slips to blades, laceration, knives. Sharp edges that can part skin and leach the bilge until the world grows dim. The idea of blue steel against her skin seems suddenly, achingly beautiful. Isabelle makes a fist and views the underside of her wrist dispassionately. The veins are deep, just a faint blue tracery under her porcelain skin. The moment of contact with the blade would be climactic. Benedictory.

Her muscles bunch into autopilots, knots of un-yielding gristle that shunt her down the hallway to slam the bathroom door locked against the locked cabinet where she keeps razors and the sharpest of her kitchen knives.

Thwarted, The Black Place demands movement, height, swirling eddies of air. They rip through the flat to the landing, round the stairwell and through the door. The ledge at the north-eastern corner of the concrete expanse is the launching pad from which all the despair, all the anxiety can disintegrate on the ground below. It is a perfect sharp wedge between worlds. Isabelle wants to give herself to the dusk air, the ground and nothingness. She curls one leg over the barrier. Then the other. She is dimly aware of the slap of a skipping rope beneath her, a child chanting. Her fingers blanch against the railing under the strain of holding her to this world. The Black Place screams the sound and fury of its death song around her, willing her to release. Still she clings to the barrier.

It is gone, and Isabelle is crying.

She is too shaky to climb back over the railing safely so she just cleaves to it, hanging awkwardly. She has wet herself a little. Urine mingles with her sweat to produce a tangy, ferrous odour. The stench of The Black Place.

From below, the chant of the child skipping at number three drifts upwards.

> *Mother, mother, I am ill*
> *Call for the doctor over the hill*
> *In came the doctor*
> *In came the nurse*
> *In came the lady with the alligator purse*
> *Measles said the doctor*
> *Mumps said the nurse*
> *Nothing said the lady with the alligator purse*
> *Out goes the doctor, out goes the nurse*
> *Out goes the lady with the alligator purse.*
> *One, two, three, four...*

Isabelle concentrates on the child's counting. On eleven she hurls herself back over the railing, falling heavily onto the concrete. Isabelle imagines that she is steaming like a hot iron on damp cloth as her blood and bone reform. Then there is a tsunami of relief – a wave of analgesic flooding her body. She lies there on the concrete, crying, watching the blurry stars take up their positions in the night sky.

Isabelle's doctor says that The Black Place is actually a panic attack at full velocity. A fight or flight response so extreme that her body is literally taken hostage by adrenalin. 'Like a drug-induced psychosis. But you, Isabelle, are manufacturing the drug.' It sounds perfectly plausible. Until you experience it. How can I *make* this, she wonders?

Isabelle has her own theory. She thinks The Black Place is an ancient force that has slipped between worlds into life here, now. She imagines it – a miasma – looking for a human to inhabit to give it shape and form. Why is her body so permeable, so vulnerable?

Isabelle stays there, spread-eagled on the concrete, for a long time.

There are many dread things about The Black Place: the physical pain of the attacks, the constant fear of the next haunting, the vicious tussle to keep her purchase on her body.

But the worst thing, absolutely the worst thing is how memory-less it is. Once in possession there is no agency, no goodness, no hope and no memory of what it is to be anything other than The Black Place. No matter how many times Isabelle suffers the experience, in the moment of it, it is impossible to recollect that it has happened before and that it passes. That there are good days on the other side. It is pure, concentrated Thanatos stretching forward and backwards around her life, an unbroken, unbreakable thread.

NINE

A day passes. And another. Isabelle is under the sea of a sticky fever purchased over the pharmacy counter. Not prescription drugs, just garden-variety analgesic and Restavit tablets. She punched out a few pills, locked the rest in her cabinet and took them methodically, one after the other, to lock out the ringing phone, the fear and the impossible question of what to do next. At some point someone (Evan?) banged on her front door. Whenever wakefulness prods her she kicks away from it, plunging down, down into the blue, calm deep. Faces swim at her – Jack, Mrs Graham, Evan, Karl – but she folds back into the Lethe water and escapes them.

Isabelle wants to stay there in that blank place but bubbles of adrenalin are forcing their way through her calm. They stream to the surface of her consciousness and burst there. The bubbles co-opt other forces like hunger, her bladder and the accursed ringing phone until she surfaces. She half-rolls, half-flops out of her bed and staggers for the bathroom door that Jim forced open on her return from the chemist. Her urine, utterly corrupted by drugs and fear, smells foul. She splashes water on her face and brushes her teeth, careful not to look herself in the eyes.

There on the kitchen benchtop are the desiccated remains of her sausage roll experiment, a cluster of flies feasting on the scabrous pastry. She sweeps the rolls into the bin. *Food. I should eat.* She makes toast but her stomach rejects it, too occupied with straining pills, mucous, tears and the acrid waste product of The Black Place.

Christ, what am I going to do?

Isabelle demands that her thoughts come to order but they skitter around her skull, adhering to nothing. She tries to sequence the steps required for a script of top-flight amnesia from her doctor. First, phone the clinic and make an appointment. Isabelle tries to recall the number but the digits dissolve in her mind's eye before she can make out the threes from the eights. Phone book. Where is her phone book? The cupboard? Her dresser? She stands up to go searching for it but her head spins and she falls back onto the couch. She gives up the attempt to organise her thoughts. Perhaps it is best that she doesn't get her hands on those fatal candies.

Isabelle's mind is a complex network of one-way streets and witches' hats. As the fastidious overseer of the system, she directs thoughts about Karl and Cindy, 'the incident' and her despair at The Black Place along back roads, aware of their dim rattle but doggedly attentive to what's in front of her. But like a bankrupt state, Isabelle has no reserves to maintain the system. She can almost hear the clitter-clack collapse of her mental discipline. Suddenly unshackled, her circuits spark and fizz, unsure which forbidden zones to tear through first, which fresh tracks to explore. Images flash and fall at random in the free-for-all.

There is Evan hugging her when she had shown him her engagement ring. He had held onto her tightly and said, 'I hope you'll be happy.' He had said it so fervently that she realises now he had known it wasn't likely. Why hadn't he said anything? Would she have listened?

Cindy, wildly overdressed in a pencil skirt and chiffon blouse, determined to engage Isabelle in conversation at a soccer barbecue. She had swamped Isabelle with her overpowering jasmine scent and ceaseless small talk until Isabelle found herself backed up against the wall near the men's toilet.

Evan bringing his new girlfriend over for dinner, an earnest, socially awkward churchgoer named Lea.

'Lea. Like Leaf but the "f" is silent,' she had said when introduced, and then collapsed into ringing, screechy laughter. 'You hear my joke, Evan? Lea, like Leaf but the "f" is silent.' Evan had smiled and given a brief nod. The muscles that connect his arrow-sharp cheekbones to his ears twitched slightly. That one subtle gesture was enough to tell Isabelle that Leaf-but-the-'f'-is-silent wouldn't be around for long. Unseen by Evan or Lea, Karl had made an 'L' with his thumb and index finger and stamped it to his forehead.

And Karl.

Of course Karl.

It was Karl who had set her on the path of what Jack euphemistically calls 'the incident'. 'You've got to send signals,' Karl had been telling her, 'that you're ready for the next step.' Carol Anne had called in sick on the day of a board meeting and her underling was on a training course. Ready or not, Isabelle had sashayed into Jack's office and offered herself as a replacement executive officer. Ambushed, Jack agreed, putting aside his reservations about Isabelle's inexplicable amount of sick leave. She had the carefully typed notes on his desk that very afternoon, surprising him with her diligence. Which led to Jack's invitation to remain on the project full-time.

Blooming under Jack's sunny approval, Isabelle tracked down elusive reports, disinterred data that had long been given up for dead, and marshalled the important people into the right meetings. Karl was almost bursting with pride and satisfaction. He had been promoted several times since they had left the graduate program where they met. Now, Isabelle felt worthy of him. As if she were fulfilling part of an unstated bargain. Energy zapped through her. Not the dark, draining current that sometimes overturned her but something expansive and white. As if she were mainlining sunshine.

A thought began to form in her mind, just a low, throbbing pulse at first but becoming more and more distinct as the days passed. Little by little, Isabelle began to admit the possibility that The Black Place, which had haunted her since high school, had been exorcised. Perhaps in Karl's love and her nascent self-belief she had found forces powerful enough to overthrow it.

Four months after joining the team, Jack asked Isabelle to brief the board on their progress. Isabelle gave a muted, modest response to keep from ruffling

Carol Anne, but inside she was dancing. She laughed at herself. It wasn't like she was rescuing children from floodwaters or developing a cancer vaccine, but she was doing her small part well and the pleasure this brought her was immense. Isabelle approached the board meeting with the meticulous planning most people reserve for a wedding. She typed out what she intended to say and practised it at home in front of the mirror until she could deliver it without notes and with a plausible air of spontaneity. She and Karl bent over sheets of butcher's paper predicting the questions she was likely to be asked. She felt silly, but Karl was earnest. 'You can't be overly prepared for this. This is the kind of exposure most people would kill for. You've got to maximise it.' He was all about maximising things.

Karl splurged on a new suit for her. It was sharp and elegant and she felt ten points smarter just putting it on. She paraded up and down their living room in the suit. 'The key is strategic alignment,' she told Karl, mimicking Jack's gestures. 'We'll blue-sky the vision then run it up the flagpole before synergising the available opportunities.'

'I'll synergise you,' Karl laughed. Then he turned suddenly serious. 'The suit's missing something.'

'Yes, about half a metre of material. Look how tight it is across my butt.'

'Your butt is amazing. It's not that. It just needs some sparkle.'

He produced a small blue box from his pocket. 'It twinkled at me when I walked past the store,' he said as he threaded the ring onto her finger. 'Marry me.'

Isabelle held her hand to her throat, overcome. The glacial light from the diamond accentuated the faint white pinstripe running through the black material of her suit. They made love on the kitchen table, Isabelle's new skirt hitched up around her waist.

Two weeks later she rode the lift to the executive floor, having stopped in the bathroom to straighten her collar and her lipstick. A message beeped through on her phone from Karl: 'Knock em dead baby xo.' Carol Anne came out of the boardroom to meet her. Isabelle took a seat at the enormous marble table and placed her supporting charts and graphs in front of her. Jack gave her a conspiratorial wink.

'Gentlemen, this is Isabelle Northwell, my data analyst. Isabelle has been taken offline for the last few months to work on the project and has unearthed some preliminary results that I think you'll find very interesting. Over to you, Isabelle.'

'Thank you, Jack. Good morning, gentlemen.' She paused and gave them a wide smile. 'As you know, the stakeholder project has been running for eight months now and we're in a position to make a preliminary assessment of its effectiveness.'

The x-axis on the graph facing Isabelle curved sharply upwards, bending the paper. She blinked and the graph settled flat on the page.

'We're principally concerned with stakeholder perceptions of our fidelity to the core strategies, to which end we developed a written survey.' Isabelle held the survey up for the board to see, trying to ignore the fact that sound was sucking in and out of the room.

'The key message is…is clearly…that…'

Suddenly the blue and red stripes on the tie of the gentleman sitting opposite zoomed large and small with the sound of her voice tuning in, tuning out.

Carol Anne placed a hand on Isabelle's shoulder. 'Isabelle, are you all right?'

'Yes, excuse me a moment. I just need some water.' She spilt a little carrying the glass to her lips, light from her ring dancing on her trembling hand. She sensed the men's discomfort but won them back with another smile and a slight tilt of her head.

'Excuse me. As I was saying, the striking finding from the survey is that our stakeholders think we need to stick closer to the reform agenda and steer clear of…'

The urge to vomit choked the rest of Isabelle's sentence. The room glittered and she felt as if the invisible bonds that held her body and soul together were peeling away. She closed her hand on the water glass to still the urge to throw it high in the air. She felt compelled to laugh, to shriek, to gallivant about the room in a freakish corporate bacchanal. How she held her seat she doesn't know. She never knows at such times.

'I'm sorry,' she stammered, 'I'm not feeling well. Would you excuse me?'

Isabelle left the room walking heel-toe, heel-toe in a determined, upright fashion. Once the door closed behind her she ran down the corridor and into the lift. When the building was built there had been no need for a ladies' toilet on the executive floor. Isabelle got out at the next floor down and hurried for the bathroom. By the time she got there the tears were already running hot and unstoppable down her face. She locked herself in a cubicle, closed the toilet lid and sat down with her head in her hands, sobbing. She tried to imagine that she was filling with orange light from her toes, the way the doctor had taught her, but her mind was rushing in and out like the sea at the shore. She had wanted, she had so wanted, to pull this off. For Karl to be proud of her. To be proud of herself. The first thing was to regulate her breathing. She looked at the second hand on her watch. In, two, three, four. Out, two, three, four. Her lungs fought back, wanting more air.

The bathroom door opened.

'Isabelle, is that you? It's me, Carol Anne.'

For a moment Isabelle remained silent, then said, 'I'm in here.'

'Can I get you anything? Would you like some water or aspirin?'

'No, I just need a minute.'

Isabelle waited to see if Carol Anne would go away but she could feel her out there, hovering.

'Do you need me to call a doctor?'

'No, I'm all right.'

Isabelle stood up and quietly opened the toilet lid. She made some convincing retching noises then flushed the toilet. She unlocked the cubicle and tottered out, wiping her mouth with her hand.

'God, you look awful.'

It was true. Isabelle's face was shiny with sweat. Mascara had pooled along her cheeks like some strange pox. Visible only to herself were the bulging seams of her body as The Black Place nestled after its lengthy absence. A panic attack was far from the worst The Black Place could do. But it was enough.

'Come on, let's get you to the sick room. Do you think you can make it there without vomiting?'

Isabelle nodded. Carol Anne took Isabelle's elbow and guided her from the bathroom. There in the corridor was Jack, waiting. The concern on his face doubled Isabelle's shame. She had failed Jack. Jack, who had singled her out from the horde of slogging, jostling junior policy analysts and would now have some explaining to do. How would Karl react? She began twisting the ring back and forth on her finger.

'What's wrong, love?' Jack asked in a kindly voice.

'Gastro. Food poisoning, I think.'

'She's been vomiting fit to burst,' said Carol Anne.

'I'll drive you home, if you like,' offered Jack.

'What about the board?'

'They can wait. They're taking a break now anyway. It's all right, come on.'

As ill luck would have it, they shared the lift with the board members making their way down to the coffee shop. Isabelle stood there in all her snotty, panda-eyed glory and felt she would combust with shame. She caught Magnus Miller, the crazy head of Finance, give Jack a wink and she knew exactly what that wink was meant to convey. *Jack, you old dog. Always a sucker for a pretty little thing in a suit. No matter how inept she is.*

Jack murmured encouraging things on the drive to Isabelle's townhouse, offering to stop at a chemist or duck into the supermarket if she needed anything. He pulled into the visitor's spot at her complex. They listened to the engine tick down. Tap, tap, tap, circle went Jack's finger on the steering wheel.

'Do you want to talk about it?'

'No.'

'Would you like me to come in with you? Is there someone you can call?'

'I'll be fine.'

Isabelle returned to work after three months. Jack told everyone she had suffered a vicious case of gastro-enteritis. It was a plausible reason for her thin frame and pallor. 'My finger got too thin for it,' she said when asked where her engagement ring was, too stricken to admit that she had dazedly handed it back to Karl when he had moved out. It was weeks before she could tell anyone the relationship was over.

There was a get-well card during her absence and a welcome-back afternoon tea on her return. Carol Anne baked a sponge cake that Isabelle dutifully spooned to her mouth even though she wanted to choke on it. To be fair, Carol Anne did refrain from preening over the fact that the project had been reassigned to her. 'Just until you get back on top of things,' Jack had said to Isabelle. They both knew he was lying.

Some atavistic urge is drawing Isabelle to the rooftop. She needs to see it stripped of her illusions. Isabelle hugs her knees to her chest and rocks back and forth until she has enough momentum to swing into a sitting position. Crosses sparkle across her vision, evaporating when she tries to catch them. When the last of the crosses dissolves she takes a series of deep breaths. She visualises the cool orange light pouring through her ankles and filling her calves. When she is brimful of orange she slips on her thongs, leaves her flat and walks steadily to the stairwell.

She pushes open the creaking door and steps out into the bouncing sunlight. The light makes everything slightly stark and unreal. Unease tremors through her. She hurries towards the incinerator and steadies herself against it. Then she forces herself to look – to really look – at the rooftop. It has magnified since she was forced up here by The Black Place. Looking at the tables and chairs floating in the glare it seems to her they only emphasise the vast, flat expanse of rooftop. In a subconscious effort to swallow some of the space she had placed the chairs wide apart – too wide for comfortable conversation. There are nowhere near enough plants to create the green oasis she had seen in her head and convinced herself she had created. Instead the effect is lonely. Lonely and pathetic. Her scrubbing and painting has effaced the shabbiness, yes, but it has replaced it with an antiseptic quality. Everything is *bright, bright, bright!* in the glare. Shiny railings. Gleaming bollards. Sunlight tripping off the scrupulously clean roof. Isabelle regrets covering the crude engravings – at least they gave the rooftop a character, a sense that something human was here.

It shimmers like a mirage. Like medical equipment. The instinct is to run from it and take refuge in the shade of the stairwell. The bamboo torches border on frightening – more light, more heat. But most pathetic of all are her little plants. They seem to her to be making a valiant effort. She has the feeling that if she turns her back they will let out a collective sigh and wilt. They are straining to bring oxygen and colour and verdure to the blankness, but like everything else she has painstakingly created they serve only to make the rooftop blanker.

She feels dumbstruck.

And she feels scared.

There is something unsettling about the scene. Something out of kilter. She imagines her guests trooping up the stairwell, noisy and high-spirited. She listens to the dissipating bustle as people seat themselves. *Soooooo. Here we all are.* Then the inevitable sloth that comes with heat. An awkward sipping of drinks to cover the silence. An attempt at pleasantries that desiccate and crumble in the dry air. And quietly, creepingly, a feeling of menace. The spaces between the chairs growing wider. Voices too low to bridge the gap. Each of them falling into their own expanding universe.

I haven't reclaimed the rooftop from The Black Place. I have ceded it entirely.

Isabelle may as well have strung up garlic bulbs at the mouth of hell and tried to douse the flames with shot glasses of holy water. Now, with a casual yawn, The Black Place swallows Isabelle, her plants, the torches and the polish, and belches the stench of what it really is. What it will always be. One of Jim's phrases comes to Isabelle: *Polish a turd.* She has polished a turd. She has stuck a shiny red bow on a steaming turd and thereby illustrated how immutably a turd it is.

The party cannot go ahead. She couldn't bear to offer her guests as sacrifice to a bloodthirsty God. Isabelle walks slowly to the chair in the most shade and flops into it. She covers her eyes with her hands and cries. Or tries to. But there is something, in retrospect, so inevitable about this moment of defeat that she cannot summon the surprise and disappointment necessary for tears. *Extravagant fictions*, she thinks, *my curse is extravagant fictions*. The signs don't hold. Work, Karl, the rooftop, goodness…they fall away, fall away.

'Belle?' Evan shouts from the stairwell. She hears the pelt of his feet on the hateful ground. He crouches down next to her. 'What the hell's going on? I've been trying to get in touch with you for days.'

'Evan,' she says softly.

He drags a chair – one of the ridiculously distant chairs – and sits next to her, drawing his face towards hers. Aware that a vestige of vomit and bed-sweat clings to her, she flinches and looks away.

'You look bloody awful.'

'Charmer, you,' she says ruefully.

She feels him scrutinising her as she tries to keep her face averted. He reaches for her cheek and gently turns her to face him.

'Have you been on a bender?'

Isabelle cannot help but laugh. 'Oh yeah. I've been having a whale of a time. Dancing on tables. Snorting coke. You shoulda been there.'

'Can we drop the flippancy? I'm really worried about you.'

'No need to worry. We'll rebuild her. Faster, stronger —'

'Enough, okay? Enough. You disappear for days. I don't know where you are. You don't return my calls. You don't get to joke about this. Not with me.'

'But no one else appreciates my humour.'

'Yeah, because finding you blue and unconscious on the floor, that really brought the house down. Good times.'

There's a second after a lightning strike when everything strobes, as if the trees and the roofs and the outline of the hills cannot withstand the illumination and might break apart. Evan has spoken the thing they are careful to avoid, kicked up the leaves and debris they've papered over the ravine, and pointed to the pile of hurt and fear she has forced him to sweep there. His breath comes ragged and sharp. Unaware that she is doing it, Isabelle runs a tentative hand over the arch of her foot. From somewhere she smells smoke.

'Have you ever played what happened from my perspective?'

'Please. Please, I can't do this now, Evan. Not now.'

But Evan doesn't hear her. Won't hear her. What had she said to Jack? *You've uncorked the bottle now and the genie cannot be stuffed inside.*

'I found you.' He waits for the words to impress themselves on the air. 'I. Found. You. Do you know what that was like? You were curled up on the floor and you had your fist to your mouth in the way babies do when they're chewing on their knuckles. You were breathing. But the breaths were far apart. Like it was an afterthought. You'd gone blue around the lips and your chin. I didn't even think it was possible for a human being to go blue. But they can.'

'I'm sorry,' she whispers but he waves it away.

He's compelled now to get it out. To lay it all out in front of her and force her to look, to really look, at what she has cost him. 'Don't you think it's weird that I knew? I mean, I didn't really know. When you called and said you were bailing on the movie because you wanted to check out some apartments I thought that was fair enough. I knew you were desperate to get out of the place you shared with Karl. There was nothing suspicious in your voice. No meaningful goodbyes. But all through soccer training I felt weird. Like there was something I'd forgotten. We were doing the warm-up jog and I remember running through what I'd done as I left the house. Had I left the stove on? Forgotten my keys? I even,' here he gives a bitter little laugh, 'thought maybe I'd forgotten my undies and the mouse was out of the house, so to speak. I pretended to be readjusting my waistband just to check. After training I told myself I was driving home but almost without knowing it I turned off to go to yours. I stood out the front of your door thinking, "What the fuck am I doing here? She's out looking at rentals. This is seriously weird behaviour." So I open the door and there you are. Blue and going bluer and all those damn pills in the bowl. I shoved a couple of the tabs into my pocket, picked you up… and that's the last thing I remember till a few hours later. I don't remember a single fucking thing about getting you from your place to the hospital. For a million bucks I couldn't tell you what roads I took or what I said to the doctors when I got there. Don't you think that's weird?'

'Oh, Evan.' Isabelle wipes away a tear with the heel of her hand.

'But I remember the colour of the pills. I remember they were in a blue ceramic bowl. And I remember that you were drinking cranberry juice straight from the bottle.'

Evan has protected her from these details until now. Before she left the hospital he had come over and cleaned up. He had done a covert sweep through her house, too. All the medication he had been able to find he had thrown out. Even her Panadol and Naprogesic. At the time she had felt like pointing out to him that replacing the pills was a fairly easy business with all the scripts she had. But as it happened she hadn't taken another pill until the latest episode. And even then not prescription drugs. Not *real* drugs.

'You ended up in hospital after Karl left,' Evan says quietly, so quietly that she struggles to hear him. 'Imagine what I thought when I told you he was engaged and then I couldn't find you.'

'Oh God, I'm such a scumbag. I didn't think. I just didn't think.'

Evan runs his fingers over his temples, eyes closed. He looks nearly as bad as she does.

'I really am sorry,' she whispers.

'I hate that Karl has this power over you. I hate it and I don't get it. You're such a smart woman and he's such a douche.'

'It's not Karl. There are bigger things than Karl, although he doesn't help. There's...there's a lot of other stuff going on. Sometimes it just gets too big for me and I have to bunker down for a while.'

'I wish you had more confidence in me.'

'I have every confidence in you,' she says, shocked. And it's true. She does. Evan sits so high in her estimation he's barely human any more.

'You have no confidence in me as a friend. A close friend. You'd rather sit up here on a rooftop howling to yourself than call me and talk to me.'

'It's not easy to explain.'

'Try me. I'm a virgin with a raging sex drive, a science degree and a belief in the big guy upstairs. I think I can cope with complexity.'

Isabelle looks out over the rooftop, at the plants she and Evan potted, at the scrubbed chairs and painted flue. How can she make sense of it all to someone else?

'Something happened up here. On the rooftop. Something bad.'

'To you?'

'Yes.'

The fatigue in Evan's eyes holds for a second then a rage she has never seen before creeps up through his iris and elbows his pupils wide apart. 'Someone hurt you?' He speaks with forced calm. 'Up here on the rooftop? Can you tell me what happened?'

Isabelle shakes her head, at a loss as to how to describe The Black Place and what it does to her without sounding completely mad. *Perhaps*, she thinks, *I am completely mad.*

'Why are you protecting him?' Evan's voice cracks under the strain of maintaining a calm he doesn't feel. 'Who was it? That's it. We're going to the police. Right now.' He stands up from his chair, clenching and unclenching his fist. It suddenly strikes Isabelle how *big* Evan is, like he's materialised in his true form.

114

'It's not like that. It's nothing I can report.'

She can almost smell the violence in his blood. Only a desperate self-control stops him from picking up one of the odd assortment of table legs and smashing it against the concrete until it splinters into dust. She has never seen him so animal, so brutal.

'Women often think that but the law's changed. It's much more supportive of victims than it used to be. There are specialist units for violence against women. They'll know what to do and you know I'll support you. Anything you need I'll do. For as long as it takes.' He pauses, breathing in and out. She can tell that he is counting his breaths. 'But I want to know who he is.'

Isabelle shakes her head.

'Oh Christ,' the blood drains from his face. 'Oh Christ in heaven, it was Karl, wasn't it?'

'No, Evan, no.'

'I'll kill him. I'll fucking kill him.'

'No. Stop.' Isabelle stands up to still his hands but the motion makes her dizzy. She paws at the air as if trying to get a hold on something. Evan holds her by the elbows, steadying her. She can feel the hot tremble of his fury through her cartilage.

'It's not like that. No one's tried to hurt me. Not Karl. Not anyone. It was…' She stops, unsure how to continue. 'Nothing human.'

Evan stands quite motionless, still holding onto her. 'Go on.'

'I wanted to take this place back. To claim it for myself. That's why I've spent so much time up here. The plants and the painting and the cleaning. It's like

I've been trying to make something beautiful. Do something good. That's why I wanted to have the party.'

'Australia Day?'

'Yes.'

'So what happened?'

'It's not beautiful, Evan. It's nothing like I pictured it in my head. It's just barren. Barren and antiseptic and ugly and…and…not good. I feel defeated. And I feel sick, like I've been tortured. I'm exhausted.'

Evan listens intently, as if he is trying to dig into her words and find their centre. Then he drops her elbows, turns and begins slowly, carefully, walking the perimeter of the rooftop as if he is mapping it out. At the north-eastern corner he reaches out and touches the railing with his fingertips. He immediately retracts them then keeps walking, heel to toe, until he has marched the entire circumference. Isabelle likes the idea of a trace element of Evan shining at every sentry point.

She has a dim sense that she should be worried about what he makes of all of this. Does he think she has cracked up? Or started dabbling in occultist things like divining negative auras and spiritual space-cleansing? The invitations have all been sent. Everyone in the apartment block knows about the party. Tomorrow Isabelle will begin issuing her apologies, bad liar or no.

She thinks of Jack, meditating on his face, his hands, his watermelon and cinnamon smell. But she can conjure up no more than an echo of desire. Before she can stop him, Evan has folded her in his arms. He gives her no room to pull away – not that she has the strength to. 'Whatever you need, Belle, I will do. Anything. But right now I want you to come with me.'

'I can't. Please just leave me be. That's what I need right now.'

'I need you to trust me. Give in to me. Just this once. Please.'

How can she refuse him after what she has put him through? She doesn't say anything but lets herself go limp. Sensing her complaisance he leads her along the roof and holds open the door to the stairwell. They pass the landing and keep going to the ground floor. Still holding her hand, Evan leads her past Mrs Graham's apartment and to his car. He opens the door for her.

'Where are we going?'

'Just hop in.' Too drained to resist, she does as he asks. They turn out of the car park and head west. Isabelle rests her forehead on the window. Evan doesn't try to make conversation, he just drives. Dazed, she stares out of the window. She didn't think it was possible for her to feel worse, but she does. She has maintained a trenchant silence about the hospital, refusing to discuss it no matter how gently Evan has tried to press her. No matter how much he had needed to talk about it. She had given her word that she would never do such a thing again and begged his silence on the subject. She turns from the window and watches Evan as he drives. His usual calm assurance is frayed but she can tell that he is unburdened. Lighter. She puts a hand on his leg and rests it there.

'I don't know what I'd do without you, Evan. I really don't. I love you to pieces.'

'Ditto.'

They drive past the university, genteel and timeless, then the manicured streets of Claremont. She dozes, and when she wakes they are driving up and down rolling hills lined with tall, straight pines. A triangle of ocean appears at the rise of a hill, shining and blue. They turn left at the Ocean Beach Hotel.

There's barely an uninhabited patch of grass to be seen. Everywhere she looks there are picnickers, toddlers, and bronzed glamour girls tottering out from the pub for a cigarette on the dunes. People spill from every balcony and every retaining wall. If Isabelle wound her window down she would smell salt tang, zinc, sweat and beer. Human, social smells.

Evan drives slowly through the meandering crowds. A young, board-shorted man thumps playfully on Evan's bonnet as he walks past. He gives Evan a big, toothy grin and a thumbs-up. Evan waves. This should be happiness, right here. Glorious weather. A beach. Some beer and friends to share it with. That's the mix. The alchemy for contentment. *I'll come here*, Isabelle thinks. *When I'm back on top of things I'll come here with Evan and a picnic and I'll listen to everything he needs to tell me.*

The crowd thins out and Evan picks up speed. After a while he turns into a car park. They sit there for a moment, staring at the ocean. Evan leans across her and opens the glove compartment. He puts his wallet and sunglasses in and closes it.

'Come on.'

'Where are we going?'

'Swimming.'

'I haven't got my bathers.'

'You don't need them.'

Evan walks around the car and opens the passenger door. He half-pulls, half-carries Isabelle from her seat. 'Easy. Easy.' She swoons a little from lack of food, drug hangover and the syrupy, warm air. When she is steady he folds an arm around her waist and leads her towards a white path cut into the dune.

After a winding thirty metres or so they emerge at a wide flank of beach. Isabelle turns to look behind her. The gorse-grassed dunes rise up, blocking the road. It is hard to believe that all that revelry continues on the other side. The sand is barely footprinted. Half a dozen bodies bob gently in the blue swell. Isabelle struggles through the sand, which sucks at her feet. She looks up when Evan gently pulls her to one side to make room for a leathery older man to pass them. Her casual glance is ill prepared for his nakedness. He walks past them, unperturbed. Salt water is drying in sticky rivers across the matted hair on his chest. A roll of fat almost obscures the cold-water–shrivelled penis idling from his body. Isabelle suppresses a shocked urge to laugh.

'Don't laugh,' Evan whispers.

'I won't. It's not that it's funny. I just wasn't expecting it.'

'The first few times I came down here I was really careful to keep my eyes front and centre. You know. *Tackle alert*. But after a while I stopped caring. Now I'm just stunned by how little we are. Real human bodies clambering out of the surf. Look at them. There's something so…I don't know…'

'Tender about it?'

'Yeah. I guess you could say that. I was going to go with *pathetic*. In the true sense of the word.'

'Pathetic. Yes.' Isabelle watches the few tiny humans bobbing up and down in the limitless blue. 'That's it exactly.'

'Coming down here always puts me in charity with the human race.'

'I thought you were always in charity.'

'Well, that's where you'd be wrong. I have my dark side.' He pretends to fold himself into a cape and juts his canines over his lower lip. He chooses a spot a few metres from the shoreline and slips out of his shoes, pulls his T-shirt over his head and tugs his shorts to his ankles. He wears no underwear. Isabelle is used to seeing him in various states of undress. When they swim he wears board shorts or hugging lycra down to his calves. On their summer sleepovers he often wears nothing but his soccer shorts. But she has never seen him entirely naked. The white, upturned curve of his buttock is stark against his coffee tan. His abdominal muscles bite, V-shaped, into his groin. He has not dematerialised to his former size; she remains conscious of the sheer bulk of him.

'Come on.'

'You want me to get naked?'

'Yes. I've plotted and schemed for just this moment to get your gear off.'

Isabelle looks dubious.

'You said you'd trust me. Look,' he puts one hand over his eyes and stretches out the other, 'take my hand when you're ready. I won't peek, I promise.'

120

Isabelle kicks her ballet flats off and unties the long batik skirt folded around her waist. She draws her red T-shirt over her head and unhitches her sodden, yellowing bra. Her knickers have barely any elastic left in them and are held up by the dent in her hip and the glue of her sweat. They clump into a tight ball as she drops them on top of her other clothes. She reaches for Evan's outstretched hand and together they walk towards the breaking waves. The sunlight tingles her white breasts and buttocks. She feels innocent, untarnished. The rooftop is still with her – cavernous and desolate – but she cannot be insensate to this. The feeling of the cold water over her bare toes, her sticky hand tightly clasped in Evan's, the sheer novelty of public nakedness. Evan squeezes her hand.

'I'm going to count to five, and then you and me are going to run in and dive under the first wave. Okay?'

'No. Just give me a minute to get used to it. This water's cold.'

'The only way to get warm is to dive in and keep swimming.'

'No! Just give me a —'

'One.'

'Evan!'

'Two.' He tightens his grip on her hand and Isabelle knows he is going to tug her in with him whether she wants to or no. She emits an uncharacteristically shrill, girlish wail.

'Three.'

'No. Evan, no!' Isabelle kicks at the water as if to run away from him. But his grip is firm.

'Four.'

She braces herself.

'Five!'

He plunges forward and takes her with him. She hauls her knees out of the water and plashes her feet down. The spray on her stomach and lower back is excruciating and delicious. They take a deep, synchronised lungful of air and plunge under a wave. She feels like she has been upturned into a shaken bottle of soda water. Bubbles stream by. Somewhere in the tug of the wave Evan and Isabelle have uncoupled. They surface together and wipe the salt water from their eyes. Then both of them laugh. A chortling, gasping, five-year-old laugh, as if they have greased an ancient, primal axle of pleasure. The glare from the sun is intense. Isabelle raises her hand to shield her eyes.

'Are you still cold?'

'No.'

Evan smiles and deftly tucks himself into a somersault. The curve of his bottom waggling in the sun makes her laugh again. They swim out another ten metres to clear the break. The current is gentle and buoyant. It takes only a slight egg-beating of the legs and arms to bob like a cork. Evan flips onto his back and floats there, his eyes closed.

'How long have you been coming here?'

'A few years. It's strangely addictive.'

'To think. All this time you've had a skinny-dipping fetish I never knew about.'

Evan cups water and trickles it onto his head. 'I prefer to think of it as a baptismal fetish. I always leave feeling

122

reborn and…' he pretends to be distracted by something on the shore, 'Would you look at the norks on that?'

Isabelle splashes him then stops kicking and sinks beneath the surface, exhaling bubbles until her toes find the coarse sand. Her hair floats around her like sea-weed in the current. How she would like to stay there, cocooned in the gentle water.

She drifts reluctantly back to the surface, emerging into a shrillness that takes her a microsecond to process as sound. Evan is quicker to respond. He tucks his knees quickly to his abdomen and shoots into the vertical.

'Go, Belle. Go!'

'What?'

'Shark alarm.'

Before she can process these words into fear or surprise she is freestyling for the shore. Her natural communion with the water finds an even deeper intimacy as she speeds and decelerates to catch the waves at her back. She keeps her eyes closed under the water. Whatever is beneath or behind her, she has no wish to see it. After exhausting the momentum of each wave she quickly raises her head and opens her eyes to be sure that she is tracking in a line to the shore. She pounds her legs and arms against each outward drag of the current, hauling against the undertow. She is all rush and vitals, as if her heart is pumping pure espresso.

The siren call is a two-second crescendo on endless repeat. It starts on a down note and expands to an unbearable pitch. The sound travels underwater, waves within the waves. Through the swirl of sound and adrenalin and the thrashing of her limbs, Isabelle tries to get a feel for where Evan is. In all likelihood, behind her. The next time she jerks her head above the water, only metres from the shore, she looks for other swimmers hauling themselves out of the surf. An inconvenient fact telegraphs across her head: most shark attacks occur in one metre of water or less. *I'll be naked. Naked fish dinner. How bloody undignified.*

Isabelle kicks from the frothing surf. As soon as dry sand crumbles beneath her toes she turns to look for Evan. Around her the solitary instinct of the nude bather has been forgotten in the collective panic. Some people have retrieved articles of clothing or towels but most stand around in alarmed nakedness. Orange-capped lifeguards attend to an older swimmer in respiratory distress. A zodiac skids across the water, harrying the fish from the beach.

'Belle.' Evan is beside her. She throws herself at him and they stand in a tight embrace. The thud of his heart in his chest is echoed in the pump and roar of Isabelle's own body. Her heart is at maximum throttle, practically high-fiving his. Adrenalin has cleared her blood to the sides of her veins. Isabelle has to grip her wrist with her middle finger and thumb to keep her grip around Evan's wide, slippery back. Abruptly, the siren ceases. Evan and Isabelle still cling together. The pulse in her stomach appears to have knotted into a tight, hot cordon of muscle that feels like it is gouging her. With absolute astonishment Isabelle realises that the gouging is, in fact, coming from Evan.

They uncouple, springing back from one another. Evan looks stricken, as if he might die of shame.

'Evan.' But he won't hear her. He hurries to their pile of clothes, his hands crossed awkwardly across his groin. He tugs on his shorts. Isabelle follows him, utterly mortified for him but also tongue-tied by his childish response. 'Evan, wait for me.'

'Are you ready to go?' His voice is forced and his face flushed an angry, splotchy red. Isabelle pulls on her coiled underwear and quickly towels herself off with her skirt before tying it around her waist. She doesn't bother with her bra. Perhaps a pair of outrageous head-lights will defuse Evan's terrible embarrassment.

'They're closing the beach.'

'How do you know?'

'They're putting up signs.'

'Oh.'

'Let's go.'

'Wait, I think we need to talk about this.' She bends down and snatches up his car keys to delay him. 'Evan, please.' He looks determinedly out at the ocean, rather than at her. 'Evan —'

'I don't want to talk about it.' His bottom lip curls outwards and wobbles slightly.

Isabelle hesitates. In all the years she and Evan have been friends she has never struggled to interpret his feelings. He's always been a tight emotional ship, steer-ing ever towards the reasonable, with only occasional digressions into frustration or annoyance. This petu-lance is on no chart she is familiar with. Before she can think of a response he turns and makes for the path through the dunes. She calls after him, but he doesn't turn around. She trudges up the hill to where he waits for her by the car, pretending to study the unfolding drama. A helicopter whirs overhead, pursuing the shark. News reporters are assembling and the panic is morphing into the excitement of unexpected celebrity.

'It really doesn't matter,' Isabelle says nonchalantly as she hands him the keys. 'I'm not remotely offended or construing meaning of any kind out of it. Adrenalin does strange things to the body.'

He nods briefly. 'Mmm hmmm.'

'Evan, please. Why are we making an issue of this?'

'Can we just drop it?'

'Of course. Consider it dropped. But —'

'I want you to go ahead and have the party.' He speaks to the ocean rather than to her.

'What? Why? The party's got nothing to do with this.'

'I want you to have the party that you'd planned. And I want to come.' Still he doesn't look at her.

'I can't.'

The seismic shifts in their conversation – in the whole day – are making her dizzy. *How did we leap from awkward erection to reinstating the party?* Evan's bargain is clear, though unstated: they can move on from this awkwardness only if she backs down on the rooftop. It is an underhanded trick and she is shocked that he – whom she has always thought scrupulously ethical – should stoop to it. One of them must cede power for equilibrium to be restored.

'Okay. Okay, I'll have the party.'

He looks at her, some of the redness gone from his face. 'Good. That's good. One other thing.'

'What's that?'

'Promise me you won't go up to the rooftop until I come to collect you for the party.'

'What? Why?'

'Just promise me.'

'Fine. All right.'

They drive home in silence.

TEN

Jack will probably be astonished to receive a seemly analysis of the day's transactions, but Isabelle is too numb for satire. She has chewed through the emotional tasting plate so fast over the last few days that she is stuffed full. She adds a trend line to a graph and suddenly there is order from chaos. Jack catches sight of her from his office and leaps from his chair. He bounds out of his door and is pelting towards her when propriety lassoes his instinct. He turns sharply and collides with Carol Anne's desk.

'Good God, Jack, what is it?'

'It's just occurred to me that we didn't send out the action items from the ministerial meeting on Tuesday. The board will be sweating on them.'

'I've done it, Jack, remember? They went out two days ago.'

'Did you? Oh yes, that's right.' He affects relief. 'You're too efficient. I should know better than to doubt you.' Carol Anne preens and gives her P3 thumbs up. Having bought off the guard dog with a sticky treat, Jack ambles to Isabelle's desk.

'Isabelle. Nice to have you back.'

'Thank you. It's good to be back.'

He settles himself on the edge of her desk and leans towards her. 'Are you all right? I've been worried.'

'I'm okay.'

He quickly scans the office and then says in a low voice, 'You didn't return my calls.'

'I'm sorry. I just wasn't well enough to.'

'Yes, I told everyone you'd called in sick. Was it… you know…*that issue*…that you have?'

A cloud passes across her face. She doesn't answer.

Jack stands up from the desk and pulls a chair over as if to read from Isabelle's computer screen. 'This is novel,' he says, gesturing to her perfectly orderly charts.

'I like to keep you on your toes.'

'That's not where I want you to keep me,' he whispers. Leaning further towards Isabelle he murmurs, 'I missed you.' Immediately the scent of him floods her hollows and fills her up, as she had hoped it would.

'I missed you too.'

'Can I see you now?' His soft tones lick all the follicles along her spine and neck. She slips her hand under the desk and squeezes his large, warm hand.

'Right, then,' he says in a louder voice. 'Let's go through this report. Meeting room in five minutes?'

'No problem.'

The lift is crowded so Isabelle can lean into Jack with impunity, pressing her hip against him. She craves the warmth of him, the smell of him. Now that the rooftop has deserted her, Jack is the entirety of the anti–Black Place. The heat between them suffuses her cells, and for a brief interlude of forgetfulness pushes everything else away. *Oh, Jack. Strong, scented, earthbound Jack.* The lift opens and they walk to the meeting room, which is in use.

'Bugger. How about we go grab a coffee somewhere since all the rooms are booked out?'

'Good idea.'

They walk out to the car park, saying little and keeping their distance. As soon as they are in the car, Jack turns to her. He watches her intently.

'Oh, Isabelle, Isabelle.'

'Not here,' she days. 'Drive.'

The hybrid silently shifts into gear and they glide out of the complex. 'Keep driving,' she says.

'Where to?'

'Melbourne. Drive to Melbourne.'

'No, no,' he says. 'South. Let's go south. Let's make love among vineyards.'

'Lazy days in the sun. Naked. Drinking wine. Swimming in the ocean. Licking the salt from each other's bodies.'

'I know a great place in Margaret River. A beautiful studio apartment right on the beach. When the sun sets it feels like the horizon is at your window. They bring dinner to the apartment. Crayfish. Champagne on ice.'

'Perfection. Let's go there. Just drive. Don't stop till we get there.'

'Oh, Isabelle. I wish we could.'

'Why can't we? I'm ready. Go to my house so I can pick up a few things. We can make the booking from there.'

'You sound serious.'

'I'm completely serious.' She swivels in her seat to face him. 'How often in your life have you done what you want to do without reference to anybody else? Just said, "*Fuck it*, this is what I want and I'm going to have it"?'

'Isabelle. Isabelle. I can't.'

'Give me one good reason why not.'

'Only one? Work. I'm expected at meetings. I have deadlines.'

'Do you really believe that the world will stop if you take a few days off?'

'No. But without notice. And if you're not there too. It might raise suspicion.'

'Who cares? Let them think what they like.'

'And I have commitments. Obligations.'

Unable to ignore her any longer, Isabelle says, 'You mean Kate. Your wife.'

He glances briefly out the driver's window. 'Yes,' he says softly. 'Yes.'

'I think...I think that Kate is separate to us. Distinct. You have your life with your wife. I don't want to intrude on that. I won't intrude on that. But this, *this* – whatever it is between us – it deserves four days out of your whole life. Do you want to turn your back on it and always wonder?'

Jack is silent for a moment. 'It wouldn't be easy. Organising four days away.'

'I know. But surely you can figure something out. You're a sovereign being, aren't you?'

'A sovereign being.' He repeats the words slowly and softly. 'A sovereign being,' he murmurs again, as if much struck with the phrase. 'Well,' he says with

131

affected jocularity, pulling into the side street near the Coode Street Cafe. 'It's not quite Margaret River but they do great coffee.'

'Wonderful,' Isabelle says flatly.

'Be reasonable. What do you expect me to do?'

She feels like she is falling down a well, further and further from the place she wants to be and the man she wants to be there with. 'I expect…I expect you to honour this God-given thing between us.' She feels her way around her words carefully, scrabbling upwards. 'To do otherwise would just be cowardly. And all because of stupid convention. "Oh, what will the neighbours say?" It's sickening.'

Isabelle sweeps out of the car and imperiously slams the door. Jack shuffles out after her, though she doesn't turn to see it. The idea of the two of them locked on one another in that apartment near the beach has colonised her mind. She needs it with a junkie's intensity. Needs it like air. She strides into the cafe, leaving him – chastised, wrong-footed – hurrying after her, scurrying for a way to even the ground between them. She doesn't wait for him to catch up but chooses a table at the rear of the cafe and stares out the window.

Jack drops his keys and wallet on the table, making a hustle and bustle of activity. Isabelle ignores him. 'Would you like peppermint tea, Isabelle?'

She nods, but other than that gives no sign of having heard him. Presently he returns from the counter. She feels the heat from his stare, but she is stoic, immovable.

'You're being unreasonable,' he whispers. 'Getting mad at me because I won't run off with you is just ridiculous.'

'I'm not mad at you.' Isabelle turns her face to the waiter as he places their drinks on the table. Just to emphasise to Jack what he has forfeited she gives the waiter her lovely smile. 'I'm disappointed. I thought I'd found a kindred spirit. Someone tough. Passionate. Elemental.' She lets her eyes melt so Jack can see how deeply she had loved that vision of him. 'I was wrong.' She blinks and a tear falls from her brimming eye. 'You're the worst of all possible worlds. A lecherous company man too weak to master his inclinations and too gutless to see them through.'

Jack flinches so violently that Isabelle knows she has located the soft, tender underbelly of his ego. 'What do you want me to do, Isabelle?'

Isabelle affects a childlike, petulant voice. *'What do you want me to do, Isabelle? What do you want me to do?'* She gambles that a lie will resurrect him in her image. 'I don't want you any more, Jack. I'm past wanting you. You know, in my fantasies you were always half-naked. In a field harvesting wheat or tacking a sail on blue seas. Self-reliant. Strong,' she laughs. 'But you're so conventional. So beige.'

'And you're cruel.'

'No. I'm not cruel. I'm just honest. It's one of my few virtues. Let's go. I can't stand to look at you.'

They drive back to the office in barbed silence. The car is barely at a stop when she gets out and strides to the entrance of the building, impervious to the questioning stares of her colleagues. She is implacable for the rest of the day, even when she completes the daily statistics report and drops it on Jack's desk. He is all false bonhomie. She senses him feeling for cracks in her demeanour so he can prise it open, but she is as hard and smooth as an oyster's roof. She leaves the office without saying goodbye to him, though she waits until he has her in full view before she turns off her workstation and glides out, saying goodbye to everyone else within earshot.

She knows she is being a bitch, but she needs him. Needs to be drunk on her idea of him. Anything to stave off The Black Place. Her vision of Jack fills her body to its limits, making it seem impossible that other forces could lodge there. So she must engineer it so that she can have him. This is the best way, instinct tells her. Goad him, trample on his ego. Flatten him down so that he has to make an eruptive gesture to win her back to him.

Anticipating how Jack will respond is a good distraction for her as she faces the other salient fact of her life: preparing for the party Evan has bargained her into. She picks up supplies on the way home, unpacks them onto her kitchen workbench then flicks on Rachmaninov. Something dramatic and portentous to inspire her. She has bought the ingredients to make quiche, sausage rolls, sandwiches, fruit salad and a pasta-and-bean salad. At least, she thinks she has. She owns only one cookbook, an old-fashioned ring-bound volume an aunt gave her for her eighteenth birthday that she has barely looked at. Her own mother loathed the necessity of providing food. 'Can't you bloody kids feed yourselves?' she had joked. Dinner in their home was a rushed interlude between school and bed, usually served to Isabelle and her brother as they sat cross-legged in the lounge room watching *Teenage Mutant Ninja Turtles*. There was never anything as grandiose as 'planning a meal'. Cupboards were raided for tins that could be served with bread – spaghetti on toast or tomato soup with a bread roll. Isabelle remembers thinking there was nothing so delicious as packet chicken schnitzel with oven chips and tomato sauce. Karl teased her for being a domestic disaster, but as he liked to cook there had been no need for her to learn.

She doesn't know if she has bought too much or too little. The right thing or the wrong thing. It all seems like a moot point now anyway. The very idea of the party paralyses her. She is scared of the rooftop. Scared of another attack. Scared that Mrs Graham has invested so much in the party that Isabelle will seem a terrible disappointment. And perhaps most of all she is scared of the growing awkwardness between her and Evan.

They have spoken on the phone a couple of times since the beach but it was strained. She could feel both of them trying not to think about his – er – mishap. But the more they don't think about it the more space it takes up, elbowing them apart. To Isabelle, Evan has always been a near-perfect being. She has never seen him be cruel or vain or belligerent. Yet he manoeuvred her into having this party, into voluntarily putting herself on that rooftop for hours at a stretch. It gives her the uneasy feeling that there is a side to him he has kept from her or to which she has been wilfully blind. She remembers that moment on the rooftop when he thought she had been raped, the fury he had tried to hide and how it seemed to transform him. Isabelle is tall herself and Evan a few inches taller again, so of course she *knows* he's tall. She had just never *seen* it. The physical reality of him. He's been a constant so constant that she has ceased to think of him. Until now.

Over the course of that day at the beach the way she thinks about him, the way she carries him in her mind's eye, teetered. It is as if she has knocked a Ming vase over in a museum and is holding her breath to see whether it is going to shatter or right itself. She pokes a finger into the packet of flour on her benchtop. *Why didn't I just buy frozen pastry?* It is as if she has a residual pulse of extravagance, a place that has not caught up to the rest of her.

'Hello. Isabelle, are you there?' Mrs Graham's cheery voice floats on the still, hot air.

'On my way,' Isabelle bellows, giving the flour one last poke. She opens the flywire to Mrs Graham, who is dressed very neatly, as usual, in a twin-set that must be far too hot. She holds two large tins in her hands. Instinctively, Isabelle takes the tins from her.

'Thank you, dear.'

Isabelle shoulders the flywire open for Mrs Graham as she steps in.

'Ahh,' Mrs Graham notices the groceries on the benchtop. 'I see I have interrupted your preparations for *la grande soirée!*'

'Not at all. My preparations are not proceeding very fast. Or at all, really.'

'Well, I promise I won't hold you up but – would you believe it – my electric tin opener has chosen this very moment to die and I haven't owned a manual one

136

for years, what with my hands being next to useless a good deal of the time.'

'Would you like me to open these for you, Mrs Graham?'

'That would be wonderful, dear. I'll be out of here in a jiffy.'

She speaks and looks her utter certainty that Isabelle is a domestic goddess interrupted in the preparation of mighty victuals. Mrs Graham's tins are name-brand pitted cherries with price tags that make Isabelle wince. She hacks at the lids with her tin opener.

'What are you making, Mrs Graham?'

'Well,' she bustles over, 'I wanted to keep it a secret, but the best laid plans…I'm making a cherry and choco-late cake for the party.'

'Good Lord, that sounds fancy. Much fancier than anything I'm planning! You really didn't need to go to all this trouble.'

'I know, dear, I know.' She reaches over and pats Isabelle's hand as she grinds through the stubborn tins. The veins crisscrossing her hands remind Isabelle of the root systems on oak trees. 'I know you are Lady Patroness and I don't want to encroach, but this was my husband's favourite. I haven't made it in years.'

'These might be a bit tricky to get back down the stairs. Shall I pour them into a bowl?'

'Please, dear. It's rather a lengthy process, this cake. I had doubts about the chocolate frosting in the heat, but Patrick – Mr Graham – did like it so.' Isabelle upturns the cherries into a clean, empty ice-cream container and presses the lid down.

'I have no doubt the cake will be a triumph. You just didn't need to go to all this trouble for me.'

'Trouble?' Mrs Graham smiles, the light from her eyes bouncing off the walls and the ceiling. 'My dear, I haven't been invited to a party in six years.'

'Well,' Isabelle says purely for something to say, because she feels humbled and grossly inadequate, 'best you put your glad rags on then.'

'Oh, of course,' Mrs Graham replies earnestly, as if aggrieved that Isabelle believes she is not approaching the party with sufficient seriousness. 'I'm setting my hair tomorrow. I shan't do anything to disgrace you, my dear.' And with that she takes the cherries and floats out of the room.

The first attempt at quiche is not a triumph. The pastry is dry and cracked but the filling is jelly-like. Isabelle eases it onto a plate and walks down to Mrs Graham's flat.

'Hello,' she yodels through her flywire.

'Hello, Isabelle. Come in.'

Mrs Graham's preparations are clearly proceeding better. Four separate slices of cake are in the process of being carefully iced.

'I've made my first experimental quiche but it's a bit squidgy. Can you try a mouthful for me and let me know if it's edible?'

Mrs Graham washes and towels her hands and takes the sloppy wedge of quiche Isabelle spoons onto her plate. Mrs Graham chews carefully. 'The filling is actually really tasty but the consistency is not quite right. More egg, I'd suggest. To bind it.'

'Why is the pastry so hard? Look at this.' Isabelle taps on the unyielding crust with a fork.

'Maybe you didn't brush enough egg and milk onto it.'

'I'm supposed to brush it with egg and milk?'

'Yes, dear. That's what makes it go brown but will stop it burning.'

'Oh.'

'And keep your oven nice and hot. That's the secret to browning.'

'Bugger. I was checking it every five minutes. All right. I'll try again. Thanks.'

'Any time, Isabelle.'

The second attempt is much more successful. The quiche is cookbook-picture golden brown with a firm centre. The pasta-and-bean salad is less successful. Isabelle cannot force it to taste of anything. After pouring in a few different sauces she ends up with a soggy mess. *Pfffffttt*. Her mother always said that the function of food was to soak up alcohol. Isabelle puts the limp pasta salad into the fridge. Perhaps once it is chilled it will solidify into something a little more appetising.

Isabelle has kept her word to Evan and not been up to the rooftop. She both does and doesn't want to go up there. She is worried about her plants, how they are going to fare without water for two days. Part of her feels that she needs to see it before the party, to grind out a half-metre where she can stand in tolerable distress until the fireworks are over and her neighbours retreat back to their flats. Yet every time she decides to head for the stairwell the promise she has made to Evan binds her.

The rest of the food preparation can wait until tomorrow, she decides. She upturns half the failed quiche into a bowl and douses it with tomato sauce. Between them, the oven and the summer afternoon have made her flat a furnace. She takes the quiche to her bedroom – the coolest room in the house – and spoons it to her lips while studying Czech Republic travel guides.

Jack sends her the first text at seven thirty, enough time for a few drinks to have convinced him that he can be the silverback she needs. It reads: 'Happy Australia Day for tomorrow. Fly the flag and enjoy yourself. Jack.' Ah, the transparent *I can explain this one away if I have to* first text. The one before the libido, the alcohol and the ego really kick in. The one he can shrug off if his wife finds it or it is intercepted by a work colleague. Isabelle doesn't respond.

Three-quarters of an hour later the second text arrives. 'Are we not talking? x' Isabelle takes the kiss as her cue. She carries her dinner plate to the kitchen then makes for the bathroom, shedding clothes along the hallway as she goes. She takes a long shower, lathering herself from head to toe. Unhurriedly, she shaves her legs, underarms and bikini line. Towelled down, she piles her brown hair on top of her head and fastens it with a Japanese ornament. The ornament has a bauble in the shape of a lantern at one end. Fronds of beads fall from the lantern, making Isabelle tinkle slightly when she walks. She emerges from the bathroom to find another text. 'When can I see you? xxx.'

Isabelle pumps moisturiser onto her hand and runs it over her legs, cursing slightly at a shaving nick above her right knee. She opens a cupboard and retrieves a silk pouch from behind a kickboard. She loosens the pouch and upturns various pieces of lace, fishnet and PVC onto the bed, all of them presents from Karl. She selects the lavender-coloured bra and French knickers that had been Karl's favourites then pours herself a glass of wine from the cask in the fridge. The sun is almost set. Soon it will shed six or seven of these infernal degrees. Isabelle opens up her flat to the encroaching evening and lingers at the door. The slight breeze is delicious on her still-damp hair and skin.

She refills her wine glass and returns to the bathroom where she paints dark-grey kohl around her almond-shaped blue eyes. One, two, three coats of spidery black mascara. Red lipstick. She appraises herself in the mirror. Isabelle is not vain, but she is grateful for the genetic accident of her beauty. It camouflages some of her other deficiencies. At nine thirty, when it is dark, Jack sends another text. 'I have to see you. Come over?' She types 'Kate?' then, unable to bear how it personalises things, instead writes 'Anyone else home?' Almost instantly her phone bolts blue: 'No. Home alone.'

Isabelle pulls on a long, clinging, navy-coloured dress with spaghetti straps. Two minutes later Jack sends her the text she has been waiting for: his address. She pictures him waiting for her. He will be drinking imported beer, a little wedge of lime forced into the bottle, and pacing in his garden. 'Sovereign being,' he will be repeating to himself. 'Sovereign being.' *Don't drink too much, though, Jack*, she thinks. *You're no good to me drunk. No good to me at all.*

As Isabelle heads down the stairs she bumps into Jim, who is shouldering three large bags of ice. 'Isabelle. Hi.' He pauses and adjusts the bags slightly. 'You look nice.'

'Thank you.'

'Got these for tomorrow,' he glances at the bags. 'Going to be bloody hot up there on the roof.'

'Yes, you're right.' Ice. She had forgotten ice.

'I'll bring a couple of eskies.'

'That'd be great.'

'Hey look, er,' Jim looks about nervously, 'do you mind if I bring someone tomorrow? To the party?'

'No, not at all. The more the merrier.'

'Cool. Well, I'll catch you tomorrow.'

'Bye.'

Jack's house is in a winding East Perth street near the picture-postcard foreshore that barely anyone besides the residents knows is there. Isabelle drives slowly along Jack's street, looking for the prearranged signal: flickering green fairy lights in the front yard. Isabelle keeps driving until she comes to a small row of bays at the front of a park as Jack has instructed. She kills the engine and steps out into the darkness. It is so warm. Warm like velvet made air. The street is whisper-quiet. Behind her she can hear the soft lap of the river on the shoreline. Despite having engineered the meeting, she feels all the sweetness and electricity of chance. She slips her shoes off to keep them from echoing on the pavement then drifts through the muted, pearly street light towards Jack's house. Jack emerges from the darkness. Where Isabelle dangles shoes, he carries a bottle of beer.

Watching him approach, Isabelle feels a pure, powerful desire. With every step her certainty grows and The Black Place recedes. She locks Kate away in the chamber where she keeps Karl and Cindy. This thing between her and Jack, it's alchemical and destined. Surely the universe has conjured this moment, thrown herbs and nettles into a cauldron and summoned long-forgotten seers – women, all of them – to secure it for her. Perhaps it was Libussa, the prophetess and leader who foresaw the creation of a great city where Prague now stands. *She has incanted this for me, breathing her magic down the centuries to the one person left alive who still believes in her.*

'Hello, Isabelle,' Jack says.

Isabelle has never really liked her name. She is used to hearing it pronounced with an Australian inflection that renders it twangy and harsh. *Izza Bell?* Like a question, rising on the 'bell'. But that is not how she hears Jack say it. To her ear he pronounces it low and mellifluous, like a benediction.

'Hello, Jack.' Isabelle reaches up and cups her hand around his neck, drawing him to her. He groans slightly as they meld together.

'Isabelle. Isabelle.'

They kiss and it is as if all of the floors of Isabelle's being become accessible to her. Every internal highway and byway The Black Place ropes off is illuminated. Jack tangles his spare fingers in her hair, the bottle taps against her leg. He pulls away slightly, his nose against hers.

'Thank God you came. I was going crazy without you.'

For answer, Isabelle sweeps her tongue delicately along his top lip.

'Isabelle,' he groans.

It is remarkable, she thinks, the way a voice can lock so perfectly into an aural receptor that the sound seems to come from within. She wants to sink into his voice, under it, the way she had sunk underneath the waves and tried to grip the sand with her toes that day at the beach with Evan.

'Come with me,' he says. He takes her hand and they cross the road, walking past the trimmed verges of the beautiful houses. They come to a stop at a square two-storey house. A light is on in one of the upstairs rooms.

'This is my house,' Jack says into her ear, the emphasis on 'my'. She runs her hand over the inside of his denimed thigh, pressing her palm into his crotch. He exhales. A cocktail of beer and provocation has led him here to this declaration of independence. The manicured lawns and the weed-free pavers of ordered, wedded life bear witness to Jack's refusal to be constrained.

'I'm a sovereign being,' he says. 'I have to have you.'

Isabelle turns away from his house (their house) and faces him. 'I know. I know.' Jack encircles her waist with his hands and steers her across his cool, soft lawn to a side gate. He lifts the latch and gestures to her to walk through. They walk along the side of the house, the swept and scrubbed limestone pavers scratchy beneath her feet. Between the rush fence and the path there is a profuse terraced herb garden. Isabelle has a sudden ridiculous urge to ask for a cutting for Mrs Graham. They keep walking to the back yard, where a rectangle of glimmering blue is cut from the dark-green lawn. Other than the cobalt shimmer from the pool there is very little light. Isabelle can just make out a basketball hoop on the back fence and a jumble of dumbbells. Jack snaps something from one of the trees and holds it against her nose. She inhales the citrus tang of lemon.

There is a tall timber screen running against the far side of the swimming pool. Jack delicately navigates her past it, one hand on her shoulder, another on her hip, and then behind it, out of view of the house. On a patch of lawn he has arranged a picnic rug. A tea light glows against a bell jar. An open bottle of champagne sweats in a silver ice bucket. Two champagne flutes are laid down in the grass. She drops her shoes onto the lawn and lies down on the picnic rug, propping herself up on an elbow. As she sinks down, a faint smell of bergamot rises to meet her. Even the picnic rugs in this house are laundered, she thinks. Almost more than she wants to feel Jack on her she wants to unzip her dress and slip into the cool, blue slab of water. Jack pours her a glass of champagne. 'Thank you.' They clink their flutes together, cocooned in the little hideaway Jack has contrived between the screen, the wall of a garden shed and the boundary fence. He reaches across and strokes the side of her face, the strands of hair that have come loose from the lantern ornament, her bare shoulder.

'I'm so glad you're here.'

'Me too.'

They lean in and kiss. And kiss. And kiss. Isabelle is actually feeling each sensation. Instead of the blunted rough-cut of approximate feeling she is immersed in each tone and quaver. Nothing escapes her. A sudden nostalgia for all the quavers she has missed because they have been swamped by The Black Place causes a terrible loneliness to lap at her throat. Tears spill down her cheeks.

'Isabelle, darling. Angel.' Jack tenderly wipes the tears away with his thumb, crooning at her. 'Don't worry,' he whispers, 'we'll be together. We'll find a way.' But the tears aren't really for Jack. They are a eulogy for all the things missed, glimpsed, guessed at because she cannot take her eyes off The Black Place for even a second. She clamps her hands around Jack's face while she kisses him as if to mine everything she can from his mouth. Jack pulls away and grazes her throat with his lips. He gently lowers the straps of her dress and leaves a long trail of kisses on her breasts. He buries his head in her bosom, emitting satisfied gorging sounds. Isabelle wriggles out of her dress and unclasps the lavender-coloured bra. 'These,' Jack cups her, 'are beautiful.' Her breasts are pearly white against his ruddy skin.

'Thank you.'

'You're beautiful.'

He gently pulls the lantern ornament and watches her long, dark hair rearrange itself around her bare skin. Suddenly, Jack is tense and primed, looking up towards the house. 'What was that?'

'What was what?'

'I thought I heard a noise.'

Isabelle listens carefully against the darkness, but the only sound she hears is the low whirr of the pool filter. 'I don't hear anything.' He remains alert for another couple of seconds and then releases his full weight onto her.

'You're right. It's nothing.'

Free of the constraint of her clothes, she wraps her legs around him and grinds her hips under him. Without uncoupling their lips, between them they manoeuvre Jack's jeans off. Isabelle curls her toes around the elastic band of his boxers and drags them to his ankles. She reaches for him, but something about the angle of their bodies denies him to her. She reaches again, and finds only a scraggle of pubic hair. Exasperated she pushes him off her and over onto his back. She pauses to take a deep draught of champagne. With their eyes locked she draws slow circles on his chest with her index finger spiralling downwards. She lingers at his pubic region, smiling impishly at him, before closing her hand over him.

Jack gives a satisfied sigh and closes his eyes. Isabelle squeezes then, disbelieving, squeezes again. He fits, entirely and comfortably, in her palm. She looks down. His penis is rigid, eager and tiny, a twenty-five-watt bulb that thinks it is a lighthouse.

In the time it takes to drain the last of her champagne the Jack she has created wavers, splinters and dissolves. The Jack who threshed wheat at harvest and crafted knots to sling over moorings. The Jack who was powerful enough to repel The Black Place. The real Jack remains, throbbing ineffectually in her hand.

'What are you thinking, Isabelle? Tell me.'

His voice is thick with lust. He wants a filthy answer, one that, five minutes ago, she was equipped to give him. She looks down at herself, naked except for the flimsy underwear Karl bought her, hiding behind a fence from her boss's wife like some petty thief. She lifts her hand from Jack and drops her head into it.

'Fuck,' she says.

'Yes,' Jack mutters. 'Yes, baby.'

There is a creaking noise as of a door being opened and a soft tread on the paving stones. Jack's eyes fly open, wide with panic. He raises his index finger to his lips in a 'Shhhhhhhhh' gesture and stands up. He takes a few cautious steps and darts his head out around the screen. His bare white bottom glows in the darkness.

'Jack? Jack, honey, are you out here?'

Jack turns to look at Isabelle. Even in the blue-tinted darkness she can tell that he has gone white. He walks out from behind the screen. 'I'm here, babe.'

'What *are* you doing?'

'Oh, I was…I was about to go skinny-dipping. Beautiful night for it. What are you doing home so early?'

'Turns out we got the wrong night. The film's not till next week. Can you believe it?' Kate laughs. 'So we just had a drink and called it a night. I think I'll join you for a swim. No chance of sleeping in this heat. I'll just go get a drink.'

The door creaks shut and Jack bolts behind the screen. He dives to the rug then half-shoves, half-throws Isabelle's clothes at her. 'Here. Put these on.' Isabelle dresses hurriedly and then realises her dress is on inside out. 'No time,' he hisses. 'Please. I'm sorry.' He places his hand firmly on the small of her back and squires her out of their little hiding place. He rushes her past

148

the pool, almost pushing her over. 'Hurry, hurry. For God's sake, be quiet.' When they reach the limestone pavers, which are beyond sight of the back door, he grabs her hand and pulls her to the gate. He lifts the latch and bowls her through it. For goodbye she has only the peremptory click of the latch as it falls back into the groove.

Stunned, Isabelle stands there for a moment staring blankly at the gate, listening to Jack scurry through the garden and back into the life he has made for himself.

'Do you want a glass of wine?'

'Yeah, brilliant.'

'Sauv blanc or chardy?'

'Is there any of that pinot left?'

'No, we finished it up last night.'

'Sauvignon blanc then, babe. And could you put a couple of ice cubes in it?'

There is a pause in which Isabelle imagines Jack scurrying to pour out the remains of the champagne bottle and bundling up the extinguished candles, the bottle and the flutes into the picnic rug and stashing them in the shed.

'Here you are, honey.'

'Thanks, honey.' Jack's voice is calm and assured. It occurs to Isabelle that this is not the first time he has done this, or something like this.

A splash, then another.

'Oh, it's so lovely in here.'

Isabelle balls her underwear into her hand and walks, dazed, back to her car. She puts the key in the ignition and turns it. The radio blasts out into the stillness.

Looking for some hot stuff baby this evening. Looking for some hot stuff baby tonight. She has to laugh. Once she starts she cannot stop. She is hunched over the steering wheel, cackling. It is the kind of laughter that might turn without warning to tears. The wrack of her chest sets off the horn. Isabelle imagines the outrage of all these solid, middle-class folk at such an unruly noise blaring through their neighbourhood. The tears are streaming down her cheeks. She wipes them away with her hand and winces at the smell. She stinks of watermelon and cinnamon and saliva.

She kills the engine and leaves the car, follows the sound of the lapping waves through the gum trees in the park. The crescent of beach glows white in the moonlight. There is no breeze. The only sound is that of the water in conversation with the shore. Right now she should be lying in Jack's arms, satiated and stunned from a love-making to which her bones have barely stood up. Instead, she is alone with the river. She thought she would leave Jack's in a warm, drunken glow, not as a fugitive scrabbling at her clothes.

The moon crooks her bony finger at Isabelle across the river, a silver strip on the black. She wants the smell off her. Jack's smell. She pulls at her inside-out dress and stands naked in the soft night air. She runs at the water and dives in, Jack's spit and smell sloughed off in the slipstream. She splits the surface and treads water in the milky moon-sliver. From across the park comes the sound of voices, laughter. Car lights sweep along the bridge. Isabelle sinks under again and tries to think. She remembers the last time she struck this pose, at the beach with Evan. When the siren sounded her body shut down to the essential service of staying alive. She zeroed in on that shore with the same intensity she had felt for Jack. She flips onto her back and looks at the night sky. Perhaps it is the same urge that bolts her bathroom door against the lure of the razor and locks her fingers, seemingly of their own accord, around the rooftop railings when The Black Place wants to throw her overboard. Isabelle raises her hand in the milky water and watches the silver droplets merge back into the river, rinsing the last of her self-induced fever for Jack away.

ELEVEN

'Hello, Belle.' The hesitancy in Evan's voice imparts a particular static over the wire.

At his first word Isabelle sees him projected along the walls of her flat. He is naked, scanning the sparkling line of blue horizon, shading his eyes with his hands. He digs his toes into the sand, making the muscles in his legs and bum pull taut as he balances himself. Isabelle pauses before she answers, afraid something in her voice will bounce the image down the line.

'Hello.'

'How are you?'

'Fine.'

'Look, about tonight. I know the party doesn't start until six but I was wondering if I could come over at five and hang out with you for a while.'

'That won't work, Evan. I've still got a lot to do. I'm busy. I have food to prepare.'

'I know. I won't hold you up. There's just…just some things I need to talk through with you.' A long pause. 'Please.'

A thousand butterflies land in Isabelle's stomach. She wants the conversation if it means they can wipe the stench of sex from the orderly, pristine house of their friendship. If Evan will climb back onto his pedestal, bodiless and predictable.

'All right. I'll see you at five.' She hangs up.

Isabelle presses play on the CD player. The stirring music from the barricades in *Les Misérables* prompts her into action. She takes the pasta salad from the fridge and sticks an experimental fork into it. It still tastes of nothing but it is a more solid kind of nothing than yesterday's damply depressing nothing. She prepares a snack of cheese and Vegemite sandwiches. She pokes Australian-flag toothpicks into the soft bread, bunching the sandwiches on the platter to make room for the potato crisps she will pour over them later. She and her brother had loved these when they were kids, and she has Samara and Max, the adorable children at number three, in mind as she makes them. She cuts chicken and gherkin, and brie and rocket baguettes. She slices fruit, juliennes vegetables and chills wine. She paces between the fridge, the sink and the cupboards, inventing jobs, but the contents of her kitchen are shape-shifters. The rounded base of the salad bowl becomes Evan's white flank in her hand, the blood-groove of the chopping board those sharp bites in his lower abdomen. Exasperated, she wipes her hands clean and picks up her brochures and books on Prague. The complex maze of streets that dissects the city never fails to hook her mind. As she traces the gridlines with her finger, divining routes, her mind whitens.

Evan knocks on the front door at four fifteen, his form dark against the flywire. He colonises almost the entire space, the sunlight squeezing through the gaps between him and the frame. Isabelle flicks the lock and lets him in.

'Hello.'

'It's good to see you.'

He walks through the door and into the kitchen, slipping the esky he carries from his shoulder to the floor. She tries not to notice the way the sinews in his forearms move or how his grey T-shirt moulds to the curve of his bicep. 'I brought a couple of bottles of that wine you like. The chenin.'

'Lovely, thanks. You're a bit early. I'm not quite ready.'

'I know. Sorry. I really wanted to talk to you.'

She takes a deep breath, girding herself. 'Well, here I am. All ears.'

'Drink?'

'Sure. Why not.'

He takes a bottle of wine from the esky, twists the top and turns to take two glasses from the cupboard. He wears jeans, a gunmetal belt slung low through the loops. Through the thin material of his shirt, Isabelle knows, is the simple dark cross tattooed on his shoulder, the stark line at his abdomen where his tan stops. She jerks her head from side to side, the way a child might shake an Etch A Sketch to clear it.

He pours the wine and hands a glass to Isabelle. 'Cheers.'

'Cheers.' They clink glasses, lightly brushing fingers. Isabelle takes a step backwards.

Evan drains his glass and pours another. His fingers curl around the stem.

'Planning a big night, Evan?'

'Dutch courage. Look, about the other day…'

The butterflies in her stomach all take off at once. 'Don't worry about it, Evan. It's really not an issue.'

'It is an issue. I owe you an apology.'

'Apology accepted. Can you taste this pasta salad for me? I've poured every ingredient I can think of into it and still can't get it to taste of anything.'

'You're avoiding the subject.'

'Not at all,' she protests, face reddening. 'You apologised, I accepted. Case closed, yeah?'

'Not quite. I feel like a complete tool. I handled it badly. I should have just told you then and there that —'

'Adrenalin. Believe me, if I had a willy – can I say *willy*? – it wouldn't have been at half-mast. You know when I got home my hands didn't stop trembling for an hour? It takes ages to get all the fight-or-flight hormones out of the body. Now, about that salad.'

'It wasn't that.' He runs a hand through his hair, flustered. 'Don't you know how I feel about…that I'm…' The rest of his reply is drowned by the shrill ring of her phone. He picks the phone up from the benchtop and glances at the screen. 'Someone called Jack.'

'Leave it.'

'You sure?'

'Yes.'

He puts the phone down and they stare at each other across the scant few metres of her kitchen.

'I'm sorry, Belle. Genuinely sorry.'

She watches him intently, as if this clothed Evan can imprint himself on her retina and that other Evan be filed away in the vault where she keeps Karl and her grief. 'That's okay. Let's just forget it.'

'Thank you.'

Her phone erupts again. He picks it up and, without glancing at the screen this time, bowls it to her. It is Jack again. She turns the phone off.

'Who's Jack?'

'My boss.'

'He's dedicated. Why's he phoning you on a public holiday?'

'The system falls apart without me. Speaking of which, how's your new job going?'

'Good. Really good. I'm enjoying it.' He shuffles his right foot awkwardly on the floor. 'I have something for you.' He keeps his eyes on the floor as he speaks. He focuses on the cranberry-juice stain in Isabelle's rug that anchored him when he told her Karl was getting married. 'I'm not sure if it's the best idea or the worst idea I've ever had...I hope I've done the right thing.'

'What is it?'

'I have to show it to you.'

'How intriguing.'

'You'll need to come with me.'

They exit the flat and walk towards the stairwell. Isabelle expects that they will go down the stairs but instead he takes her hand and begins leading her sky-wards. She pulls back. 'It's all right,' he says soothingly.

'Where are we going?'

'The rooftop.'

'No.'

'Please?'

She stops dead on the stairs and wrenches her hand from his.

'I'm not going up there.'

'Well, you'll have to go up there for the party.' He reaches for her hand but she stumbles backwards down two, three, four stairs. He follows, arms outstretched. She cannot navigate the turn at the landing from her backwards-facing position so comes to a halt at the wall. Feeling trapped, she starts to cry.

'I didn't even want to have this party,' she sobs. 'You made me. You keep…keep forcing me into these corners. Just stop…' she wants to say *doing things I don't expect*, 'stop playing God.' She sinks down to the stair and rests her head against the wall.

He sits next to her and is quiet for a moment. 'Do you ever pray?'

'No.'

'It might help.'

'How?'

'There's something releasing about it. Almost like you're handing the burden to something bigger than you to carry for a while.'

'Right. God as emotional Sherpa.'

'I'm being serious.'

'So am I.' She wipes the tears from her eyes with the heel of her hand.

'I don't pretend to know what's happened to you Belle, what it all means. But I know it's got to do with the rooftop and that you have to take the rooftop back in some way.'

'Don't take this the wrong way, but you can't help me. Not with this.'

'I don't think we necessarily get to choose where help comes from,' he says softly. 'Sometimes it just comes.'

'How are you helping me?' She twists on the stair so they are facing one another. Anger amplifies her voice so it bounces off the stairwell. 'How are you helping me?'

'Will you please come up to the rooftop with me?'

'No.'

'Please?'

'No. Stop asking me. You don't understand anything.'

'Can't you explain it to me?'

'No.'

'Do you tell Jack?' he asks.

'What on earth does Jack have to do with this?'

'Come to the rooftop with me. If it makes no difference, if I've done the wrong thing, then you can berate me and then I'll get in my car and drive away and not contact you till you're ready to talk to me again.'

'I'm not a broken chair that you can fix. And I don't need saving.'

'I know, but —'

'If you're so keen to be the issues superhero then deal with your sexual hang-ups, Church Boy.'

It is the first insult that has passed between them in the six years they have been friends. It sits there, twiddling its thumbs and staring awkwardly at the ground, an interloper in the comfortable, familiar grooves of their exchange.

'Fuck you, Isabelle,' he says quietly, so quietly she barely hears him. 'You know what? I'm done. You want to be Ms Self-Sufficient? Knock yourself out.'

He walks down the stairs and doesn't look back. She listens to the purr of his car as it leaves the visitor's car park. She is heavy-limbed, as if she might be coming down with the flu. Evan and his 'help'. Jack and his 'incident'. Karl. For a fleeting moment she wants to package up some of The Black Place atoms in her hand like a snowball and hurl it at Evan, at all of them. *Here's a small taste of what I battle every day. Feel, just for a moment, this despair wriggling into your bloodstream like a leech. Muster your rational self against this malevolent force a thousand times older and stronger than you are. Crumple in a heap because you've got nothing in your oh-so-sensible artillery that will even make a dent in this thing. Then tell me what help you can offer.*

Immediately the thought occurs to her, she repents. She wouldn't wish The Black Place on anyone, least of all Evan.

'Sorry,' she says to the stairwell, the air. God.

Getting back down the stairs to her apartment seems monstrously difficult, so she just sits there. Waiting. Everyone in Perth is inside, soaking up the air conditioning before they descend on the South Perth foreshore and Kings Park armed with eskies and picnic rugs and gallons of insect repellent. The energy from the rooftop is at her back. She can feel its cold fingers snarling around her organs. Soul-eating, goodness-eating space waiting for her and everyone else to tumble into it.

She anchors her mind on her maps. The route to the Charles Bridge from Staré Město along Na Poříčí. Onto Zlatnická, Soukenická and then walk along Revoluční until you hit the Vltava River. A left turn will take you past the lesser bridges, Letná Park tall against the skyline. A light breeze enters the stairwell. Something red flutters past Isabelle and comes to settle on the stairs below her. Then another. Then another. She bends down for a closer look. They are petals. Rose petals. Blown from above her. She stands up and rounds the corner to the final row of apartments and there are dozens of petals on the stairs, thickest near the door to the rooftop. She bends down and picks one up. It is soft and delicate. The petal is a very deep pink, almost red. Hesitantly, she closes her fingers on the latch. The purple *Do Not Enter* letters that she forgot to paint over hover there like a dare. She turns the latch, steps out into the illuminating sunlight and walks the seven steps that carry her level with the horizon.

The entire rooftop is carpeted with petals. Not an anaemic, wedding-celebration sprinkling of petals, but an ankle-deep pool of red and white petals across the entire space. She slips her shoes off and takes a few steps. The petals are soft and cool. They dance around her ankles as she picks through them. The mass of red petals is mingled with a smaller spray of white ones. She picks a silky white petal and holds it to her nose. It is from a frangipani, sweet and satiny. Evan has detonated the wasteland with thousands upon thousands of petals piled thick on the no-longer-visible rooftop.

Isabelle sinks down into the flowers and thinks about Evan's injunction to prayer. Even in her blackest moments she refuses to utter God's name. When she woke in the hospital, still singed and wild with terror, she didn't throw herself on his mercy. She never begs celestial aid when The Black Place crushes the life from her. The closest she comes is her attachment to Good King Wenceslas. She knows Evan thinks she is proud, pathologically self-reliant even. She cannot tell him the real reason she refuses to pray.

There is nothing in the world more terrifying to Isabelle than the idea that The Black Place does not have its equal and opposite force. She is silent not for fear that God will respond, but that he won't.

She returns to her flat to phone Evan, apologise and beg his return.

At five minutes to six Isabelle collects Mrs Graham. She barely has time to tap on the front door before Mrs Graham throws it open.

'Wow. Mrs Graham, you look sublime.' The older woman has abandoned her traditional twin-set in favour of a long, loose blue dress that hangs to the floor. Wound around her arms is the most spectacular pashmina Isabelle has ever seen. It is midnight blue, shot through with gold and silver thread in a moon and stars pattern. It shimmers and flows around her, as if Mrs Graham cut a rectangle from a perfect night sky and folded it to her shoulders.

'Thank you, dear. Mr Graham bought the wrap for me many, many moons ago, pardon the pun. In Istanbul, I think. I almost never have a chance to wear it.'

'Well, you look beautiful.'

She beams. 'Do you think I'll need a hat? Only, I've set my hair.'

'No. I've fixed up a shade umbrella for you.'

'Thank you, dear.' Mrs Graham touches a finger to her crinoline wave. 'This took me hours.'

'It was worth it. You look an absolute picture.'

Mrs Graham's cake is rigged up in a large white plastic box. Isabelle takes the box in both hands and Mrs Graham lays a delicate, gnarled hand on her elbow for support. She has painted her nails a frosted shell pink.

'Is that nice young man of yours here, dear?'

'That nice young man's name is Evan and he's not mine. As you bloody well know. But yes. He's here.'

Mrs Graham and Isabelle meet Mr and Mrs Lumb and their two children on the stairs, all of them travelling skyward. The children are intoxicated with excitement.

'Is this the fireworks lady?' the littlest one asks Mrs Lumb, pulling at her sari.

'Yes. That's what she calls you, Isabelle, since we received the invitation. Samara thinks you are single-handedly responsible for the fireworks.'

Samara looks at Isabelle with unvarnished awe. 'I've never seen fireworks before,' she says earnestly. 'How do you do it?'

'I'm afraid that's a secret.'

'You can tell me,' she says wide-eyed. 'I can keep secrets.'

'Pfffft. No you can't,' says her brother. 'You can't keep any secrets. Remember when we found the train set in the park and we decided to keep it and take it home and you ran straight to Mum and said I'd *stolen* it. Which I never.'

'Which I *didn't*,' Mr Lumb corrects him.

They step out onto the rooftop, Samara and her brother heatedly discussing her capacity to keep confidences. As they draw level with the surface, the argument abruptly stops.

'Wow,' says Samara. 'Wow. I never knew there was a garden up here.' Her brother scoops up a handful of petals and throws them over his head.

'Oh my,' says Mrs Graham. 'Oh.' Her hand drops from Isabelle's elbow and she walks a little way into the floral carpet. The late sun catches the iridescent blues and silvers of her wrap as she moves. She looks to be levitating through the petals. 'It's even more beautiful than I imagined it would be.'

'You knew about this?'

'I had an inkling. Your Evan came to my house to see if I knew where he could buy petals. Lots of petals.'

Samara kicks up a flurry of petals and laughs, delighted. Her brother follows suit and the two of them become the centre of a storm of red and white. 'Now, children,' Mrs Lumb says seriously, 'remember what we talked about before we came up here? Promise me you'll stay away from the edge. Promise me.'

'We promise.'

Evan takes the cake box from Isabelle's hand and places it in one of the tubs of ice he's rigged up under the incinerator flue. Isabelle makes introductions then shows Mrs Graham her handiwork with the plants, feeling foolishly proud of herself.

'Ah,' Mrs Graham puts a fluttering hand to her chest. 'You planted my list. Ixora. Echeveria. And you've kept them alive up here in this heat!' Mrs Graham drops her

163

hand and encloses Isabelle's fingers within hers, shaking them slightly as if overcome.

'Let's get you in the shade. We can't go and spoil your do now, can we?'

Isabelle hands Mrs Graham into the reclining chair that Becca found for her and adjusts the umbrella above her head. Evan pours her a glass of chenin with ice cubes and she looks as if life could furnish nothing finer. The Lumbs decline wine, but pour orange juice and soda water from a tall jug.

Samara curls her little hand into Isabelle's. 'Did you make this garden on the roof?'

'Yes. But my friend Evan brought the petals up here. How did you manage that, by the way? It must have been a monumental pain.'

'It was. They sell the petals by the garbage bag. I had twenty of them. Up and down. Up and down. I thought if anyone sees me they'll think I'm disposing of body parts in the incinerator.'

'Why did you make a garden up here?' Samara asks.

'Well,' Isabelle puzzles over what to tell her, 'for one thing I live on the second floor so I don't have any garden. I've always admired Mrs Graham's garden. And I used to come up here a lot. It was so ugly and barren that it bothered me. I wanted to make it good. To make it beautiful.'

'It's like a fairyland,' Samara whispers softly. 'What will you do with the petals after the fireworks?'

'I don't know. I hadn't thought about that. I guess we'll sweep them up and put them back into garbage bags for the green waste collection.'

'Oh no, you can't do that, Isabelle. That would just spoil it.'

'What would you like me to do with them?'

'I think you should throw them off the side of the roof. On that side,' she points to the north-eastern corner, 'where we live. And I'll stand underneath on the ground while all the flowers are falling and I'll twirl and twirl and twirl until I'm so dizzy I can't stand up any more. That's what I'd do.'

'I think we can arrange that.'

Samara nods seriously, clearly believing Isabelle can do anything. Jim arrives, hauling two eskies onto the roof. Somewhat to Isabelle's surprise, his companion is not the tanned, short-shorted lady she was expecting but a studious-looking thin man.

'Isabelle, this is Peter.'

'Lovely to meet you,' she says, extending her spare hand. (Samara steadfastly refuses to let her other hand go.)

'Bloody Nora,' Jim looks around. 'You haven't tricked us into coming to a wedding, have you, Isabelle?'

'Hah. That'll be the day. Just the fireworks, I'm afraid.'

One half of the speed-freak couple that lives between Jim and Isabelle arrives. She pauses at the top of the stairwell, nervous. Isabelle walks towards her, hand outstretched.

'Hello. I'm so glad you could come.' Isabelle knows her neighbour's name. She has often heard it bellowed by her husband – usually preceded by an expletive. 'We've never properly met. I'm Isabelle.'

'I'm Jacinta. I brought these,' she says, handing Isabelle two large packets of chips without looking her in the eyes. There is a thick smear of foundation in the crook of her arm, barely concealing her raw, red track marks. Isabelle hopes Samara doesn't notice them and ask her what they are.

'Thank you, that was nice of you.' Isabelle takes the packets and gently propels Jacinta towards the rest of the group. 'Can I get you a drink?'

Jacinta shakes her head. 'I'm kind of trying not to drink.'

'Would you like a soft drink?'

'Yes,' then, as an afterthought, 'please.'

'We have orange and soda,' Samara pipes up. 'It's really nice. I'll get you one of those.' Samara releases Isabelle's hand and toddles off to get Jacinta's drink. Jacinta scratches at her arm and shifts her weight from one foot to the other. 'I've never been up here before. I didn't even know you could get up here. It's pretty cool.'

'Yes. Perfect for the fireworks.'

Jacinta nods. 'I haven't been to see the fireworks since I was a kid. Should be cool.'

Samara returns, hands Jacinta her drink and faithfully closes her hand in Isabelle's again.

'Will your husband be joining us?'

'Nuh-uh. He moved out.'

'Oh. I'm sorry,' Isabelle lies. 'Maybe it's for the best. In the long run.'

Jacinta momentarily ceases her scratching and fidgeting. In her sudden stillness she looks young and achingly vulnerable. 'Yeah,' she says. 'I know. It's hard, but. Starting again.'

'I know. It's awful. Beyond awful.'

166

'You been there?' Her eyes plead for reassurance. 'Do you get through it?'

'You do. You absolutely do. A year from now you'll look back and be amazed how far you've come.' Red lines thread around Isabelle's cheekbones and temples, a hieroglyphic that says *I am lying to you.* 'You'll be a different person a year from now,' Isabelle insists. She says it with such vehemence, almost violence, that Jacinta flinches.

Jacinta threads her hair around her index finger and draws the chewed ends to her mouth. 'Yeah. Just gotta get through it. And get off everything else.' Her eyes well red.

Samara pulls gently on Isabelle's hand, beckoning her to bend towards her. 'Is that lady okay?' she whispers.

'Yes, honey, she's fine.'

Samara nods, as if she understands the situation perfectly. 'Did you know that Isabelle makes the fireworks?' she asks Jacinta, her voice thick with awe.

It strikes Isabelle that, in a way, Samara is right. Today Isabelle is the medicine woman wielding the power of fire. To Samara she is little less than a god. To Mrs Graham, harbinger of the first party in years. To Jacinta she offers a few hours' distraction from her itching need. At this moment, Isabelle may be the equal and opposite force of The Black Place. Allowing herself to feel some pride in what she has done, she scoops up a handful of petals and pours them on Samara's head. The child giggles.

As dusk descends, Isabelle and Evan set out the food. They share the unconscious coordination of a longstanding couple, Evan wordlessly gravitating towards the cutlery and glasses and Isabelle laying out the sandwiches and salads. Samara helps them arrange the feast on the wobbly vinyl tabletop. Her brother Max repeatedly asks Isabelle when she will start the fireworks.

'I can only work my magic when it's completely dark.'

'Can't you make it dark?'

'No. My power doesn't extend as far as that.'

Max pulls a face, as if Isabelle's powers are unspeakably lame. He occupies himself by filling the tray of his toy truck with petals, pushing the truck to the other end of the roof and emptying the tray. His parents tense every time he approaches too near the edge.

'Jacinta, would you mind standing guard between Max and the railing?' Isabelle asks.

Jacinta smiles. 'Sure thing.' Isabelle's request gives Jacinta an excuse to pace. Up and down she goes as Max and his truck tear up the petals. Isabelle shows Samara how to make the ultimate Oz sandwich, prising the butter-and-Vegemite–filled bread apart and loading it up with chips, then pressing the top down again.

'I used to eat these when I was little. It was my favourite.'

'I like it!' Samara announces triumphantly.

'I'm not sure,' Max says, pausing to take a bite in between his trips to the edge and back. 'It tastes like splinters.' He puts his half-eaten sandwich back on the plate and zooms his truck through the petals, Jacinta in hot pursuit.

Mrs Lumb produces a platter of tandoori chicken wraps that are devoured in seconds. 'It's not that I don't like the Vegemite and chips,' Samara explains to Isabelle in between mouthfuls, 'it's just that I'm more *used* to this.'

'Shall I cut your cake, Mrs Graham?' Evan offers.

'Please, dear.'

Evan passes around generous chunks of cake oozing chocolate and cherry. Max's eyes grow wide.

'What do you say, Max?' says Mr Lumb.

'Wow.'

Everyone laughs.

'Besides wow?'

'Thank you, Mrs Graham.'

'You're welcome, dear.'

'Fuck me, this is good,' Jim says to himself, summing up everyone's sentiments.

Samara looks shocked; Max giggles.

Jim raises his eyebrows, realising too late that he has verbalised his thoughts. 'Sorry,' he says.

Samara climbs up onto the same chair as Isabelle, keeping one steady eye on her plate of cake.

'Samara, give Isabelle a moment's peace,' her mum says gently.

'She's fine,' Isabelle assures Mrs Lumb. 'Really.' Watching Samara wriggle up against her and tuck into her cake, Isabelle tries to retrieve a memory of her and her brother on similar outings but it eludes her. She knows such outings existed. She has seen the grainy eighties snapshots that prove it. But she cannot penetrate the flatness of the photographs to the days they represent. Sometimes she wonders if The Black Place has corrupted her memory, like a filter that streams out joy and pleasure.

Samara hands Isabelle her wedge of half-eaten cake. 'Have you had enough?'

Samara nods, a thick smear of chocolate and cherry around her mouth. 'I think I could finish it later. I'm just too excited right now.' Mrs Lumb hands Isabelle a tube of moist towelettes and Samara sits patiently as Isabelle scrubs at the cake around her mouth.

'I'll have Samara's if she doesn't want it,' Max pipes up.

Samara's eyes flash. 'I *do* want it,' she shouts. 'Just not this immediate moment.' In the heat of her indignation, her precise English lapses so that 'immediate' sounds like 'midget'. Her father frowns. Samara pushes her fork into her cake and moves it around her plate, refusing to look up.

Mrs Graham, the consummate diplomat, glides over the awkwardness with assurances of the abundance of cake. Max is distracted from teasing his sister about her accent by another wedge of dessert. Evan, Peter, Jacinta and Jim all have more too. Jacinta eats as if her body has been starved for months and she has only just woken up to the fact of her hunger. She eats standing up, rocking from one foot to the other like a metronome. Wordlessly, Mrs Graham hands Jacinta a third piece of cake. Mrs Graham raises her empty glass for more wine and laughs at her queenliness. Evan refills her glass and adjusts the umbrella. Every time he does something solicitous of her comfort, Mrs Graham gives Isabelle a significant look as if to say, *All this could be yours, my dear.* Isabelle pretends innocence as to the meaning of these looks.

'Samara, can you help me get ready for the fireworks?'

'Of course, Isabelle.' Samara gives her brother a superior smile but Max is distracted by cake and chooses not to retaliate. A battery-operated radio sits on the rickety plastic table next to Mrs Graham. Isabelle tunes the station. Samara offers advice as to the clarity of the reception from various vantage points on the rooftop, Jacinta placing herself between the child and the edge.

After a few delicate semi-rotations of the tuner the music beams out clearly. There is a crackle of rising excitement from Samara and Max. Isabelle asks Samara to stand a little distant as she lights the bamboo torches. She cups her spare hand around the flame while it takes, then steps back and watches the torch flare against the darkening horizon. *A scene to burn witches by*, she thinks. For a millisecond she smells smoke and feels the ice-like burn on the arch of her foot. She squints her eyes shut and shakes her head. When she opens her eyes, Evan is watching her quizzically.

'You all right?' he mouths. His lips, like his cheek-bones, are sharp-cut. His face is saved from the aloofness of perfect angles by a spray of freckles on his nose. 'Belle?' he says aloud and steps towards her, placing a hand on her shoulder.

She jumps. 'Yes. I'm fine. Sorry. Senior moment.' Evan drops his hand but Isabelle can feel him there, still.

'Wait till you get to my age,' says Mrs Graham. 'Senior moments can last all day.'

'I don't believe you for a second,' says Isabelle. 'You're as sharp as anyone I know.'

There are only a few fingers of sunlight left. Most of the rooftop is in darkness now. A little bubble of excitement hovers over the group.

'It's going to start soon, isn't it?' says Samara.

'Yes.'

Samara climbs back onto Isabelle's chair and wedges herself into the crook of Isabelle's arm. Mrs Lumb gives Isabelle an apologetic look, but Isabelle is enjoying being made such a favourite. Evan refills Mrs Graham's glass then moves his chair next to Isabelle and Samara. He sits so close that Isabelle picks up his heat in the hairs along her arm. At the first sparkling anemone bursting in the sky, Samara and Max scream with pent-up expectation and excitement. The fireworks crackle and plop like sonic champagne corks before exploding in colour. Purples, blues and oranges erupt in the sky, hold their shape for a second or two and then open up like flowers, trailing their sparks down to earth.

The radio crackles out a succession of songs by Gang Gajang, Midnight Oil and INXS. Jacinta, Jim and Peter seem to know all the words. With each successive explosion the adults shed their composure and soon they are *ooohing* and *aahhing* as unaffectedly as Samara and Max. Even Mr Lumb sets aside his polite reserve to exclaim 'Marvellous!' two or three times. Midway through the radio broadcast, the announcer asks everybody to turn off their lights and candles.

'Quick, Isabelle, come with me,' Evan says. He extends his hand. After a second's hesitation she takes it. Samara leaps up too.

172

'Samara, I think you'd better stay here,' cautions Evan. 'It might not be safe for you.'

Samara's face flares with indignation. Mrs Lumb calls Samara to her and the child reluctantly goes. Evan guides Isabelle to the incinerator then laces his fingers together.

'Step into my hands and lever yourself up.'

'No, you'll never be able to take my weight.' Their eyes meet and Isabelle knows they are both thinking the same thing. *I carried you to the hospital.*

'Don't worry. I won't drop you.'

Evan launches her onto the top of the flue. She balances herself against the rickety pipe. He pulls a chair up and clambers up after her.

'Exactly what am I looking at?'

'Wait a moment.'

Suddenly, the embankment at Kings Park lights up with tens of thousands of torches, sparklers, lighters and candles, all held aloft at an instruction from the radio announcer. The lights seem to be suspended in space like some celestial message.

'It's so beautiful,' she says.

'Like Tinkerbell's school reunion.'

They stand there together watching the dancing lights, falling under their mesmeric sway. Evan reaches for her hand and holds it. She feels so disembodied she might float towards the lights and join them. She remembers Evan telling her about his synaesthetic experience and feels as if she might understand it. Evan's warm hand, the lights, their suspension in space, the music on the radio…they merge into joy.

Then, as suddenly as they appeared, the lights are gone. Isabelle feels a little stab of grief as her impressions diverge and separate. Evan jumps nimbly from the incinerator then climbs onto the chair.

'Bend down and give me your hand.'

She scrambles onto the chair, losing her footing slightly. Evan steadies her, drawing her towards his chest. He smells of sandalwood and salt. Isabelle pretends an urgent need to cough.

'Excuse me,' she steps down from the chair and coughs into her cupped hands. She hopes her blush is invisible in the dark.

'What was it like?' demands Max as she rejoins the group.

'Like watching the most enormous carols by candle-light from space.'

'Cooool.'

'I think there was probably room for all of us up there,' Samara says icily, before taking Isabelle's hand and pointedly turning her back on Evan.

'Our turn now,' says Evan. He hands sparklers around to the group and at a signal from the radio they light them and toast their unseen counterparts on Mount Eliza with their fiery message sticks. Isabelle watches the half-lit, half-shadowed faces of her companions in the spluttering fire of the sparklers. The adults have shed the masks of their maturity and glow with the unselfconsciousness of their four-year-old selves.

The fireworks resume. Colours tumble one atop another. The cascades of falling embers blend together.

The lowest tier still glows before the next head of colour bursts hundreds of metres above it. They look like hands of fire that might snatch the group from the rooftop and slingshot them into the night sky. The excitement is too great for Samara and Max to maintain sitting positions. They stand together in the middle of the circle of adults, holding hands. Their little bodies are primed as the staccato rumble runs across the sky and then, as the coronas burst into shards of fiery colour, they raise their joined hands in triumph and shout.

As the announcer declares the last song, Isabelle feels a glimmering joy. She has accomplished what she thought she could not. She has reconnoitred far into the territory of The Black Place and she has stared it down. Isabelle watches Samara and Max throw their arms skywards and let out a yawp of pleasure. They are hiving a memory that will live between them long after Isabelle has exited their lives. For the first time in her life Isabelle understands why people toil to prepare Christmas and birthday extravaganzas even though the effort means the moment itself contains little enjoyment. The joy lives in the afterglow of recollection, the invisible threads of memory that can bind even a group as disparate as this one.

As the final shards glow and die, Max and Samara let out a shared cry of thanks.

'That,' says Max decidedly, 'was aaawwwe-sssome.'

'Did you enjoy it?' says Mrs Lumb.

'It was the bestest thing ever.'

'Max?'

'Best, then. Best thing ever.'

Samara runs at Isabelle and throws her arms around her. 'Thanks, Isabelle. Will you make the fireworks again next year?'

Isabelle picks her up and returns her hug. 'We'll see, shall we?'

'Thank you, Isabelle.'

'Thank *you*, Samara.'

Samara looks at Isabelle quizzically. 'I didn't do anything.'

Evan and Isabelle stand either side of Mrs Graham and help her down the stairs, though Mrs Graham barely needs it.

'I feel positively buoyant,' she says.

Max and Samara leap down the stairs, then run back up to the adults who are carting leftover food, drink and utensils back to their flats. They part at their respective landings, all effusively thankful for Isabelle's efforts. Isabelle overhears Jim invite Jacinta back to his flat to hang out with him and Peter. Isabelle and Evan escort Mrs Graham to her front door, where Mrs Graham startles Isabelle by sliding off her beautiful pashmina and draping it around her shoulders.

'Thank you, Isabelle.' Mrs Graham leans toward her and kisses her tenderly on the cheek. 'I can't remember when I've enjoyed myself more.'

'Mrs Graham, I can't take this. It's beautiful. Very beautiful, but I can't accept it. Mr Graham gave it to you.'

'I'd like you to have it. Isabelle of the Moon and Stars, conjurer of fireworks. It suits you.'

It tears at Isabelle's heart that Mrs Graham is so grateful for a simple act of inclusion that she would give her this beautiful object. She doesn't want this loneliness for Mrs Graham. She doesn't want it for anyone. The shawl is light and soft against her shoulders. She returns Mrs Graham's kiss and gives her a hug. Her body feels frail and birdlike, but there's a supple vine of strength there too.

'Don't put it away in a drawer and save it for best like I did,' Mrs Graham whispers. Isabelle shakes her head, too overcome to speak.

Back at her flat, Evan and Isabelle parcel up leftover food and put it in the fridge. Isabelle keeps the pashmina around her shoulders, pausing every few moments to admire it. When the last of the food is stored, Evan pours two glasses of wine from one of the remnant bottles.

'You did a good thing today, Belle.' He clinks her glass. 'Thanks for inviting me back. I wouldn't have missed it for the world.'

'Thank you for coming back. You'd be quite within your rights to still be angry with me.'

'I'm a forgiver,' he strikes a superhero pose, fist in the air as if flying, 'being Church Boy and all.'

'Ouch,' Isabelle grimaces.

'Too soon to be funny?'

'Yes. Leave it till next week at least.'

She takes a gulp of the wine, which has grown warm from the night air.

'I think this needs ice.'

Evan takes her glass and places it on the sideboard next to his, but he doesn't open the freezer. Instead, he clamps his hands down on the benchtop and holds himself rigid, staring at the wine glass. The intensity of the stare is alarming, as if he is scrutinising the glass for traces of poison.

'Is something wrong?'

He whirls from the benchtop and Isabelle can no longer follow his movements because she is in and of them. One of Evan's hands is around the back of her head. Another presses into the small of her back. She is pinned between the wall and Evan, completely enclosed. The rapidity of his movements overtakes her capacity to think. His mouth is so alive it stuns her.

Sandalwood. Salt.

The flex and fall of the black cross on his shoulder as he reaches for her breast, her thigh, her hand.

The Ming vase spins, teeters and shatters.

II
Prague

Mark my footsteps, my good page
Tread thou in them boldly
Thou shalt find the winter's rage
Freeze thy blood less coldly.

– 'Good King Wenceslas',
traditional Christmas carol

garlanded by white-shuttered windows. It looks like a wedding cake. Human figures in coal hug chimneys and clasp hands around railings. Little stone balconies, hardly larger than window boxes, adorn the walls. To the left of the wedding-cake building is a boxy dirty-white hotel with mean blue rectangles for balconies. Drab and utilitarian, it sulks next to its more beautiful neighbour.

When the sun has irradiated all that Isabelle can immediately see, she leans far out of the window, straining for a glimpse of the dozing street. To her astonishment, the window has no grille, not even a flimsy net of flyscreen. It simply opens to the dawn air and the plunge to the road beneath. There is nobody about. Below her, at street level, the shops – an ice-cream parlour, a jeweller's and a clothing store – are trussed up in chains and mesh. Isabelle breathes deeply of the air. It is cold. A kind of cold she has never experienced: lung-shocking and white-winged. She reaches far out from the window to touch the damp bricks on the outer wall, marvelling at how old everything is by her new-world standards.

Broiling with excitement, she retracts her head and surveys her room. It is a neat, clean rectangle of bed, desk, fridge and bedside table, bare and sparse as a monk's quarters. The only flourish in the room is the drawing Samara made for her after the party, tacked up on the wall above the desk. Samara used thick, creamy art paper, the expensive kind with a gilt edge, to draw the flowered rooftop. Dozens of swirling petals in deep crimson practically leap from the page. There's a kinetic energy to the petals that make them look as if they are twirling down from the sky. If you look closely at the crayon you can see the lead-pencil outline of the stencil Mrs Graham – whom Samara has taken to visiting in the afternoons – made for her to painstakingly trace over: *Isabelle of the Moon and Stars*.

Only Mrs Graham and Samara know that at this moment Isabelle is far from Perth, savouring her first Prague morning. She hadn't trusted herself to tell Evan.

'Evan.'

She speaks his name to the empty room as if she might conjure him. She permits herself two delicious minutes of remembering his fingers pushing the stray hair from her face, his lips in the hollow of her neck. Then she shakes her head, banishing him from her thoughts. She removes her clothes and steps, with some trepidation, into the bathroom. When she'd arrived in the early hours, dazed with jet lag, her pupils had almost burst in the white glare of the room. Gleaming white tiles cover the floor, the walls and the ceiling. She has the uneasy feeling that it might have been an interrogation room in a former life, easily hosed down of blood, faeces and tears and now rehabilitated in the service of hospitality and tourism.

In one corner stands a large cylinder. Isabelle peels back the hemispheres and steps into the cylinder, closing the doors behind her. She looks up, half-expecting to see a chute on the ceiling through which she might be sucked into another world. But there is only an innocuous showerhead. She listens intently for the collected memory in the room, as if she might weigh the good and ill done there. The sobbing of tortured dissidents. The sound of samizdat leaflets being shredded. Guilt. Betrayal. The kind of heroism of which Isabelle thinks herself incapable. But the room, for now, is silent.

The steam from the hot water has no escape from the cylinder, so soon she is swaddled in a dense white cloud. Her limbs emerge from the fog as if they belong to someone else. She notices how thin her arms have become over the last year, how bony her ankles. She towels off and dresses for the day ahead in black Converse boots, beanie, jeans, two jumpers, Mrs Graham's pashmina and a red anorak she can shake dry and ball up into her bag if need be.

Isabelle leaves her room and rides the juddering lift to the ground floor. The grumpy man who had checked her in the night before – she has christened him Grigor – is gone. In his place is a young, pretty woman dressed two decades too matronly.

'Good morning,' she says pleasantly.

'Good morning.'

'You are early.'

'Yes.' Isabelle feels unaccountably embarrassed.

'Breakfast is through there,' she gestures behind her. 'Not too long. Ten minutes maybe.'

'Thank you.'

'Where are you from?'

'Australia.'

'Long way.'

'Yes.'

'And in the winter too.' The young woman shakes her head. 'I hope you will not be freezing.'

184

'It's a change for me. I've never been cold before. Really cold, I mean.'

'You must come back in the summer. Best time to see Prague. But of course is even more busy. Everyone come then.'

'It wouldn't matter to me if it snowed the whole time I'm here. Just to be here is enough.' *Just to be away, away from the whole bloody mess, is enough.*

The dining room is empty of guests, save for Isabelle. Soon, Prague will wake and go about its business and Isabelle will be there to see it. Anticipation makes her feel light, as if she is gliding some inches from the ground. One of the staff gives her a gesture indicating that she can eat. Isabelle is aware of a gnawing sensation low in her stomach but she can't be sure it is hunger. *Eat*, she tells herself. *I must eat because today I will walk. I will walk and I will walk until my feet mould themselves to the cobblestones. Until I have inhaled gallons of native air and part of me has become Prague.*

She pokes through the dishes, searching for something that sparks her appetite. She puts some dark bread, cheese, apple and a boiled egg on her plate. Her heart lurches slightly when she spies the coffee urn. Brown, murky coffee spurts into her mug. It is weak and tepid, no more than coffee-flavoured water. *Do they still ration coffee*, she wonders. *Should someone tell them the war is over?* She picks at her food as she studies the map, testing her recall of the streets.

Four young English men in soccer jerseys enter the room and take the table next to hers. They are full of sly humour about the debauches of the evening before, signs of which are still evident in their hair and clothes. 'Morning, darlin',' one of them winks at her. She nods once in acknowledgement and drops her head to her map. The waitresses eye the men warily.

'Where you from, love?' one of them asks her.

She shakes her head and cups her hand to her ear. 'No English.'

'Russian?'

She shrugs dumbly then returns to her map.

'Well, it's not like I want to talk anyway,' says the English boy to his friends. 'I speak,' he affects a Latino accent, 'the universal language of love.'

Isabelle computes the time difference between Prague and Perth. Is Jack wondering what's happened to her? Or is he just relieved she's gone? She had dragged herself to work after the Australia Day holiday. She dreaded seeing Jack, but she dreaded the waiting to see him even more. When Carol Anne said he had called in sick, Isabelle felt she might snap on the rack of her anticipation. When he phoned in sick the next day too, she toyed with the idea of arranging a private meeting away from the curious eyes of their colleagues to clear the air. When he was still away on the third day she asked Carol Anne what was wrong with him.

Carol Anne looked up from her computer. 'Ummm, migraine, I think. That's what Kate said.'

'Jack doesn't suffer from migraine.'

Carol Anne removed her spectacles, folded them and placed them on her desk. 'How do you know?'

'Well, I don't. It's just that he's never mentioned it.'

'I was unaware that Jack's health was of particular concern to you.'

The two women looked at each other for a long moment.

'Who should I give the daily stats to?'

'What's that?'

'The transaction data I provide to Jack every day. Who should I give it to?'

Carol Anne smiled thinly. 'Send it to me. I'll give it all the attention Jack does.'

From the other side of the partition someone sniggered.

'Anything else? Other crucial information about your work I should know?'

Isabelle swallowed hard. 'No. There's nothing else.'

Carol Anne retrieved her spectacles, unwound them, returned them to her triumphant face and continued typing. As Isabelle walked away, Carol Anne or the person behind the partition muttered something. Isabelle cannot be sure, but she thinks it was 'slut'.

She stopped asking if Jack was coming in. Perhaps, she mused, the delay was for the best after all. The more time they put between his throwing her out of his garden and now the better. Let the memory recede until the sting died to a bruised awkwardness. When Jack did return they were mutually ingenious at avoiding one another. A glance across a corridor was enough to remind them both of urgent meetings, unreturned calls and compelling scuffs on their shoes. When Jack strayed into Isabelle's field of vision, his suit and tie did nothing to erase the image of him, flushed and naked, on the picnic rug. She felt again his faint frog-pulse in her hand and had to wipe her palm clean on her skirt. She wondered what he saw when he looked at her. Probably the look on her face as he closed the gate on her half-dressed dishevelment.

Friday morning found Isabelle at her desk, pecking away at the daily stats (correctly) when she was assailed by a cloying smell. She looked up to find Jack bending over her seat in alarming proximity.

'Hello, Isabelle.'

'Jack. Hello.' She inched her chair away from him.

'I'd like to see you in my office when you have a moment.'

'Oh, I'm just…I haven't finished the dailies yet. I'm sorry, I'm a bit slow today but you should have them by one. Will that be all right?'

He dropped his voice. 'It's not about the dailies.'

Oh God, she thought, *here it comes, the mortifying moment when we have to 'talk about it'*. But what could possibly be said to set all to rights? What words could magic away what they had seen? Isabelle locked her workstation and followed Jack to his office. She was aware that an alert silence had fallen over the floor, a silence so total that she could hear the swish–swish of her skirt as she walked.

'Could you close the door, please?'

Reluctantly she did so.

'Please take a seat.'

Jack sat in his chair, the desk between them. He swivelled slightly on his seat, his fingers pressed into a steeple. He looked at her with no sign of embarrassment. Could it be that he had assimilated it already? Was he ready to move on without an agonising verbal post-mortem?

'I have something for you.' He reached for one of his management texts (*Be the Change You Want to See in the Office*), flipped it open and drew out a slim rectangular object wrapped in silver paper and tied with a tiny iridescent bow.

'What is it?'

'Open it.'

His eyes twinkled. His mouth contorted into his lopsided grin. Isabelle pulled the thread of the bow and peeled back the paper to reveal a long ivory-coloured envelope. A letter of resignation, she thought. He's resigning. Or having me transferred. She saw herself banished to Finance with crazy Magnus, pretending to care about measuring outcomes. *Maybe it won't be so bad*, she thought. *A fresh start. New people. No Jack.*

She opened the envelope and drew out an elegant black card engraved with silver script. Isabelle read:

Dear Jack and Isabelle,

We are delighted to confirm your accommodation at Casa di Cuore in Margaret River. For five nights you will enjoy the sumptuous luxury of our beachside accommodation. Our friendly and discreet staff will deliver breakfast to your door in time to enjoy the sunrise from the beach. We can organise tours to the surrounding award-winning vineyards or if you just want to relax and unwind we can source an extensive selection of fine wine for you. Don't feel like moving beyond the beach and your fully equipped apartment? Let us bring a delectable range of gourmet delights to your door.

We at Case di Cuore are here to ensure your getaway is as romantic and relaxing as possible. We look forward to welcoming you as our guests.

'We leave tonight,' Jack said triumphantly. 'I didn't want to say anything before. I wasn't avoiding you, I just wanted to make sure everything was perfect before I told you. I have bottles of champagne chilling in an esky in the car. I've pre-ordered the crayfish dinner. If we leave right after work we can be down there for eight thirty. A swim at the beach tomorrow before breakfast. Make love. Lunch at a winery. Back to bed. Make love. Swim. Four heavenly days, just like you said.'

At the words 'make love' he was under her hand again, a thin straw of plasticine that might divide under the rolling pressure of her palm.

'We can call in at your place on the way. You won't need much, just a swimsuit and a sarong. An evening dress or two for dinner.'

'I can't go with you, Jack,' she said, unable to meet his eyes.

'I know, I know. You're worried about work. But I've got this all planned out. I'm not the director of strategy for nothing. You can phone in on Monday and say you've come down with flu and need to take a few days off. Just quietly, I've doctored your leave allocation so you won't get any problems from Human Resources. I've arranged to work from home to look over some new corporate strategy reports so they won't miss me here. I've told Kate I'm going fishing in the south-west so I'll collect some fish fillets for the esky on the way back. It's perfect.'

'You changed my leave records?'

'I interpreted them creatively.'

'Jack, you could lose your job for this. You could be sacked. What about P3?'

'Fuck P3. Anyway, who's going to know?'

'Jack, I think Carol Anne knows. I think everyone knows.' Isabelle looked up through the glass walls towards the neat rows of desks. Sixty pairs of eyes darted downwards.

Jack's voice swelled with rebellion. 'Why should we care what other people think? We're different. Chosen. Sovereign beings, remember?'

Isabelle realised he had been rehearsing the speech and enjoyed delivering it. She forced herself to meet his imploring eyes. She had never seen such craven entreaty before. If she said no and refused him then the facts were irrefutable: he was a dodgy, middle-aged public servant with a wandering eye who had risen as far as his management-speak would take him. Isabelle did not want to be the instrument of that fact. She wished she could give him the gift of his fantasy, but the only caress she could offer him was a slightly pitying, maternal pat on the head.

'Isabelle. Please.'

One of the cruellest things in the universe is asymmetry of desire. It is horribly sad and horribly cruel. Isabelle had a visceral memory of standing in her old bedroom, naked, as Karl stuffed clothes into a bag and spat insults at her. She had felt so weak she had spilt juice from the glass she was holding.

'Please,' he said again, low and tremulous.

Isabelle didn't trust herself to speak so she slipped the card back into the envelope and put it on the desk in front of him, her hand trembling. His mouth contorted, as if there were twelve different beginnings of sentences vying for the first syllable. But he knew it was hopeless. Even as Isabelle rose to go it was as if his belly spilt over his belt and his hair thinned. Tomorrow there would be liver spots on his pate and a tightening of his bones. Floundering for a way to leave Jack all the dignity she could, she extended her hand across his desk.

'Peace,' she said.

He looked at her hand like it was a foreign object he didn't recognise and couldn't trust. 'Why? Why won't you come?'

'Whatever was between us Jack, it wasn't real. It was infatuation, nothing more. We were both foolish. Thank God we didn't actually,' she cuts the air with her hand, 'you know. You said yourself that you love your wife.'

'Yes, but —'

She raised her hand and left the room. *Please don't cry. Please don't cry. Please don't cry.* Isabelle silently repeated the mantra over and over as she took the walk of shame from Jack's office back to her desk, as if by dint of repetition and vehemence she could salve his pride. In the end the only gift she could make to him was the removal of her presence.

Isabelle leaves her breakfast table, drops her key in the box at reception and steps outside into the chill air. There is a supernova in her chest: fiery, white and ecstatic. She cuts through the Náměstí Republiky heading for the Vltava River. She feels a smug sort of rejoicing in being able to predict which streets will emerge under her feet from her years of devouring Prague guides. When the Soviet tanks rolled into the city in 1968 the Czechs tore down the street signs to confuse the invaders. *That wouldn't have fooled me.*

To Isabelle's surprise she has the ancient streets to herself, save the odd taxi and empty bus sweeping its headlights along the damp road. It is profoundly quiet. The only sounds are the squeak of her shoes on the smooth black stones and the trickle of water through drains. The roads rise up and around her, shunting her into lanes and squares and archways. What a flat, bright city she lives in by comparison. A city of horizons in all directions. Here, Isabelle is walled in, corralled. She longs to know what lies behind the iron gates she passes. She is itching to scale the walls and nose around in those courtyards, walk into those old rooms and stare out at the skyline from a kitchen window.

She wonders what it would be like to live with the inescapable past in your walls and hallways. To move through rooms that have seen war, occupation, resistance and revolution. Does the past gather there, amplifying with each passing decade? Are you subtly changed by the weight of collective experience gathering dust around you? *I might have been different in such a space.* The Black Place might have found it harder to gain a toehold, competing with all those ghosts. Maybe The Black Places have deserted the old world and come shrieking across the ocean to the blank, open vistas of the new.

She rounds a building and suddenly the Vltava River is before her, rippling between the bridges. Empty wooden pleasure-steamers bob in the water, waiting for the tourists. A pair of ducks make clumsy landings between two boats, then set to squabbling with one another. Isabelle gasps at how comparatively paltry are the magazine images upon which she has fed herself, now that the original is here before her. She pulls off her glove to touch the damp stone wall that runs astride the river. The cold bites into her fingers but she trails them along the wall as she walks, pulling Mrs Graham's pashmina tighter for warmth.

The casual omnipresence of gorgeousness is slightly asphyxiating. Every building, every statue, every window box holds something that could make her weep. As she saunters through the empty streets, all this beauty to herself, she feels as if she is watching a gorgeous human being slowly divest themselves of their finery to reveal their perfect nakedness. The metaphor brings Evan before her: taut and shining with sweat on her bed. Evan who had knotted his fingers in her hair and…

No. Stop.

Isabelle shakes her head as if she is sluicing trapped water from her ear. She has to ration her thoughts about Evan carefully or they will capsize her.

She speeds up. Still she has the city to herself. She pauses at the entry to the Charles Bridge. Behind her in Staré Město there is an occasional clatter of chains falling as stores open for the day. Malá Strana beckons her from the other side. With its turrets and towers, it looks like a giant hostel for fairytale characters. Isabelle puckers her lips to her still ungloved hand and then places her fingers tenderly on the first of the statues that line the bridge.

'I'm here,' she whispers. She zigzags the bridge, skipping between the statues on each side. A shaft of weak sunlight irradiates some letters above the statue of the Christ. She walks towards it until the glittering bronze letters clarify. 'I.N.R.I.' The Christ is on the cross, his head dangling from the bunched muscles in his neck. In the amplifying light every curve and lineament of his suffering, slender body is magnified. He looks painfully thin. Isabelle could almost encircle his waist with her hands. Only the nails keep him upright, and they threaten to slice through the tendons in his hand, leaving him in freefall to the hard cobbles of the bridge. Isabelle finds the torture of the image slightly shocking. *Why do we think that suffering is redemptive*, she wonders. *And how much suffering? Do I get any credit for surviving The Black Place?* She reaches for the statue and splays her fingers across his feet.

And that's when she hears it – a low, droning sound like a swarm of bees hiving nearby. The sound rises and rises, coming towards her on the bridge. She leaps backwards as the buzz resolves into hordes of people boring across the bridge from both sides of the city. She feels the solitary, ancient Prague with which she has been communing turn tail and dive deep within itself, leaving her alone on the bridge with the rampaging hordes. She is caught in the net of people before she can find safe passage. They come sweeping over the bridge, ensnaring her. She shuts the door to herself and folds into the crowd.

They are a bobbing, weightless thing that curls like a wave over the bridge and into Malá Strana, hurtling from shop to shop. From between the whirling limbs, Isabelle glimpses strings of marionettes hung from doorways and trays of garnet rings stuffed into windows urging 'Sale!' and 'Last Chance!'. They swerve around carts of celebrity matrioshka dolls blocking the pavement. Every second someone darts out from the net to make a purchase before being reeled back in. They gather jewellery and postcards and pashminas and shiny green bottles of absinthe. It starts to rain but the drops barely touch Isabelle as the crowd lifts a tarpaulin of individual umbrellas. Their numbers swell with the late-rising, hung-over and recently arrived.

Through the gaps between the umbrellas, Isabelle sees that the Charles Bridge, so still in the post-dawn, is thick with people. Sketch artists lay out easels as hawkers hang up photographs and jewellery and puppets. From somewhere the smell of strong, fresh coffee drifts down the street making her salivate. She wants to follow the smell but she is trussed up in this crowd with no apparent means of escape. They move again, compacting themselves into a tight stream through the narrow streets. They are weighted now with more things and more people. Isabelle is struggling to breathe. She has to flee this mob. They don't understand Prague. They are aliens here, too loud and busy and cashed-up to hear the real city whispering to them.

Isabelle takes a deep breath and throws the full weight of her personality into the crush. People bounce off her and the crowd parts. She tears back over the bridge towards Staré Město and turns right. She quickens her pace, following the curve of the river away from the city. The roads are now clogged with trams and cars and tour buses. The honking of horns and sigh of breaks erupts around her. She walks fast, almost runs. After about twenty minutes the city loosens and she finds herself in a neighbourhood with the air of a sleepy fishing village. The steep flank of a hill rises to her left, houses clinging improbably to its side. To her right the Vltava curves, grey and cold, around the outcrops of rock. In front of her an imposing chunk of mossy rock chomps into the riverbank.

Isabelle knows she is approaching the ancient fort of the Vyšehrad and that somewhere above her on the top of the cliff is a church. She pauses to study the hillside, looking for an entranceway up the steep embankment. Every time a car passes her she smothers a childish urge to hide, as if the encroaching century is all that prevents her from returning to the cradle of sullen stone. She decides her route, crosses the road and is swallowed into the snaking green tendrils of the park.

Despite being so fit, she finds it hard going up the sharply angled walkway. Her feet disappear into the coiling fog at her ankles and her breath comes jagged and white. She stops at a bench halfway up the cliff to catch her breath. Too little food and fatigue are beginning to cloud her mind. For an unsettling moment she cannot recall what day it is or how long it has been since she left Australia. The glimpses of traffic between the beech trees and the tumbling vines strike her as anomalous, an image spliced out of time. She can feel the centuries at her back.

It might have been this very place where Libussa had stood, entranced, when she prophesied that a great city would emerge in Hradčany. With a twist in the frequency Isabelle, too, could be a seer, a lightning rod for dreams and visions instead of darkness and panic. She imagines Libussa before her, falling deeper and deeper under the sway of the revelations unfolding behind her eyelids. She senses the mix of awe and terror Libussa inspired in her people. Feels them holding their breath, waiting to see if Libussa will awake to prophecies of pestilence and war, scattering them across countries in search of sanctuary. Or will she thrill them with tales of fat crops and thriving babies? Isabelle feels their excitement when Libussa awakes – the vision still wet behind her eyes – and shares with her court the city of surpassing beauty she has seen. Of towers and spires and stone bridges across the river, grape vines on the hill opposite and gracious squares for music and dancing. What would it be like to have visions so dazzling it set courtiers and peasants alike hewing it out of the rock around them?

Isabelle understands why Libussa chose a farmer for a husband. A man who could make things grow. An earth to her moon. Perhaps he planted the parents to the very saplings under Isabelle's feet. She gives up her battle against sleep, pulling her beanie lower over her head and winding the pashmina into a pillow. She zips her anorak and curls up on the bench, nestled tightly in the wood of seers and prophets.

THIRTEEN

From: evan117@hotmail.com
To: IsabelleNorthwell@dppar.wa.gov.au

Dear Belle

I went to the pool tonight but it's not the same solo.
I'm slow and demotivated without you there to push
me. (I can hear you in my head laughing and saying,
Evan, you're slow and demotivated with me.) I managed
about twenty laps and then I got bored. I don't know
if it's the boredom or the heat or whatever but I can't
settle to anything. I'm restless. Jumpy.

Do you ever think back to those days at the
Department for Civics and Arts? (Mimics and Tarts,
Karl called it. And he was right. All those wannabe
Scorseses and Atwoods slumming it as bureaucrats.)
You, me and Karl were the refugees from the sciences.
'The numbers people', the rest of the grads called us.
At least, that's what they called you and me. Karl –
always the chameleon – was accepted as one of 'them'.
The arty types who clogged up meetings talking

about 'communities of practice' and 'the exegesis as research artefact'. I've still got no clue WTF that means.

You, me, Karl. We were a natural group of outsiders with only Karl moving between all the factions. Karl and I both liked you. We even talked about it once, about how we were going to handle it. (Please don't think we talked about you like a piece of chattel. We didn't. We barely mentioned you, in fact, after our bald declarations of attraction.) It was all very blokey. We'd still be friends no matter what and no hard feelings and, after all, the decision was up to you and you might like one or neither of us. 'And Isabelle's broad-minded,' Karl said casually. 'Maybe she'll be into a ménage à trois.'

That's vintage Karl. The offhand remark you can't pull him up on without looking like a tool but that kicks you in the guts all the same. He'd zeroed in on the fly in my ointment. The sex thing. If I pursued you, stayed in the game instead of leaving the field to Karl, sooner or later you and I were going to have to confront the sex issue. All I could offer you at that point was relationship-lite.

So I stood by and watched you and Karl get together. I didn't last long at Mimics and Tarts after that. Even my Catholic masochism has its limits.

You need to know this. What happened between us on Australia Day wasn't some freak thing I

haven't thought long and hard about. So if you're
worried about me being impulsive and regretful,
forget it.

Let me know when you're ready to talk. What do
you think about my idea of getting together on
Sunday for takeaway and beer?

Love,
Evan

After ten hours of ceaseless motion Isabelle drifts into
a cafe near her hotel with the unlikely name of Bob's.
She steadies herself on the barrier that leads down the
stairs. She knows she must sleep and she must eat if she
is to arm herself against dark things. But the lightness
in her body and the whiteness of her hibernating mind
are seductive. Addictive.

A pixie-like waiter, small and deft with pointed ears
and an adorable snub nose, brings a menu to her table.
Isabelle gestures to an item she thinks is soup. Instead,
the waiter brings her a glass of wine so acidic that she
flinches at the first few sips. Around her the orange-
walled cafe fills with cigarette smoke and rapid-fire
Czech. Occasionally someone uses an English word,
making Isabelle feel as if her camouflage is dissolving.

An elderly gentleman in a bumblebee-striped jumper
pauses on the landing to survey the cafe. There are very
few spare seats left and four of them are at Isabelle's
table. He gives her an inquisitive, almost hostile look, as
if she has appropriated a table on permanent reserve for

him. As he makes wheezing progress down the stairs, the pixie waiter greets him by name. Isabelle looks away, back towards the tourist brochures she has collected during her restless crisscrossing of the city. She thumbs through her options for day trips: Kutná Hora. Karlovy Vary. Terezín. She briefly considers the last destination, a concentration camp, before deciding against it. Perhaps later, when she is feeling stronger.

The wizened gentleman pulls a chair out and sits down opposite her. He gives her a slight nod across the table. Wordlessly, the pixie brings him a tall stein of dark beer. The froth collects in the salt-and-pepper bristle of his beard as he raises the glass repeatedly to his lips. Isabelle is fascinated by his silvery-grey eyebrows, which refuse to lie flat against his brow but point in all directions like a crazy weathervane. He takes a fresh packet of cigarettes from his pocket and carefully winds back the cellophane. His nicotine-stained fingers are nearly as orange as the stripes on his jumper. He looks above Isabelle's head to the window where the booted feet of Prague clatter past, and smokes.

Isabelle wonders what he makes of the seismic changes in his city over the last fifty years. Is he glad the communists are gone, or could the fluttering banners for Benetton and L'Oréal that line the streets be May Day garlands for all he notices or cares?

'English?' he asks, his eyes still at the window.

Startled, Isabelle shakes her head. 'Australian.'

He takes a deep, satisfied draught from his glass. 'Long way.'

'Yes.'

The wine makes Isabelle feel even lighter, as if she is a wraith that might dissolve into the thickening smoke. The pixie gestures towards Isabelle's empty glass. She nods, soup forgotten. Three people collect at the entrance and look around for a table. They seem too chic for the venue in their caramel coats and high-heeled boots. The old man looks at them, then at the empty chairs at their table, then at Isabelle. A shrewd calculation is evident behind his rheumy eyes.

'You like Prague?' he asks her, drawing the vacant chairs in against assumptions of a communal table.

'Very much.'

'Is like Sydney?'

'I'm not from Sydney. I'm from Perth. But no, it's very different.'

'Perth?'

'Western Australia.'

'Australia is not old,' he says matter-of-factly.

'No.' *Well*, Isabelle thinks, *not old for the whitefellas.*

The seatless Czechs continue to survey Isabelle and her companion. Isabelle thinks furiously for a sentence. 'Do you like Prague?'

He shrugs. 'I've always lived here. I don't know.'

'You've never lived anywhere else?'

'During war.'

Isabelle does a rapid calculation of his age. 'Where?'

'Places,' he says, his gaze wandering above her to the window again.

The patrons waiting for a table take slow, deliberate steps towards them. The clatter of their boots draws the old man back. 'Do you like Prague?' he asks again. Isabelle wonders if he has dementia or is merely determined to keep the conversation on endless loop until the people eyeing off their seats go away.

'I'm in love with Prague. In my city, the streets are choked from seven in the morning. Shops are open. People take calls. Here, it's whisper-quiet. I could have been the only person on earth. I walked to the Vyšehrad. The church was closed, but I walked through the cemetery and put a flower on Smetana's grave.'

'Tomorrow?'

'I'm not sure. Maybe Josefov. Or the Petřín Tower. Or the Museum of Communism. I think that's nearby. Have you been?'

He laughs. At least, Isabelle thinks it is a laugh. 'No. I *am* Museum of Communism.'

The stylish Czechs have found their own table so Isabelle and her companion are free to lapse into silence. The pixie brings the man another beer immediately he finishes the first. This one is accompanied by a plate of soft white bread and feta cheese sopping in oil, lemon and peppercorns. He deftly manages bread, cheese, cigarette and beer all at once. He times his repast so that the last mop of oil is followed by the final mouthful of beer. He pushes his seat out from the table, gives Isabelle a sharp nod and leaves.

From: evan117@hotmail.com
To: IsabelleNorthwell@dppar.wa.gov.au

So you're not returning my calls. Not responding to my emails.

I haven't heard a word from you since the morning after the party.

What do you think this does to me, Belle? Leaving aside the fact that we've had sex for the first time and haven't spoken about it, what do you think not hearing from you for days on end does to me?

So I went to your flat with a crowbar and a coathanger to break in. I was sweating like a bastard. Terrified about what I might find.

I saw Samara on my way up the stairwell. 'Hello, Evan,' she says cheerily to me. 'I thought you'd be in Prague with Isabelle.'

WTF?????

I asked Samara when you left. She told me five days ago. She said she gave you a drawing to remember her by.

What am I supposed to do with this, Belle? You up and leave without so much as a word. I find out about it accidentally. You know what finding you did to me, and here you've gone and done it again.

This is totally shitty. It's unforgivable. If you need space or time, fine. No problem. But you don't just up and leave like this without a word.

I've always known that things were unequal between us, that I love you more than you love me. But it never occurred to me till now that you don't really give one gram of a f*ck about me. So what am I? A convenience? A crutch? Habit?

If you get this message FFS say something. You owe me that much.

FOURTEEN

A gibbous moon clambers through the open window and wakes Isabelle up. She opens her eyes to find herself in a silvery pool of light. In her feverish dream she was back at the Vyšehrad, a wild creature gathering vines around her for a bed. She was digging into the earth, becoming indistinguishable from the trees and the frost and the river.

Isabelle throws off her blankets and showers in the dark. She tears open four coffee sachets and empties them into her mug while the kettle boils, then takes a rough-haired blanket from the cupboard and winds it around her, drawing the wicker chair close to the window. She feels the empty, moonlit street sigh and open up, relieved that all the jostling, buying, gorging tourists have retreated to their heated rooms to sleep off their excesses. That a city of this many people could be so quiet astonishes her. Always in Perth there is the sound of a car backfiring, a rumbling train or barking dog. Perhaps it is the sticky weight of history that pulls eyelids shut and stuffs the mouth. Even the flabby English boys here for stag nights and football wind-ups are silent.

Isabelle sits there drinking coffee until the daylight creeps up Na Poříčí towards the Náměstí Republiky and the city folds in on itself. She rides the braying elevator to the breakfast room, wondering if the lift is powered by a donkey high above her in a turret. Yes, she thinks, Grigor would have had a donkey, his faithful companion on the collective farm. When the revolution came sweeping the collectives away and flooding the cities with people looking for work, Grigor couldn't bear to leave his donkey behind. So now the donkey, Agnes, earns her keep pulling the levers that operate the lift, receiving European Union baby carrots for reward.

'Thanks, Agnes,' Isabelle speaks skyward as the lift lurches to a halt.

She takes her seat in the dining room and waits for the signal that she can eat. Perhaps today the coffee rationing will end. But no, the urn spurts the same tepid, muddy water into her mug. She spoons quivering eggs, pale bacon and dark bread onto her plate. She manages a few reluctant mouthfuls then leaves.

Grigor glances up from his newspaper and cigarette as Isabelle enters the street, tightening her pashmina around her. She heads for the Charles Bridge, struggling to keep her footing on the slick cobblestones. The bridge seems to float on the fog. Beneath her, she can hear the slap and suck of the boats at the water but she cannot see them. She parts the fog with her mittened hands until she finds the statue of the Christ. Impelled by a sudden surge of loneliness, she tugs at her glove, kisses her fingers and places them lightly on his feet.

From somewhere the tantalising aroma of brewing coffee folds into the mist. Isabelle circles, her nose upturned, trying to divine where it is coming from. Eyes partly closed she walks hopefully in the direction of the smell. Perhaps she can find a cosy spot with decent coffee and the Czech equivalent of Mrs Graham to chat to for an hour or so. Searching for the source of the coffee she finds herself corralled in a narrow street hardly wider than a cupboard that eventually spills her out at a park. The licks of fog dissolve in the gathering light. Disoriented, she tries to anchor herself on a landmark but nothing is familiar.

A phone booth materialises from the fog. It floats there, a ghostly reproach. Evan doesn't know she is here, Evan who had found her (blue and going bluer) and somehow got her to the hospital. Did he hoist her onto his back and drop her onto the back seat, blindly running red lights the whole way? Was he calm? Frantic? Dumb with fear or yelling at her to wake up? There is a blank in his mind where this information should be. She imagines the fact of her disappearance echoing in the chamber she has carved out.

The morning after the fireworks they agreed to give each other a few days apart to collect themselves. To think seriously about what they wanted from each other. Even as she had agreed to this she was preparing to run. She has left her mobile phone at home on the kitchen bench to make contact impossible. She imagines him now, increasingly panicked, as his calls and emails go unanswered.

'I'm sorry.' The words come white out of her mouth. 'I'm so sorry. But I can't give you what you want. What you deserve.'

The night of the party he took her by surprise. He had pinioned her against the cupboards, flooding her with his salt and sandalwood smell. There were a few seconds of shock, where she could not reconcile the hot, probing mouth determined to find her tongue with Evan's mouth. With this Evan who was hitching her skirt up and breathing close into her ear, making her stomach liquefy. That shock was her window, the moment when she could have done something different. After a few seconds she offered no resistance. She had none. The magnificent sculpture that was Evan turned flesh-pink and pulsating under her hands.

Later, lying on her bed, sweat-drenched and happy, he collected her to his chest and said, 'I love you.' She ran her fingers along the ridge of his brow, the curve of his lips. The simple cross tattooed on his shoulder. She waited until his body slackened in sleep and then she wept, holding herself rigid against her sobs so as not to wake him.

The last thing Karl had said before walking out was that loving her was like hugging a shadow. Isabelle couldn't bear for Evan to discover this about her. How insubstantial she was, how limited. How disappointing. As she was silently crying, she thought about the exchange the American Indians made for their land. How long did the shiny beads distract them from what they had lost? She had watched Evan as he slept, loving him more and more. What a pathetic trade he had made for her. His virginity. His goodness. And for what?

Her mind tracks backwards to the time in Perth. She should call him. She *must* call him. But only to tell him she is safe. Two minutes. Three at most. Any longer and she will succumb to her craving for him. 'You've thought about this,' she said, astonished, as Evan knotted her hair in his fingers and grazed her neck with his lips. 'A thousand times,' he said. Her desire answered his. If she lets herself think about him her body and heart scream for him. She lacks the strength to resist if she is in the same room, the same town, the same hemisphere as Evan.

If this were a film or a novel love would conquer all and The Black Place would shrink to a quirky bit-player while she and Evan set off into the sunset. But it is not. Her only hope is the ocean between them – a cooling draught to chill them back into sustainable friendship. Anything else would mean losing him and that is unthinkable. Unbearable. Almost from the first they had fallen into an easy, uncomplicated intimacy. One of the other grads told her about Evan before she had met him. 'Drop. Dead. Gorgeous,' she had said. And she was right. But it was Evan's playfulness rather than his looks that drew her. Where the other grads fell quickly into pole position, jostling for attention and promotion, she and Evan held back, faintly amused by the whole thing. They had invented a game called 'Lights on, eyes open' to entertain themselves during the interminable meetings where nothing was decided and the outcome was always to 'consult further'. The game involved imagining having sex with the least attractive of their colleagues with the lights on and their eyes open, suggesting less and less appealing prospects until one of them was forced to choose death. He protested that she chose death too often, she countered that since for him it was entirely hypothetical she was entitled to choose death because of her better informed imagination. He had baulked. 'If I want my comeback I'll go ask your mother.' Shocked at his crassness she had laughed out loud, earning a black look and a black mark from the director facilitating the meeting.

Isabelle rummages through her purse for coins and checks her watch. Two minutes. Three at most. Keep it strictly to what he needs to know. She is safe, she is fine, she is sorry. She screws up her courage and steps into the phone booth. There is no handset. Instead, embedded inside the booth is a lump of ill-shapen concrete with a phone moulded into it, stone and inert. Isabelle squeezes her eyes shut and opens them again. But the carved phone is still there. She runs her fingers along the round nubs of numbers. She looks up, puzzled. Further along the walkway is another booth. She walks towards it to discover a shower rose for a mouthpiece.

She becomes increasingly unsettled as she investigates booth after booth with no phone in any. One booth is so small she has to wedge herself in it sideways to fit. Another is filled with straw and manure and boarded up with wooden planks. Another encircles a tall, slim birch with the word 'phone' carved into the trunk. The last of the booths is crammed with plastic 'oxygen' symbols. Isabelle drapes herself over one of the O_2 objects and talks herself down. She is locked in that dream where bizarre and improbable obstacles prevent you from getting to the exam that will determine the rest of your life.

The park funnels her out at a gate where two giant fluorescent bunny rabbits stand sentinel. Immediately she steps onto the road Isabelle is caught in the crush. In her panic she has failed to notice the rampaging hordes spilling from their hotels and hostels into the street. Unable to fight her way out of the net of people she idles her mind and the mob becomes a collage: a mouth agape there, a squinting pair of eyes here. She is swept along in a cacophony of languages that eventually collapses into a winding queue in what she surmises is the district of Josefov. The man in front of her wears a bright red shirt emblazoned with blue lettering: *Czech me out*. It begins to drizzle. Isabelle wraps Mrs Graham's pashmina tighter around her head and neck. The crowd siphons through an archway to a synagogue, some of the men pausing to take a blue skullcap from the basket hanging from one of the eaves.

Inside, the synagogue is bare and quiet, eerily so after the roar of the street. Isabelle feels slightly calmer. She knows what she must do now. She must phone Evan. Let him know she is all right. Beg his forgiveness. She sweeps her eyes over the beautiful medieval script covering every inch of the church walls. She looks around for a guide or a pamphlet that might translate the words for her but can see none. She manoeuvres herself through the crush to be closer to the wall and stares. Up close, the calligraphy clarifies. It is not a medieval script as she had thought. It is a series of names. Row upon row upon row of names, painstakingly hand-painted.

213

The names flow from the topmost corner of the wall to the floor. They spill over to the next wall, and the one after that. It is a hall of perfect names.

She wonders who painted all of these names, their face pressed up against the wall, tiny paintbrush in hand. What discipline to produce each name so perfectly, so lovingly. She turns to leave, determined to find a phone, but one name leaps out and lunges at her cornea: Adolph Schwarz. Did his parents live long enough to regret the name they had given him? Huddled together in the train heading east did they collectively decide on a new name? Or did they cling to it to the end, a pure thing not to be corrupted by the existence of the other Adolf and his madness?

'Eighty thousand people,' drawls the man to Isabelle's right. He lets out a long, low whistle, slowly shaking his disbelieving head. 'Gee whiz. Eighty thousand people.' His wife nods. 'Eighty thousand people *is* a lot of people to gas. I mean, just the logistics of it. All those bodies you gotta dispose of.'

The silence teeters, looking for a solid space to lean on, then collapses into a sharp collective intake of breath. The very walls themselves seem to contract with shock. Suddenly, the blobbish crowd resolves into disparate individuals. Faces come rapidly into focus, pale and stricken. A young man standing near the entrance throws his jumper over the stars and stripes stitched onto his backpack. The couple themselves seem oblivious. They continue to stand next to the wall, the man still shaking his head.

'Gee whiz,' he says again.

Isabelle glues her eyes to the floor and wedges past the other people out of the room. She pursues a shaft of sunlight to a grassed area outside where she is immediately locked into another queue. She has a brief moment of nostalgia for the open spaces of her home town as she waits for the line to snake around a chaotic cemetery, headstones skewing from the grass at improbable angles. They look like teeth in a badly managed jaw. Eventually the line spills out into an alley behind the synagogue. It is a wide thoroughfare crowded on both sides with stalls and shops. Isabelle buys a bottle of water and sits down on a bench to collect herself. She watches the people, silent and slow-limbed, leave the burial ground.

A couple emerge, blinking into the sunlight. Dazed, they jolt from one step to another. They pause for a moment at the bottom of the stairs as if uncertain what to do next. Then, because they must do something, he reaches into his pocket for a few crowns and buys a Coke from one of the stalls. He takes a few sips and hands the bottle to her. She looks at it blankly, as if she has forgotten what it is for, then lifts it to her lips. They pass the bottle back and forth between them, shuffling along the walkway. A few stalls along she picks up a golem key ring and holds it to the light, turning it slowly this way and that. He riffles through some postcards, selects a few and shows them to her. She counts something on her fingers, addressees presumably, and he chooses a few more.

The bottle is now empty. He drops it into a bin and buys doughnuts from a street vendor. They are talking now, between bites, and pointing to clocks and matrioshka dolls and tea towels. He picks up one of the dolls and says something, making her laugh. They buy the doll. By the time they arrive at the stairs onto upmarket Pařížská they have several bags of merchandise and are chatting animatedly. Robotically, Isabelle follows them, but the hive has ejected her.

She walks alone, past beautiful clothes in beautiful stores patronised by beautiful people. In one store window a lithe, tall model in a gold lamé gown reclines on a chaise. A whirring fan makes her auburn hair float above her alabaster face. On the other side of the window, a photographer prowls back and forth, snapping her haughty loveliness. Opposite, the statue of Kafka points an accusing finger at Isabelle.

From: evan117@hotmail.com
To: IsabelleNorthwell@dppar.wa.gov.au

Your work phoned me today. I never knew you
had me listed as your next of kin. I spoke to Jack.
He hasn't heard from you either. He mumbled
something about a 'problematic' leave application.
They're trying to trace you to get it sorted. I told
him that you were in Prague. No, I didn't know
when you'd left and no, I didn't know when you
would be back.

Then he starts crying.

He starts crying down the phone and saying, 'Oh
fuck, oh fuck, oh fuck.'

I'm trying to calm this guy down, wondering why he's getting all worked up over a leave application and then I remembered that night at your place before the party. You kept getting calls from a guy named Jack.

This Jack. This guy I'm talking to on the phone, who's having a complete meltdown and sounds like he's in even worse shape than me. So I try to calm him down, telling him nothing's wrong and that you've been planning to go to Prague for ages and I'm sure you'll be back soon (hah).

He asked me if I was your brother. I said no. He asked me if I was your boyfriend. I said, 'What's it to you?' Then he starts crying again and mumbling something about a hearing and disciplinary procedures. I asked him what he was talking about and he said nothing but to get you to call him as soon as I heard from you. On impulse I asked him if he wanted to meet me. There was a longish silence down the phone and then he said yes. He told me to meet him at the Civic Hotel at 6 pm. He'd be sitting at a table in the sports bar at the back.

I got there a bit late. It looked like he'd had a fair bit to drink already. I introduced myself. Said I was an old friend of yours.

Before I'd even ordered a drink he said, 'Are you fucking her?'

I stood up to leave, decided he was a crazy old drunk
and this was a waste of time, but he grabbed my
arm said he was sorry and begged me to stay. Said
he wasn't in his right mind. That his life was falling
apart. I asked him what that had to do with you and
he told me the whole story. His version of it anyway.

He said he was your boss. That you'd always gotten
along pretty well and he thought you had some
promise but never seemed to find your groove (his
word). Then something happened recently. He said
after a meeting you'd come onto him. 'Let me know
she was into me,' was what he said.

I'm looking at this craggy old guy across the table
from me and trying to understand what possible
attraction he could have for you. I mean, Karl's
a manipulative dick but I can see he's got some
charm. But this guy? He's gotta be in his mid-
fifties. And I hate to say this, but I get the feeling
that this meltdown he's having over you is the
most interesting thing about him. After twenty
minutes I could guess what sort of car he drives
(I was right; I checked when he left), what sort
of house he lives in, what his wife is like. He was
so beige I thought there had to be some mistake.
That he'd imagined the whole thing and your
coming onto him was nothing more than a polite
conversation in the tearoom that he'd blown out of
all proportion.

I tried to suggest this as politely as I could and he
went off. Said you'd been lovers (again, his word).
That you'd gone to his place the night before
Australia Day when his wife was out and you'd
hidden out in his back yard, drinking champagne
and carrying on. He said you wore a Japanese
ornament in your hair. I remember that ornament.
Karl bought it for you when he went to Osaka with
the Mimics and Tarts for that cultural-exchange
junket.

As soon as he mentioned the ornament I knew it was
true. It makes sense. You go into this guy's house,
the house he shares with his *wife*, wearing things
Karl gave you. What was this, Belle? Some kind of
revenge fantasy? You think that by detonating this
guy's marriage you score one against Karl? That you
get back at him somehow?

Is that what I was, too? Were you counting on me
telling Karl about us? That he'd work himself up
into a jealous fury and come beat your door down to
win you back?

Because he won't. He calls you Hysterabelle.

The clusterfuck doesn't end there. You're wanted
at some kind of disciplinary hearing at your work.
I don't know the full details (Jack was virtually
incomprehensible after an hour) but there's an
'irregularity' in your leave records. It looks like

someone's deliberately altered them. I told Jack that if he thought you'd done it he was dead wrong. That's not you at all. Then he got aggro, yelling, 'Well who else then? Who else would do it?' I calmed him down as best I could, made an excuse and left.

All of which brings me back to where I started – that I'm fucking terrified you're going to do something stupid. I'm angry with you and jealous and confused and furious and I'm also scared witless that you're going to do something dumb. You promised me you wouldn't. You gave me your word. I'll be holding you to it.

Evan

Isabelle makes her way back to Bob's and looks for a seat in the crowd. The old man from the day before – she has christened him Socialist Man – looks up from his beer and nods at her in acknowledgement.

'Hello,' Isabelle sits down opposite him.

'Hello.'

The pixie brings her the same wine as yesterday. She puckers her mouth in readiness for its astringency but cannot stifle a cough as it strips a layer of skin from her throat on the way down.

'Have beer instead.'

'I don't like beer.'

'Not very Australian.'

'No. I'm a national embarrassment.'

Socialist Man grunts.

'Can I ask you something?'

He shrugs, as if to say it is all the same to him.

'I was in Malá Strana today, near the Art Gallery. I found all of these phone booths. Well not really phone booths. Pretend phone booths. Some of them were filled with concrete. One had a tree growing out of the booth. One of them was like a shower. I don't know what to make of it. Is it some kind of joke?'

'Joke? Yes. Joke, I suppose.'

'Why?'

Socialist Man takes a deep, silent drink, his throat barely rippling, then wipes his large, orange-tipped hand through his beard for any collected froth. 'Communists put phones everywhere. Everywhere phones. And phone books. Great symbol of socialist pride. Phones, they never work. But they keep build them.'

'Does it,' Isabelle hesitates slightly, 'does it bother you? To be reminded, I mean?'

He shrugs. 'Phone booth. No phone booth. I still remember.'

What Isabelle really wants to know about is all those names on the church wall. She is wondering how to bring it up when Socialist Man becomes suddenly animated. He sweeps an accusing hand at the window above them. 'Tourist. All tourist. English. American. French. Come here. Eat, drink, get drunk. Buy every-thing. All old factory flats. Buy, buy, buy. But where they in 1948?' He mutters something in dark Czech. 'Where they when Masaryk jump? When tanks come in sixty-eight? Buy, buy, buy. Make everything better. Bah.' He curses again.

221

The pixie hurries to the table with a placating beer and a plate of cheese and bread. He gives Isabelle an apologetic smile and another glass of wine, though she is barely started on her first. She sculls a glass, wincing, then figuring Socialist Man's blood is up anyway, plunges ahead.

'I went to Josefov today, too. Accidentally, really. I got caught up in a crowd. I ended up at the Jewish Museum.' Isabelle waits to see if anything flickers in his face, but his eyes betray nothing, save his stewing anger. Socialist Man drinks his beer then embeds his cheese in his bread and begins demolishing the plate. 'They said... they said that eighty thousand Jews disappeared from the city. Most of them didn't...come back.'

He grunts and eats. 'Everyone suffered,' he says, between mouthfuls. Isabelle waits, but Socialist Man has reached his quota of vowel sounds for today. He mops up his plate with a thick wedge of crust and pushes his chair out from the table.

'Goodbye.'

'Goodbye. Are you off home?'

He shakes his head. 'Work.'

'What do you do?'

He mimics manoeuvring a steering wheel. 'Barge.'

'You drive a barge? For the tourists?' Isabelle thinks he is rather miscast as the jolly sea captain for the photographing hordes.

He snorts, a snort that might signify laughter. 'The homeless.' And with that he gives her a slight nod and leaves for his shift.

FIFTEEN

From: evan117@hotmail.com
To: IsabelleNorthwell@dppar.wa.gov.au

I don't know why I keep writing these emails. We
joke about my masochistic streak but maybe I really
do have one.

I think it's sympathetic magic. Like if I keep the
thread going, keep talking to you then you have to
be there. Have to be.

I'm not in good shape, Belle. Drinking too much.
Not exercising enough. My mind's got stuck in some
weird loop trying to make sense of us. One minute
I think I was just part of your revenge fantasy
against Karl. The next that what happened between
us completely freaked you out and you've done a
runner.

The worst was last night. I woke up at about
two. It was still hot, well above thirty, and I was
drenched in sweat. I felt like I'd forgotten something.

Something I was supposed to do. I'm lying there
under the fan going over the day when it hit me.

The rooftop.

When I found you up there, before we went to the
beach, you said that something bad had happened
to you. My first thought was that someone had
attacked you on the rooftop. It made a kind of sense.
All that obsessive cleaning and painting. You were
trying to make it go away. To make it disappear.
I was ready to hunt the prick down and make him
eat his balls. You told me I had it wrong. 'Nothing
human,' you said.

It fell out of my mind what with the party and
everything that happened afterwards. But my
subconscious kept chewing it over. It spat it back at
me in the early hours of this morning.

'Nothing human.'

He would've seemed inhuman. I get that now. Is that
why you're running Belle?

Am I the guy you thought was 'safe' who's turned
out to be like all the rest?

The thought makes me physically sick.

I'm so fucking sorry. For God's sake, come home.

Isabelle considers the string of numbers written by the receptionist she thinks of as the Nice Lady and deliberately dials each one. After a pause of a few seconds there's a hiss of static that resolves into a pinging sound. She strikes the bedclothes with her fist in frustration. She has tried every combination of numbers that might connect her to Australia but may as well be talking into the shower rose at the park. Exasperated, she phones downstairs to request assistance.

After twelve rings Grigor answers.

'Hi. This is Isabelle Northwell in room seventy-one. I'm trying to get an outside line to call Australia but I can't get through.'

'Phone zero first for line then international dialling code then number.'

'Yes, I did that but —' Too late. Grigor hangs up.

'Fuck!' Isabelle yells at the bare room.

She swings from the bed to the open window and leans out. The Saturday-night streets are thick with people. Directly opposite, tourists bunch around the pizzeria window, bundled up in their coats. There must be a phone box in one of the better hotels. Or perhaps the tourist bureau. Isabelle hesitates. The city belongs to the shoppers and the revellers now. She would rather wait for first light, but the urge to talk to Evan, to explain herself, is more than she can bear. She pads herself in her thermal vest, thickest jumpers, anorak, pashmina, beanie and gloves, glances her fingers over Samara's drawing and plunges into the street.

'Good luck,' Grigor says to her back.

Bastard.

He probably has a stash of phone manuals in perfect English locked away in a drawer somewhere. Frosty white bubbles purl from Isabelle's lungs with each out-breath. She thinks of Good King Wenceslas going doggedly against the snow to take food and firewood to the poor. She makes for the large square at the end of her street, ducking and weaving through the hordes. The chatter is incessant – a nonsensical crossed line of languages tangling through the icy air. In the gabble Isabelle makes out the odd Russian word. She thinks the Russians are brave to come here. Brave or stupid. High above the skyline in Letná Park a red needle ticks back and forth. The Czechs put it there after blowing up the statue of Stalin that used to brood over the city. Maybe the metronome sums up the Czechs' phlegmatic attitude. 'Bah,' as Socialist Man would say. Maybe the beauty here means they recover faster from historical wounds. Still, Isabelle cannot imagine that the Czechs relish having the Russians on their turf. But still they're here, with their bottomless pockets and tourist maps, like everyone else.

The shops are all open, the restaurants and bars bulging with people. At the Republiky Isabelle climbs up on one of the pillars supporting a long-forgotten folk hero and squints through the crowd. Across the square is what she thinks is a phone booth. It is only about three hundred metres away. All she need do is cut across the quadrangle. She jumps down from the pillar and forces her way into the crush. The crowd surges against her and she is barrelled past the Powder Tower and onto Celetná Street, further and further from the phone. The revelling horde mostly comprises young English men. Isabelle recognises the boys from the dining room at her hotel. They bellow football songs and seem impervious to the cold in their thin jackets. When they open their mouths to sing, a roar of beer fumes swirls past. One of them locks eyes on Isabelle. 'Hey, it's you.' He hooks his arm into Isabelle's. 'Come on, love, you know the words,' he says, then tears into a song.

Isabelle wants to cry with frustration. The crowd gobbles the road, indifferent to the drivers honking their horns in frustration. The noise is rising, rising. The banner for the Museum of Communism flutters from a pole nearby. She considers making a run for it – surely the museum will be quiet on a Saturday night – but the stretch between here and there seems impossible. Somehow the crowd has equipped itself with steins of beer. The man next to Isabelle tightens his grip on her arm and thrusts a glass into her face. It is impossible to argue – to do anything – so Isabelle takes the glass and a swig before passing it back.

'Sure, you're all right,' says the man.

The whirligig turns then, driven by some manic, impenetrable force, moves into another street. They are a human hive throbbing and swarming. The crush is so dense that Isabelle is struggling to breathe. None of these people looks human to her. Their faces contort into shadows and holes and elongated whites as they bellow and chant. Some have removed their shirts, revealing thick gooseflesh chafing against the cold. Isabelle feels trapped in a petri dish of metastasising impulses and appetites.

The pressure against her doubles, becomes unbearable, then miraculously relents. Her arm is free. They have arrived at a large square. From somewhere up ahead comes a brass and wind cacophony of folk music. Horses with red plumage line the square, hitched to glossy black carriages. With every whinny they send white swirls into the air. Isabelle looks around for the ventricle of a quiet lane to release her into stillness but the crowd behind her remains thick. She presses forward, past folk dancers in peasant dress whirling each other about. The English boys are mimicking their steps, beer steins for partners. The one who had hooked his arm around Isabelle sees her. 'There you are.' He moves towards her so she slips backwards behind a line of Italians buying coffee. 'Wait,' he yells, 'I just want to talk to you.'

Isabelle sights the spire of a church ahead of her and pushes for it. Perhaps she can hide in the church till early morning, bunkering down on a pew in a darkened corner until the appetites are sated and it will be just her and the real city. She tears up the steps, the English man following. She opens the heavy wooden door and looks around for a hiding spot. The pews offer no refuge. They are almost empty save for a couple of older women, scarves tied under their chins, bent low over prayer books.

Desperate, Isabelle opens the door to a confessional booth and steps inside. The booth is no larger than her pantry and smells faintly of incense. She opens the door a crack to see where her pursuer is. He stands by the main doors, seemingly reluctant to enter further. He steps to the side, peering into the candle-flickering space, but cannot see her. 'Fuck it,' he mouths, and leaves. Isabelle slumps against the wall, relieved.

'Bless you, my child.' The priest's voice startles her.

Isabelle doesn't know the etiquette and is stumped for what to say.

'How long has it been since your last confession?'

'I've never been to confession,' she says honestly.

'Never, my child?'

'No. I'm sorry, but I came in here to hide. Someone was chasing me.' Isabelle tries to make out the priest's form on the other side of the latticework but he is obscured. *Can he see me?* she wonders.

After a moment the priest says, 'Who are you hiding from? Are you in danger?'

'No. I don't think he's dangerous. Just drunk. Anyway, he's gone.' She pauses, wondering how to make a polite exit.

'Is there anything you would like to talk about, my child?'

'You don't have a phone, do you?' she says feebly.

'A phone?'

'It doesn't matter. I need to go now. Thank you, though. For letting me hide.'

'Wait a moment. Are you troubled, my daughter?'

Isabelle suppresses the urge to laugh. *Am I troubled?* 'No more than some.'

'Yes, I suppose it's all relative, isn't it?' He chuckles.

Isabelle has always thought of priests as chill and remote creatures. The earthiness of his laugh surprises her. On impulse, she asks, 'Do you believe in ghosts?'

'The Holy Ghost, of course.'

'No, I don't mean that. Other ghosts. Aren't there stories in the Bible about people being taken over by spirits?'

'Ye-s,' he says cautiously. 'You might be thinking about the story of Legion.'

'The man who lived among the tombs?'

'Yes. Jesus cast the spirits out of him and into a herd of pigs.'

'Why do you think he did that?'

'Why? To give the man some relief from his torment.'

'No, I didn't mean that. I meant to ask why the pigs? Why not just kill the spirits off?'

'I've wondered that myself. Was it an act of compassion? The spirits begged Jesus to let them be transferred to the pigs.'

'Pigs are considered unclean in Jewish tradition, aren't they?'

'Yes.'

'So maybe that's it. Maybe the spirits thought they'd be at home there.'

The priest is silent for a moment. 'I don't think that can be right. Evil doesn't want what is already itself. It wants to corrupt. It wants its opposite.'

'Its opposite?'

'Goodness. Purity.'

This idea is so radical, so new, that Isabelle cannot immediately digest it. It latches onto her deepest fears and tugs at them, demanding attention. She reaches out a hand to steady herself.

'Are you all right?'

'Yes,' though she sounds unconvincing.

'Take your time. There's no need to hurry away.'

But there is. Her spinning head is made worse by the claustrophobia of the confessional. 'Excuse me. I have to go.'

'You'll be all right?'

'Yes. Thank you.'

Isabelle steps out of the booth and onto the cool, smooth flagstones of the church. Remarkably, it is whisper-quiet, as if the real, ancient Prague hides here until the tourists retreat, stupefied, to their hotels. Isabelle takes a seat towards the front of the church beneath the diamonds of stained glass and the statue of the crucified Christ. The shuffle of pious feet and the soft turn of a prayer book rustle through the church. It is a comforting, homely sound like the crumpling noise of brown paper being torn from a much-anticipated package.

All around her candles flicker. A chandelier thickly crusted with wax hangs from the ceiling suckling hundreds of tiny flames. Candles in glass jars ring the pulpit. Candles lit as offerings sway in front of ornate mirrors so the room seems to be in the lee of a gentle swell. Rise and fall, rise and fall. The flames suddenly bend left, as if a wind has blown through the room. They sputter, then right themselves. Isabelle is hypnotised by the gold and blue teardrops.

The priest's words circle round and round her head. *Evil doesn't want what is already itself. It wants to corrupt. It wants its opposite.* Isabelle has always outwardly acquiesced to her doctors' precise explanations of chemical imbalance. Until she threw away her pills she took them diligently and routinely, as if she might

231

find an equilibrium of serotonin and adrenalin. But privately she thought the whole idea was ludicrous. The Black Place was too medieval for modern medicine. It wasn't an indifferent, chance amalgam of molecules but an external visitation of pure malevolence. At some barely conscious level she assumed there was a darkness in her that attracted The Black Place. The priest's idea is intoxicating. Strange and intoxicating. That she might be good, and it is that goodness that lures The Black Place.

Her last thought before her head drops onto the back-rest in front of her is how strange it was that the priest knew to address her in English. She closes her eyes. The names from the museum walls float before her. They move across her internal screen like grotesque sheep funnelling her into sleep.

From: evan117@hotmail.com
To: IsabelleNorthwell@dppar.wa.gov.au

Dear Belle

Jack called me yesterday and asked to see me again. We met at the Civic. Man, I thought I was in bad shape. I'm Gary Cooper next to this guy. His shirt was all wrinkled and he had a red-wine stain on his tie. He'd aged even from when I'd seen him last. Bleary-eyed. Shaggy-haired.

I bought a jug of beer and just let him talk. What a f*cking train wreck. You remember I mentioned about the doctored leave? Internal audit got onto it, brought in the IT guys and traced it back. It was Jack who changed it. But wait, it gets worse. Then they went sniffing around in his corporate credit card records and found a bill for some swanky five-star hotel in Margaret River.

My guess is that when they confronted him with it he didn't have the wherewithal to even attempt a plausible excuse. He just came right out with it. That the accommodation was for the two of you and that he'd changed your leave records. He said you had nothing to do with it so I guess you're in the clear as far as that's concerned.

So long story short (this all came out over nearly three jugs) he resigned on the spot rather than face the sack. His wife is furious. Threatening to throw him out and take him to the cleaners. From some hints he dropped I get the feeling they might have gone through something like this before. I didn't press for details. If his wife didn't leave him the first time I'm not sure why she would now. Maybe she feels like she's got no options. Or maybe she really loves him and can't face a future without him. It's shithouse for her either way and shitty of you to have put her in this position.

It would be different if you were serious about this guy. If you really thought you two had a future together. But I find that difficult to believe.

Obviously I don't want it to be true but I don't think I'm deluding myself here. There's just not much to Jack. He seems like one of those textbook management types we used to take the piss out of at Mimics and Tarts. Long on buzzwords, short on insight. And he's self-pitying, which you hate.

So what was it??

Which is all really just a roundabout way of asking what I really want to know. How do you feel about *me*, Belle? What is it you feel for me?

EB x

Isabelle wakes with the dawn. Something is blocking her airways, making her flail at the lifting darkness. She shoots upwards, scrabbling at whatever is groping her face, but it is only her pashmina plugging her nostrils with each intake of breath. Memory returns. She is in the church. Someone has placed a blanket over her during the night. Soft light pushes weakly through the stained-glass windows, illuminating a familiar scene. The tall figure of the Good King walks towards a fountain, the thick outline of his footprints behind him. *They've forgotten the page*, she thinks, slightly indignant.

Despite the blanket her neck is frozen rigid from the cold. She tries to turn it alternately from left to right but her turning circle has seized to a few centimetres.

If she strains beyond it a sharp pain stabs her right side. She curls her gloved hands around the pew and slowly lifts her bottom from the seat. Her feet are there on the ground, she knows, because she can see them, but they could be someone else's feet for all she feels a connection to them. She concentrates, fixing her will on her feet. She curls the big toe of her right foot in her boot, then takes experimental steps, supporting herself on the backrest of the pew. She rubs her thighs, willing the blood to thaw and move some heat around her body.

Isabelle shuffles down the aisle, opens the door and steps into the deserted square. Everywhere are signs of the previous night's excesses. An abandoned football shirt is iced to a bench. Wine bottles collect along the low stone walls. She sidesteps a suspicious-looking puddle at the base of the steps and makes for her hotel. She takes the path along the slowly materialising river, watching the land divide from the water. The city is shushed, no cars or trams or signs of people anywhere. It is just Prague and Isabelle. She walks fast, staring straight ahead so as not to move her neck.

The Nice Lady is on the desk this morning. She smiles coyly at Isabelle and drops her head. Clearly she thinks Isabelle has done the walk of shame from a tryst in some other hotel room. Isabelle rides the shaky lift to her room. 'Morning, Agnes,' she says skyward. 'You'll never believe what happened to me.' Agnes brays back, unimpressed. Agnes has seen everything.

Isabelle peels off her clothes and drapes them across the radiator, watching the steam rise from them. Everything is damp. Her very bones are wind tunnels, funnelling chills around her body. She turns the water in the shower as high as it will go and sits cross-legged with her back against the tiled wall of the chute. The hot water is an inexpressible relief on her neck and shoulders. She imagines the steel girder wedged into her back slowly melting back to a spine. She tries to order her thoughts. *How long is it since I ate properly? Have I caught pneumonia? How can I get a message to Evan?*

She towels off and dries her hair under the dryer. She slicks Vaseline across her lips and under her eyes. She looks hollowed-out, the way Jack looked as Isabelle left his office, the silver card for the resort on the table between them.

Jack.

The returning memory of him has a physical force that makes her jolt. A lecherous company man she had called him once, purely in an effort to goad him into approximating her vision of him. She speaks to the mirror, as if The Black Place might lurk there: *Even when you're not attacking me I'm still your creature. Searching always for your opposite. Inventing it when I have to.*

But then, she thinks, *I might be the opposite.* She is groping around the full import of this idea. She knows she needs to eat and rest, get herself together, square things with Evan before the idea will settle. She dresses and heads down to breakfast. The women who work there cluck their tongues at the sight of her, this strange excuse for a tourist who gets up with the dawn. Isabelle lingers in the lobby, waiting for the dining room to open.

'You are enjoying your stay?' the Nice Lady asks her.

'Yes, thank you. Very much.'

236

'Looking for anything particular?' she gestures towards the brochures that line the wall.

'Not really. I don't have much of a plan.'

'Karlovy Vary is nice. They film James Bond film there. You know James Bond?' She mimics holding a gun and blowing away the smoke. 'Or Kutná Hora. Very popular. That is where have bone church.'

'Thanks, I'll think about it.' Suddenly Isabelle recalls something she does want to see. 'Do you know anything about a barge for the homeless?'

'I am sorry, a what?'

'A barge. A ship. Apparently there is one on the Vltava for the homeless.'

The Nice Lady looks momentarily confused. 'Oh. Oh yes. But is not for sightseeing.'

'No, I know. I don't want to go on board or anything. I'd just like to see it. A friend of mine – a sort of friend – drives it. I'd like to see it.'

'Barge moves. Up and down river. Is not in one place. That way cost is shared between districts.'

Isabelle suspects she has missed something, a vital piece of information that has fallen through one of the hollow tubes in her unreliable brain. 'The people were put in a ship because no district would put them up – house them – permanently?'

'Yes. For the cost. This way, cost is shared. If you have boat for night, you pay food, you pay drink, you pay blankets.' The Nice Lady is uncomfortable. This is not tourist talk. This is Czech business.

'How many people are on the barge?'

'I don't know.'

'Where did they live, I mean before?'

'In flats. Flats go with factories. You work in factory, you get flat. Now, no more factories. So. No more flats.' She gives her wrist a slight phlegmatic twist as she says this. Half a century of history digested and processed in a small, contained physical gesture.

'Right.'

The Nice Lady opens a ledger and busies herself with it.

'Well, have a nice day,' Isabelle says.

'You too,' the Nice Lady says pleasantly, though she doesn't look up.

Isabelle piles her plate high: eggs, bacon, various cheeses, breads. Her hand wobbles a little as she moves the food to her mouth.

'First time I see you eat,' one of the kitchen women nods approvingly. 'Too skinny for Czech winter. Need some fat for keep warm.'

As she eats Isabelle can feel the fuel whizzing around her body, plumping her shrivelled organs. She has been here before. She knows that adrenalin is chewing through her fat reserves, spitting them out as electricity. She must eat and sleep to keep herself from a dangerous cycle of nervous energy and inanition. An American party enters the dining room, chatty and ebullient. They say a cheery good morning to Isabelle who feels as if now, finally, she could sleep. Another cup of weak coffee and her inner heat will be restored. Then she will seek the Nice Lady's help to phone Evan. She queues for the urn, behind the Americans happily surveying the food.

'Danish,' one of them says appreciatively. 'I love Danish for breakfast.' She puts two pastries on her plate, pauses for a moment as if considering, and then picks up a third.

'Gee whiz,' says her companion, 'I'm so damned hungry I could eat a horse. Two horses.'

Isabelle's internal turbine stalls. She returns her empty mug to the table, picks up her bag and heads out through the lobby.

'Off again?' the Nice Lady asks.

'Yes.'

Isabelle waves goodbye, a thousand 'gee whizzes' ricocheting off the name-covered walls in her head.

SIXTEEN

From: evan117@hotmail.com.au
To: IsabelleNorthwell@dppar.wa.gov.au

Dear Belle

You're not going to like this but I'm going to tell
you anyway. You need to hear it. I've downed half a
bottle of scotch. Sorry if the sense suffers but there
are some things you can't do sober.

Karl came to my place this afternoon. He swans in
just like nothing's changed since the old days. As if
we do more than say hi for the sake of appearances.
He wants to know how I'm going, how you are,
what's my take on the last game, blah blah blah. And
before I know it I've offered him a beer and we're
sitting at the table, talking. And as soon as he's got
me comfortable and playing along he springs it
on me: he wants me to be his best man.

Can you believe it? Me holding the rings for Karl
and Cindy with a carnation in my buttonhole and

a jolly little speech tucked into my cummerbund? I was gobsmacked. Couldn't get the words out. And this is the part you're not going to like. When they did come out they weren't conciliatory. I don't know why you feel the need to be so damn polite about Karl all the time. To protect him. Because, Belle, the guy's an arsehole. A bona fide, certifiable arsehole. He always has been.

I laughed in his face. And I'm glad I did. Because I don't think Karl has ever had anyone do that before. Call him on his form, I mean. I said that he and Cindy could do whatever they damn well pleased but I wasn't going to have any part of it. He acts all shocked and hurt. 'Evan, I don't know where this is coming from. If you had a problem with Cindy and me you should've said something before now.'

He's right. I should have. But the thing about Karl is, he's sucked you into his version of events before you even realise there *is* a version. You know I met Cindy a few times while they were carrying on behind your back? You probably did too. I wouldn't put anything past Karl. He brought her to an after-game drinks and he's parading her round and introducing her to people and I'm thinking, okay, this is all a bit weird. I take him to one side and ask him, 'So who's this Cindy woman? What the hell's going on? Where's Isabelle?'

He's all outrage and disgust. Can't a guy have a female friend without it being suspicious? And if I must know Cindy is a friend of his cousin's and she's just moved to Perth and Karl has agreed to show her round and introduce her to some people and if I've got a problem with it well maybe I need to take a good hard look at myself. And before I know where I am I *do* feel bad and I'm apologising to Karl and he's being all very gracious about it and I'm talking to Cindy and making all this effort to get to know her because Karl has made me feel like a prick. And the whole time it just doesn't smell right. I can't put my finger on it but it's just wrong. Out of kilter.

But I've finally figured it out. What makes Karl tick. He's got this genius for collusion. You're implicated in his stuff before you know what's going on so you can't point the finger at him without having to point the finger at yourself, too. I mean, FFS, Karl's bringing Cindy to these events and each time they're getting cuddlier and weirder and I'm telling myself it's me that's got the problem so I make even more effort to get to know her and be nice so when Karl finally leaves you he just glides right on in with his new relationship and into everybody's lives because he's already there.

Asking me to be his best man is the coup de grâce. If I do that then it's his absolution, isn't it? He gets off scot-free. Well not this time. I let him have it, Belle. And you bloody well should, too. I told him where he could stick his best man proposal. That I didn't want anything to do with him. That my loyalty was to you. That it was unconscionable the way he had carried on.

I'm sorry, Belle, but I'm going to tell you exactly what I think here: Karl wasn't that into you in the first place. It was the fact that *I* liked you that got his blood up. Nothing like a bit of competition to whip up an attraction. And it was all fine between you while you're playing up to his idea of you two as the super-couple. Climbing the corporate ladder together and hosting dinner parties and being all fabulous, dahling. And when you couldn't hold up your end of the power-couple bargain he chewed you up and spat you out. AND YOU LET HIM DO IT WITHOUT A WORD. YOU LET HIM GET AWAY WITH IT. No wonder the guy's got a god complex. No one ever calls him on being an über-shit.

So here's what I think. I think Karl figured you'd be the perfect girlfriend, with your smoking looks and your psych degree and the satisfaction of beating his friends to get by your side. That together the two of you were going to storm the corporate barricades and get a house full of funky appliances and cool art and travel the world and have impossibly beautiful babies. I don't think he bargained on your less than ravishing mental health.

I'm right, aren't I?

I'd bet my left leg Karl decided to replace you from the second you fell short of being the ultimate trophy-wife. It's so obvious. Cindy was the cookie-cutout substitute waiting in the wings. The pretty little physiotherapist who wants to open her own practice and have a honeymoon in Venice and a house in Matilda Bay.

You're better than that, Belle. So you're never going to be the poster girl for mental health. Big f*cking deal. We've all got our cross to bear. You called me 'Church Boy' once, remember? I'm lugging around a carousel of sexual hang-ups and Catholic guilt and that's just for starters. But I know I love you. And I know you can love me if you let yourself.

One more thing you need to know. I punched Karl. Hard. But I didn't throw the first one. I don't feel bad about it. Neither should you.

Evan

The bus is a spinning top unravelling from the centre of the city's maze. The further out of Prague they go, the more the drab vestiges of socialism pockmark the landscape. Square, hulking flats loom over the fields. Desolate quarries and abandoned factories crumble between cornfields. This is the first blue-sky day Isa-belle has experienced since she left Australia. It is not a candy-hard blue you could press your thumb on, but a dolorous, diffuse blue lazing all the way to space.

'Can I have a show of hands, please?' the young guide says. 'English-speakers?'

Six people raise their hands.

'*Deutsch*?'

Another four.

'*Italiano*?'

Two.

'*Français*?'

Four.

As the bus trundles through the countryside the guide switches between languages, using the same efficient, well-worn tone for all. Isabelle half pays attention to her information about agricultural yield and industrial production. She was overjoyed to find two strong painkillers in the side pocket of her bag, almost weeping with relief when, looking for hair ties, she found them. They have reduced the savagery in her neck to something approaching bearable. How long they will last she doesn't know.

'We are now approaching the Small Fortress,' says the guide. 'It was used as a prison by the Nazis for dissidents (both Christian and Jew), homosexuals and miscreants. Most of the inmates were from the nearby Jewish ghetto or "Big Fort".'

The occupants pour off the bus and collect at the start of an imposing tree-lined avenue.

'Stay together,' the guide says. 'Move to the next site when the rest of the party moves. Check that you are in the party with the right sticker.'

She waves one of the stickers about in the air. 'Does everybody have one of these stickers?'

Isabelle checks that her sticker is stuck fast to her jacket. It reads: 'Terezín. Enjoy yourself!'

If Isabelle didn't know better she would think she was approaching an English country manor, what with the wide sweep of the avenue and the stately silvery birches lining it. With a parasol and a corset she could be ambling across a nineteenth-century lawn to a tea party, except that the fields grow graves rather than roses. There is a simple wooden cross with a circular crown of thorns in the front field, in the field behind a Star of David. Here, as in Josefov, the headstones are adorned with small stones. To take in the manicured beds of headstones Isabelle must turn side on, walking crab-fashion, as she cannot turn her head.

'Are you all right?' a handsome German man asks her in impeccable English.

'Yes. Thank you. I've just strained my neck.'

The greenness surprises Isabelle, almost overwhelms her. She is used to straggling brown scrub scratching life from salt plains and sand. It is all she knows. So this… this verdure in the centre of death is almost blinding. In the unblemished sky and bouncing sunshine it takes an effort of will to convince herself it is real.

The group enters the small fort and collects underneath an archway. The guide points to the lettering on the arch: *Arbeit Macht Frei*. Work Makes You Free. *It's the sort of corporate slogan Jack would appreciate*, Isabelle thinks darkly, then castigates herself for her flippancy. The guide fusses them into a tighter circle away from the other groups milling about the archway. The guides are all young women who slip easily between languages as if unaware they are doing so. Does it change your mental circuitry, Isabelle wonders, bending your mind around different words for the same thing?

The guide stands still for a moment, gathering herself, then hoists a smile. 'Welcome to Terezín.' She gestures to the buildings behind her much as a game-show host might point out prizes. A small, bustling bird wheels above her head and darts into an open room off the main courtyard. In a mechanical voice the guide begins her recitation, a paragraph for each language.

'The fort was built under Joseph II and named after his mother, Maria Theresa. It was intended as a fortification against the Prussians. During the Second World War the town of Terezín was ordered to empty to make way for Jews being evicted from Prague and other centres. This,' she gestures towards the building where the bird flew, 'was the receiving station.'

The tour group troops in and takes in the wide, chalky wooden floorboards, whitewashed walls and sparse furniture. The guide enumerates the facts and figures on how many people were *received*. The bird is a red-breasted industrious creature building a nest on one of the ceiling beams. She jerks her head in an endless stuttering motion, taking the group in before darting out to gather more twigs. The group moves out again to the dusty courtyard, halting before open doors for more facts in various languages.

At the ablutions block one of the young German women refuses to go inside. The man who asked about Isabelle's neck talks to her in a low voice. She shakes her head and looks down at her feet, scuffing at the dirt with her heel. He runs his hand affectionately through her wavy blonde hair and says something encouraging. The ablutions room is concrete, bare and cold. Water pipes thread the ceiling, apparently perfect scaffolding for twigs and leaves. But there are no birds in this building. Isabelle wonders if they remember the pipes running hot. Or with something other than water.

Nearby is a faux model ablutions room with multiple washstands and mirrors.

'This washroom,' the guide explains, 'was built in preparation for a visit from a Red Cross delegation from Denmark. The Nazis embarked on a beautification program to convince the international community that Terezín was a model town for the Jews. Later in the tour we may see the film that the Nazis made about life in Terezín to promote this view. Move along, please.'

They pause at the front of a small holding cell.

'This cell was used to detain Jewish prisoners. Up to forty men would be held in here at a time. I am going to close the door on you for one minute to give you an impression of what it was like.'

Isabelle peers around the guide's shoulder into the dark hold.

The German lady shakes her head. 'I'm not going in there,' she says in English.

'Okay. Everyone else all right to go in?'

Throstles sing a jubilee behind Isabelle.

'Are you going in?' the guide asks Isabelle.

She clambers in after the others. The heavy wooden door is closed behind her. Chinks of daylight between the door and the jamb provide the only light in the cell. Someone laughs nervously. The Italians speak in low voices to one another. From their tone Isabelle knows they are attempting black, indifferent humour. Soon they fall silent. The bare cell has an unearthly smell. You could attack these walls with scourer, soap and paint for a century and the smell would remain. It is the fleshy trace memory of the unspeakable. Isabelle breathes shallowly. They all do. The forced, calm breathing soon becomes the only sound in the cell. Isabelle regulates her breathing by mimicking the rate of those around her but they are racing one another to hyperventilation. The breath starts to come ragged from someone to Isabelle's right, their form indistinct in the dark. They reach out, searching for a space to lean on, but stumble slightly. Instinctively, Isabelle turns to prop them up, triggering an excruciating pain from her neck down her spine and through her upraised arm.

'Sorry,' an English voice gasps.

'That's okay.'

'How long have we been in here?' comes the voice. 'That must be a minute by now.'

'Yes, it's definitely longer than a minute,' says a voice by his side.

There is a collective shuffling and coughing in the cell. Pressure is building in Isabelle's chest. She wants to take gulping, greedy mouthfuls of air but the idea of what its particles might contain keeps her mouth closed. Instead, she breathes through her nose so forcefully her nostrils jam shut. The panic in the room rises as surely as if it were water rushing a capsized boat.

'Is she there?' says one of the Germans. 'Perhaps she has moved away from the door for a moment.'

'What? She can't do that. She can't leave us here unattended. Open the door, someone just open the door. I can't breathe.'

The door creaks and groans and is thrown open. Courtesy forgotten, they all scramble to be the first out. Someone loses their footing on the way but Isabelle doesn't turn to offer assistance. Out in the bright sunlight of the courtyard her lungs pull at the air. They dart sheepish glances at one another.

'Everyone okay?' says the guide.

Someone laughs. Then they all do. Isabelle turns away so they don't see how desperately she sucks at the air. She feigns interest in the paintwork on the building opposite as she gorges on oxygen.

'That was a long minute,' says the German man gently to his girlfriend who stayed outside.

Her arms are folded defensively around her and her eyes have a guarded, cloudy look. He gathers her hair from her shoulders and deftly winds it behind her head into a bun.

'It was thirty-seven seconds. The guide says that no one ever lasts the full minute.'

They move on. The pain in Isabelle's neck is intensifying. She winds her pashmina around it as tight as comfort will allow. If she moves too quickly she is seared down her right side. Perhaps that explains why the fort begins to appear in snapshots, her consciousness a periscope surfacing between gaps in the pain to take in disconnected images. Whitewashed dark spaces. Crude wooden bowl and spoon, uniform and shoes. Bunks denuded of straw. A toilet. A washbasin. A preening throstle.

'We are going to go into the tunnels,' says the guide. 'They run for half a kilometre under the ground. The tunnels are dark and can be claustrophobic. If you like not to go in the tunnels I can arrange for you to go above-ground route.'

There is a pause as the group confers. Isabelle is the only one of the group without a companion. Her heart is still pounding after being in the cell. She worries that she will never get that smell out of her nostrils. She wants to wander off and find a patch of untombed grass in the sunshine until the tour ends and they wind their way back to Prague. She doesn't want to go underground.

'Gee whiz,' the man at the Jewish Museum had said. 'Gee whiz, eighty thousand people *is* a lot of people to gas.'

Isabelle shakes herself. She must go into the tunnels.

Half the group elects to take the above-ground route. The rest cross a bridge over a thin river. A tumble of lush green reeds banks the water. High red-brick walls run on all sides, funnelling into offshoot buildings. They walk in single file into the maze, dropping closer to the earth's core with each step. Within a few metres sunlight and fresh air become things of the past. The narrow walkway is lit with tiny lights. Small, oddly shaped 'rooms' are carved out of the stone beside them. The cells are more or less triangular, wider at the base then tapering to a rough point in the rock. It would be impossible to stand up in them. A couple of the crawl spaces contain rough wooden chairs. The pretence at domestic comfort makes the cells even more macabre, like a throw rug over an electric chair.

The German man says something under his breath behind Isabelle. The sound of his voice startles her in the dark. They walk on, past more caves. It is dank and chill. The cold tunes Isabelle's muscles like guitar strings. She is tight-wired, so each lengthening tread sets her nerve endings screaming. She takes short, sharp breaths to manage the pain. The German man lightly puts his hand on her shoulder, his warmth like a balm.

'Don't worry,' he says kindly. 'We'll be out of here very soon.'

The walkways diverge at several points but these are closed off by iron bars. Each time they turn into another tunnel, Isabelle hopes to see the exit up ahead. If an architect were challenged to build despair, surely this is what they would come up with. Locked away in these diabolical spaces you would come to doubt your own existence. It would be impossible to believe that anyone would remember you. That you were connected to parents, lovers, rivals. The only thing you could love would be death – the idea of a blankness unbounded by rough, cold stone walls and iron grilles.

Ahead of her, Isabelle catches a burst of sunlight. Despite the pain in her neck she would run for it were there not people ahead. They all quicken their pace, trying to be casual about it. Finally they step out into a broad grassy area, dazzled by the sunlight. Isabelle puts her hands to her eyes while they adjust to the light. The rest of the tour group is gathered, waiting. The sun overhead gives everything a brilliant aspect. The grasses are reclaiming the building, clambering over abandoned pylons and bricks, and licking at the high walls. Dandelions grow in clumps around the field. An orange ladybird whirls past Isabelle.

'This,' says the guide, sweeping her hand to take in the green yard, 'was the execution ground.'

Isabelle stops listening and watches the progress of the ladybird up a vine curling around the remains of a patio. She takes off her glove and places her bare hand on the wood to soak up its heat.

'Where that lady is standing,' the guide points to Isabelle, 'is the gallows.'

Isabelle retracts her hand from the wooden beam and stumbles backwards a few steps. The ladybird, disoriented by her flailing, traps itself in her fringe. She rubs her bare palm on her jeans several times and then gently disengages the ladybird from her hair. She sets it down in a clump of dandelions then picks her way across the field, sidestepping any suspicious mounds of earth.

The young guide strides through the tall grasses. Particles of light have trapped themselves between strands of her dark hair, giving her a diffuse halo. The sun is now directly overhead. Isabelle unwinds her pashmina and bares her neck to the heat. She walks behind the Germans, who are in earnest, though not heated, discussion. Their doubts, fears and rationalisations are apparent in the low and steady deliberateness of their voices. The blonde lady doesn't say very much. Most of the discussion is carried on by her companions. She strides over the grass, hugging herself, careful where she treads. Isabelle is drawn to her. They walk past the guards' quarters, the now-empty swimming pool collecting dead leaves.

'Everyone ready for our last stop?' says the guide. They are paused in front of a low, yellow-coloured building. The pain in Isabelle's neck is now so intense that stepping onto her right foot shoots pure fire through every nerve and artery in her body. She treads softly on her right side, taking most of the weight on her left. Her peculiar gait draws quizzical looks from the Italians. The blonde lady wheels off from her friends and marches away from the building. Instinctively, Isabelle follows her. 'Are you not going in?'

'To the crematorium? No. I don't think I can. Are you?'

Isabelle watches the members of the group disappear into the entrance. She wants to freeze, motionless, to minimise the pitchforks poking at her nerve. 'I think I must.' They idle there silently together for a moment. 'Would you like to come in with me?'

She regards Isabelle closely through narrowed eyes. 'Okay.'

They are the last of their group to approach the old man at the entrance. He wears dark-blue overalls and a skullcap identical to the ones he offers the men on entering. 'Good afternoon,' he says to them pleasantly. 'Could I please ask you not to take any photographs in the crematorium and to mind the step?'

'I'm Isabelle,' she says as they descend the stairs.

'I'm Ingrid.'

Isabelle wants to grip onto the walls to have them take some of her weight, but the idea of touching anything is horrifying. Ingrid looks around at the wide cast-iron ovens.

'It's like…it's like,' she pauses. 'If I didn't know better I would think I was in a bakery.'

Hearing her own thought pressed into words sets Isabelle's stomach rolling and heaving. The ovens are coated in ash. The implements used to stir the…the remnants still sit in the open hatches. Ingrid loops her arm in Isabelle's and they walk quietly into a tiled room with steel, bed-like slabs. One of the slabs suddenly levitates blue and silver in the flash from a camera. Ingrid stiffens. Her sharp, loud intake of breath mirrors Isabelle's.

'What are you doing?' Ingrid says in English to the tourist holding the camera. He ignores her and turns as if to move into another room. Ingrid drops Isabelle's arm and detains him by reaching out for his shoulder.

'What do you think you are doing?' she says. There is an edge of hysteria in her voice.

'Let go of me,' the man says, annoyed. 'It's none of your business.'

'Didn't you hear them say no photographs?'

'What's it to you?' he demands. 'Piss off,' and with that he forcibly shakes Ingrid's hand off his arm and storms into another room.

'What's going on?' Ingrid's boyfriend has entered the room.

'That, that,' Ingrid points a trembling finger at the back of the furious man, 'bastard is taking photographs.'

'Perhaps he has special permission.'

'Yes. Or perhaps he's an *arschloch*.'

Isabelle feels cut on the expletive.

The German man contemplates his girlfriend. 'I'm sorry,' he says. 'We shouldn't have come here.'

'It's not your fault.'

They leave the crematorium and make for the waiting bus. On the way, Ingrid introduces Isabelle to her travelling companions: her boyfriend Peter, cousin Anja and friend Cornelius. As the bus swings out of Terezín, Ingrid twists around in her seat to watch the town disappear behind them.

'Isabelle. Look.' She points a finger. Isabelle turns awkwardly in her seat, the pain pushing up tiny beads of sweat at her hairline. She follows Ingrid's finger to where a dozen otters frolic in a stream by the side of the road.

SEVENTEEN

From: evan117@hotmail.com.au
To: IsabelleNorthwell@dppar.wa.gov.au

Dear Belle

I was thinking today about our different childhood
obsessions. What they mean. You told me once
that your thing for Prague started with 'Good
King Wenceslas'. I just found a YouTube clip of a
choir singing it. As far as I can make out there was
a blizzard blowing and the King looked out over
his balcony to see a peasant freezing his balls off
collecting kindling in the snow. So the King asked
his servant who the peasant was and the servant said
he lived a long way off near the forest. Times must
have been hard if the guy was all the way out here
foraging.

So Wenceslas asked the servant to put together a
care package. Meat, wine and firewood. Wenceslas
and the servant head out into the storm looking for
the peasant's dwelling so they can make sure he eats

a good meal and gets warm. But they set off near dusk and the night draws in and the storm gets really crazy. The servant starts to get hypothermia and thinks he's done for. He tells the King he can't go any further and is about to die in the ice.

The King tells the servant to look for his footsteps in the snow and to walk in them (good thing there was a 'bright moon'), which the servant does. The tracks left by Wenceslas are warm. Moral of the story? Do the right thing by the poor and downtrodden, especially if you're rich and powerful, and you'll find blessing.

It's basically a twist on the Jesus story. Do unto others. Love thy neighbour. Faith, hope and charity. It's always puzzled me why you haven't gravitated towards Christianity, Belle. For the comfort of it, I mean. For the heated footsteps in the snow.

It's not hard to Psych 101 my thing for Ancient Rome. I had this wand I was given for Christmas one year, while my dad was still alive. You know the ones with the transparent plastic outside and the glittery gelatinous stuff inside? So I'd wind myself up in bedsheets, take my wand and go from room to room making laws and treaties. I developed an accord between my toy soldiers and my *Star Wars* figures. I wrote it up and everything, and tied it with a bit of ribbon to make it look like a scroll.

After Dad died I remember this sense of barely
contained panic, like we might go over a
precipice at any moment. You know that weird
thing adults do where they assume that kids
either don't listen to or don't understand what
they're talking about? Mum and her sisters would
be poring over these pieces of paper and forms,
on the phone to various people trying to make
sense of things and Mum saying things like, 'But
there's no money, Lil. There's just no money. It's
all very well to say it'll come through in three
months. But what do we eat *now*? How do we
keep the electricity on *now*?' Then she'd tell me
there was nothing to worry about and seemed to
expect I'd believe her.

No wonder I became a lawmaker. Strutting from
room to room in my toga making decrees and
restoring order. Ensuring everything ran smoothly.

But you, Belle. What about you? Why the powerful
King who could keep you safe from certain death?
What is it you needed to be protected from?

I miss you,
Evan

The bus drops the group off at the Staroměstské.

'Isabelle, we are going to get some dinner and a few
drinks at the Metropole. You will come with us, of
course.' The way Ingrid phrases it, this is not a question.

'I'd like to,' Isabelle says feebly, 'but I really have to get to a chemist. I need some painkillers for my neck.'

'Oh, don't worry about that,' Ingrid says confidentially, taking Isabelle's arm and leaning her head in towards her. 'Anja is a walking pharmacy. She's got a pill for everything.'

Anja dutifully produces a small red-and-black-striped bag and riffles through it.

'Is it a torn muscle or just an ache?' she asks, fingering a tab of blue-and-white capsules. 'Can you pinpoint the moment it happened or did it come on gradually?'

'I woke up with it. I think it's just an ache.'

'Did you sleep awkwardly?'

'Yes. Very. And I was very cold.'

'Right.' Anja puts the capsules back in the bag and pulls out a tab of white pills instead. 'Take two of these when we get to the Met. Wash it down with a cocktail or two. You'll be pain-free in about fifteen minutes.'

'You probably won't feel much of anything at all,' Cornelius says dryly.

'What are they?'

'Best not to ask,' he says smilingly. 'But don't worry. They'll work.'

The restaurant is not far from the Staroměstské. They take a table at the back, away from the stage. A waitress sporting an extreme eighties lopsided bob delivers menus to their table and unsmilingly takes their drink orders.

'Just water for me, please,' Isabelle says. She likes her new friends but she just wants to take the drugs then find a phone.

'Nonsense,' Ingrid says brusquely. 'She'll have a caprioska.'

Anja, Cornelius and Peter order beer. Mercifully, the waitress brings the beers and Isabelle's water quickly. Isabelle swallows the tablets and waits, praying for swift effect.

'Where are you from, Isabelle?' Peter asks.

'Western Australia. A small city called Perth.'

'Oh, I love Perth,' cries Anja enthusiastically.

'Really?' Isabelle is somewhat incredulous that people this sophisticated would be familiar with her isolated home.

'Yes. Corn and I went backpacking around Australia three years ago. We were in Perth in summer. I've never been so tanned.' She sighs, as if this were the pinnacle of a happiness that will never be ascended again.

Corn nods. 'City Beach. Heaven. We played night volleyball there on New Year's Eve. Thirty-two degrees at nine o'clock at night. The Germans versus the Dutch. We won!' He raises his beer and clinks it against Peter's glass.

Ingrid drums her fingers on the table. 'Where is my caprioska? God, I need a drink.'

'I think you need more than one,' Peter says quietly into his beer.

Something shimmers out of the corner of Isabelle's eye. She turns to catch it but it remains at the periphery of her vision. Suddenly she understands. It is relief. A warm, glittering relief is ambling through her, pausing to give the strained muscles and tendons on her afflicted right side the kiss of numbness. She sighs a long, languorous sigh and drops her shoulders by what feels like a foot.

'They're working?' Anja asks.

'Yes.' To Isabelle's embarrassment, tears rush, warm and free, down her cheek before she can mop them up. 'Sorry.' In the flush of her relief Isabelle is worried she will do something foolish like hug her new-found friends and declare lifelong allegiance to them.

'Neck pain is the worst,' says Anja sympathetically. 'The pills will probably last for about four hours. Maybe take two more before bed. But definitely don't take any more after that until tomorrow.'

'I won't.'

Wondrously, miraculously pain-free Isabelle turns to survey her surroundings and finds herself in a strange hodgepodge of decor. The style is twenties art deco with, to her, incongruous Egyptian flourishes. Two white pharaohs stand sentinel above the stage. The large, broad windows face onto Na Poříčí. The walls are olive green with gold trim. A mosaic of black-and-white photographs of American jazz greats runs along the back wall. The tables are highly polished jet with gold inlay at the corners. A shaggy off-white pouf sits under the table of the gentleman in front of them. Isabelle looks again. No. The pouf is a poodle chained up to his chair. The bobbed waitress bends down to put a silver tray of water in front of the dog. Incredibly, she smiles as she does so. The dog laps happily at the water. Pain and Terezín recede further and further from Isabelle's consciousness. Finally, she feels that the scabrous smell is out of her nostrils.

Peter reads his menu. 'I cannot eat another goulash or dumpling or potato soup. I want fatty, imperialist food. Ah. American-style buffalo wings with fries. Perfect.' He takes a long, satisfied drink from his beer.

'These people!' Ingrid spits out. 'They're so damn lazy. I hate this country.'

Peter laughs. 'Your caprioska is late so you write off an entire country? I don't think travel writing would be your thing, Ingi.'

The table titters, but Ingrid doesn't laugh. 'It's not the caprioska. It's these people. They're lazy. Intellectually lazy. How many Czechs did you see out at Terezín today? None. Do you know they don't even have tour groups for high-school kids as part of the curriculum? I know because I asked the curator at the museum. *Oh, the Nazis came and took the Jews. Oh, the Soviets came and took our freedom.* Boohoo.'

Anja coughs slightly into her hand. Peter and Cornelius exchange nervous glances. Isabelle wants to cushion her comfortable, glowing absence of pain from Ingrid's wrath.

'And what were the Czechs doing? Did they riot when their Jewish neighbours disappeared and didn't come back? Did they ask questions? And when the Soviets invaded, who ran the bureaucracy? The army? The secret police? Because if you let the Czechs tell it, the system ran thanks to two or three bad guys while the rest of them were wailing over Masaryk and marching two steps behind Dubček.'

Ingrid's eyes are flinty. She holds herself rigid, as if she fears she will tremble uncontrollably if she relaxes.

Perhaps Anja should offer Ingrid some of these lovely pills too.
The waitress finally comes with the cocktails. Isabelle
feels Peter, Corn and Anja tense in case Ingrid says
anything in front of her. But she doesn't. Isabelle sips
her caprioska. It is pure heaven. All minty and sugary
and limey. It dances with the pills in her bloodstream.
When the waitress is out of earshot Peter speaks.

'You don't know, Ingi. You don't know the ways in
which people resisted.'

'Or if resistance was even possible,' adds Corn.

Ingrid nods impatiently. 'I'm not a child. I know
that. Silence comes in many, what's the word, *flavours*?
But you don't hear anything about that silence, do you?
That's my point.' Isabelle is awed that they are carrying
on the discussion in English, for her benefit. Ingrid
challenges the table with her eyes. 'I mean today, at
Terezín, did you see anything about how the Czechs felt
when all these people they knew – people they went
to school with, worked with, who ran the shops they
bought their groceries from – just evaporated?'

'I don't think you mean *evaporated*,' Anja interrupts,
'I think you mean —'

'Oh really, Anja, does it matter? It may as well have
been evaporated. How did they feel? Did they notice?
Did they say anything, even if it was just to each other?'

'What did our grandparents do under the same cir-
cumstances?' says Peter. One of the instruments squeals
as the band tunes up. They all flinch, even Isabelle from
underneath her pleasant cocoon.

'They didn't do anything.'

'So, what's the difference?'

264

'It's in how it's remembered. How the silence is dealt with. I mean, how old were we when we first started to learn about the Holocaust at school? Eight? Nine?'

'I think I was eight,' says Corn.

'And then every year after that,' says Anja, frustrated. 'Maybe the Czechs have got the right idea. What good does beating us over the head with it do? It's not like we were responsible. Like our kids are responsible. But they're going to get beaten over the head with it too.'

Ingrid eyes her cousin closely. Isabelle senses that the conversation is approaching a notorious bend in a dangerous road and considers moving tables so she can enjoy her euphoria untroubled by Ingrid's angst.

'Did you think that Gran and Pa were monsters? Aberrations?'

Everyone but Ingrid drops their eyes.

'I don't see why this has to get personal,' Anja says quietly.

'But Anja, surely that's the point. It *is* personal. I loved Gran and Pa. I loved staying with them. Some of the best memories of childhood I have are of making jam with Gran at the summer cottage out by the lake. I still love them. Even though I know what they are. That's why the Nazis have everything to do with us. Our grandparents weren't freaks, a never to be repeated anomaly. They were like us. *And* monsters. We could be like them. That's why we have to go back to the past. Over and over and over again. We have to resist silence.'

Corn shakes his head. 'I could never be a Nazi.'

'Bullshit, Corn. We're all Nazis. I'm a Nazi. You're a Nazi. The Czechs are Nazis.'

'Stop. Saying. That.'

'What? Stop saying what? *Nazi*? We have to say it, Peter. We have to be able to say it.'

'Complicity,' someone says. It takes half a second for Isabelle to realise that it is she who has spoken. 'It's about degrees of complicity, isn't it?'

'Yes. Yes, exactly. I'm not saying that there's no difference between being a camp guard and being an average citizen who just kept their mouth shut and their eyes closed. There is a difference. I'm not even condemning the fact that they were silent. It just annoys me that the Czechs don't have anything to say about their silence. That's all.'

Ingrid's companions don't say anything. Isabelle says 'yes' for them.

'I think you're hard on the Czechs,' murmurs Anja. 'Suffering blunts responsibility. They had the war and then the Soviet dictatorship. You can't blame someone for just...just disappearing into themselves. Surviving. Why rake over the past looking for more pain and guilt?'

'Hmmm,' Ingrid ponders, taking a mighty slug of her cocktail. She gestures to the waitress to bring two more. 'Because of the Ossis, perhaps?'

'Aussies?' Isabelle asks, confused. 'What did we do?'

'*Ossis*,' Ingrid corrects her. 'East Germans. One minute they are the aggressors in the war and then they are under the Soviet dictatorship. Suddenly, they are victims. They don't think about their Nazi past. They don't own it. They don't talk about it. It is all forgotten. All of the Nazis were *someone else*. And where does most of the Neo-Nazi movement come from in Germany?

From the East. Those same Ossis who never fronted up
to their responsibilities, to their guilt.'

'You have a point,' Anja concedes.

Isabelle is awed by their mastery of English. She feels
gauche and hick with her one-trick tongue, and then
she is angry with Ingrid for making her feel inadequate
when all she wants to do is coast in the pleasant, dulling
amber of her caprioska and her painkillers.

'All I am saying is that you should own up to the
silence. To the complicity, however justified it might
have been. You've got to own the shame of it. The
Czechs don't. It's like they weren't even there.'

'Maybe they're not ashamed of it,' suggests Peter.

'Of course they're ashamed of it,' Ingrid's eyes glitter
cheekily. 'Why else would they be so bloody rude?'
After a microsecond, everyone laughs and the tense cord
around the table loosens and falls to the floor, forgotten.

'Capitulators are always rude,' says Anja. 'Look at the
French.' They giggle conspiratorially, four Germans and
an Australian delighting in their political incorrectness.

'You know what makes me laugh?' says Peter. *Happy
Hour.* The concept of *Happy Hour* here in Prague. You
see signs up in bars and restaurants for it but it just
doesn't translate, does it? *Slightly Less Sullen Hour*, more
like it.'

'Yes,' agrees Corn, 'or *Might Crack a Smile Hour*.'

'*Not So Dour Hour*?' Isabelle offers.

'Perfect! Let's enjoy *Not So Dour Hour*.'

The waitress brings their next round of drinks and
is obligingly uncommunicative and sulky. Isabelle has
never tasted anything as delicious as her caprioska.

Surely there has never *been* anything as delicious as her caprioska.

'We should eat,' suggests Peter.

'Yes,' everyone agrees. But somehow the impulse is lost in the rising revelry. The band starts to play an upbeat, jazzy number. The pianist throws his entire body into the performance, his face puckered as if he is eating lemons. Anja sways in time to the music. All the tables fill and the latecomers lean against the walls and the bar. Everyone smokes. The waitress moves from table to table, lighting tea lights. Only the poodle remains unruffled, occasionally lapping from his bowl but otherwise curled up asleep under his owner's chair. The caprioska and Anja's drugs hold communion in Isabelle's body. The intense pain in her neck, the suffocating dark room at Terezín, the reasons why she must phone Evan all grow fuzzy and inconsequential.

The lead singer clicks his fingers and a big brass sound explodes through the room. A swing number lifts bodies from the walls and onto the spare few metres of dance floor in front of the band. Peter whoops appreciatively. The room is alive with whirring, whirling bodies shuffling together and then springing apart. Even the waitress looks as if she might crack a smile at any moment. Isabelle closes her eyes and is in a forties dance hall, the women all curled blonde hair and red lipstick, the men all crisp army uniforms and smooth patter.

'Would you like to dance?' Corn asks.

Isabelle opens her eyes. 'Who, me?'

'Yes, you.'

268

'Sure. Why not.'

Cornelius takes her hand and leads her to the floor.

'Can you jive?'

'I have no idea.'

'Look at my feet, okay?'

Isabelle studies his feet as they back-step and shuffle, back-step and shuffle. Cornelius holds his hands up in front of his chest and she grasps them. He is warm and alive to her touch.

'Don't worry about the steps. Just go with it. Ready? One, two, a one, two, three four.'

He directs her by pressing on the heel of her palm, driving her across the floor. The room spins around as she pivots away and into him. Her body effortlessly reproduces his steps, catching every flourish and embellishment. They move fluidly through the twirling, twining bodies. To her left someone attempts a lift above the crowd but she cannot see how it ends. She is so joyful to be tipsily amnesiac and dancing with a beautiful stranger on a crowded dance floor in Prague. As the song closes on a long saxophone note, they collapse against one another in a fit of giggles. His shirt is damp and his heart is beating fast. He doesn't release her hand.

'You're really good.'

'Thanks, Isabelle. We had to take lessons at school.'

'Really?'

'Yes, didn't you?'

'God, no.'

'Then where did you learn those steps?'

'From you.'

'Wow, I'm a great teacher.'

The band strikes up again but the dance floor is now choked with so many people it is hard to move. Cornelius folds Isabelle into him and they sway together on the spot to the music. She can feel the muscles in the small of his back rippling as they move. There is a questioning in his fingers along her spine. She thinks of Evan and the way his body had melded to hers. Pleasantly drugged, Isabelle half convinces herself that Cornelius is Evan. The sea of people whirls and eddies. Cigarette and cigar smoke gather at the ceiling, but Isabelle is so anaesthetised she doesn't notice. It becomes hotter and hotter.

A hand reaches for her. It is Ingrid. 'Come on,' she mouths. 'Let's go.'

They muscle their way through the throng into the street. A victorious whoop goes up behind them as the bouncer replaces them with five more people. The cold air hits Isabelle's damp body, making her shiver. She rethreads her pashmina around her neck and tugs on her coat and gloves as they walk up Na Poříčí to Republiky. She reaches surreptitiously into her pocket to ensure the other pills Anja gave her are still there, secreted away for later.

'That place is great,' says Corn, wiping sweat from his face and neck with a handkerchief.

'Yes, but too crowded. I couldn't breathe in there with all that smoke.'

'And it was taking too long to get a drink.'

'So. Where to now?'

The soft pearly glow from the orbs in the Municipal House is warm and welcoming against the black sky.

'Don't you just love this building?' says Peter.

'I do, actually.'

'Oh, please,' says Ingrid while Anja puts her hands to her ears in mock horror. 'Not the mascarons again.'

'Anything but the mascarons,' groans Corn.

'I don't understand.'

'They are mocking my fetish for building design,' Peter explains to Isabelle. 'Apparently, some people find it boring.'

'Are you an architect?'

Anja wails and Ingrid makes as if to sprint off into the night. 'Alas no. A mechanical engineer. I took the safe option.'

'And here,' says Ingrid playfully, 'begins the tragic story of Peter's bitter, bitter life.' She leans over and embraces him in a ferocious bear hug.

'Let's get a drink at the American Bar,' suggests Cornelius. He reaches for Isabelle's hand and they enter under the dome. Somehow, between the entrance and the bar they are swept into a tour group making their way into the inner sanctum of the building. Peter gives a pleading glance to the rest of the group to beg their acquiescence.

'Fine,' mutters Cornelius, 'but you owe me a drink when we get to the bar. And Isabelle, you owe me a dance.'

They move through room after room, mingling and dispersing with different groups. Some emerge from concert rooms trailing bursts of classical music down the intricately tiled corridors. Others stand in groups of twos and threes before silver garlands and ginkgo inlay, sketching. Tourist groups thumb through laminated guides, their heads bobbing up and down from the artworks to descriptions of their provenance. Even to Isabelle's untrained eye it is clear why Peter loves the building. It is a dreamy confection of light and colour, as if a fairy, uncorked from an absinthe bottle, drew her wand across the walls. Dozens of artists followed her, ecstatically drunk, laying down parquetry and tiles and wreaths on her pencilled outline.

Isabelle floats through the rooms, tipsy and light and tingling with the press of Cornelius's hand. She knows that Cornelius is not Evan, but her dream-like state has twinned them. They amble under a ceiling of lace and frescoes where war and death are valorous and clean. Isabelle touches her free hand to gilded snails gliding along the sides of an empty aquarium. Along rectangles of sheepskin headrests. Linden leaves. Gilt-edged mirrors. Gleaming samovars. Dried coral in the grates. Stunning mosaics of green and red and gold. Cornelius bends and whispers something in her ear. She imagines Evan hears the same barely coherent sentence delivered on the breeze.

Finally, they come to a domed room the absinthe fairy did not visit.

Immediately they enter it Isabelle feels the fanciful whimsy of the other rooms lock shut behind her. She looks up at the domed ceiling where a falcon in shadow circles above them. Beneath the bird, wide Slavonic eyes stare manically from the smooth alabaster faces of seers and farmers, warriors and gypsies.

Those eyes.

They bore down from the ceiling, beautiful but unyielding. Isabelle has a powerful sense of déjà vu. She has been here before, but when? How? She drops Cornelius's hand and whirls beneath the panels. On one panel young naked men stare into the far-off distance, as if focused on the great deeds their strength will call from them. Their pale buttocks and sinewy arms are exquisite but curiously desexualised, as if the libidinous drive has been arrogated for nation-building alone. Isabelle spins, transfixed, under the exhorting blue eyes of Mucha's imagined Czechs. His silver blues radiate from the ceiling, turning the very air around them silver blue too. *I've been tricked*, thinks Isabelle. The building has lulled and disarmed her then closed her in this dock for the judgement of the universal muses that stare, unflinching, from the ceiling.

A woman robed and turbaned in white fixes on Isabelle. It is Libussa, her palms planted on the ceiling, demanding that Isabelle bring herself to account. Her wide, glacial eyes know how Isabelle came to be in Prague. She knows what Evan suffers, alone, without Isabelle and the fear that keeps Isabelle from returning his love. She understands The Black Place. All Black Places. Her gaze is merciless and unyielding. Isabelle turns on the spot, trying to spin away from the net of Libussa's stare, but her judgement has her in thrall. She turns faster and faster. The softening pills wilt in her bloodstream. There is only Isabelle trapped in the silver-blue dock and found wanting.

'My name is Isabelle,' she says, commencing her dialogue with the unseen.

And then there is darkness.

From: evan117@hotmail.com
To: IsabelleNorthwell@dppar.wa.gov.au

Dear Belle

I feel like I'm talking to the great beyond.
Sometimes I like that feeling. Like now, when I've
exhausted myself with sprints at the pool and drunk
too much. It's almost like going to confession, which
is an analogy you won't like.

Remember that day at the beach? After the shark
alarm? I know you think I made a real dick of
myself (yes, pun intended). But it's not really what
you think. Yes, obviously I was embarrassed and
I let you think that it was some weird Catholic
sexual-repression thing. But when we were out
beyond the break it was like we'd fallen into a land
of blue. Blue sea. Blue sky. A blue country with just
us in it. The sea was so warm and the light was so
intense and you looked so beautiful with your hair
floating around you that I thought f*ck it. This is it.
Do it now. No more prevaricating, no more pushing
it down. Just tell her. Tell her how you feel.

But it didn't go like that.

The alarm went off and all I could think about was
getting both of us onto the beach as fast as possible.
We got separated coming out of the surf and then,
when I saw you standing on the sand with your hand

screening your face looking around for me, I ran
over and scooped you up because I was relieved. And
then willy-gate. I know you were trying to make
me feel better but what you don't know is how much
I was raging inside. I'd finally decided to grow a
pair and then that bloody siren goes off. It was like
a cosmic joke.

I felt churned up. Like I couldn't get comfortable.
Once I'd decided that I was telling you there was no
going back on it. But how? When? That's why I was
so belligerent about you going ahead with the party.
I don't pretend to fully understand the rooftop. What
it means or what happened to you. But I do know
that we're all f*cked when we operate from fear.
When we don't stare stuff down. I know I'm guilty
of it. Maybe that's what you're doing in Prague:
finding your tracks in the snow. When you're done
I'll be here.

I love you.
Evan

EIGHTEEN

'Isabelle? Isabelle?' A blur resolves itself into Ingrid hovering above Isabelle's face. 'Are you all right?'

Isabelle is no longer in the room of silvers and blues, but in an anteroom with coat pegs and lockers. She lies on a wooden bench, Cornelius's jumper tucked beneath her head.

'Can you sit up?'

Isabelle struggles to a sitting position and takes the glass of water Ingrid offers her. 'What happened?' Her voice is a whisper.

'You passed out. Is your head all right? It looked like you might have hit it pretty hard.'

Isabelle feels nothing. She is as inert and numb as the concrete phone in the park.

'Do you need to see a doctor?'

'No, I don't think so.'

'Is your hotel far from here?'

'No. It's on Na Poříčí, near the Metropole. I'll be fine. Just give me a minute.' Isabelle tries to focus, to understand what it is she is doing there amidst the coats and bags of the Municipal House's staff, but she cannot order her memories. They circle her like snapshots from someone else's life. Evan, naked and strong at the shoreline of the cool, blue ocean. Cornelius's warm hand propelling her around a crowded dance floor. Waking in the swirling mist at the Vyšehrad. Libussa's silver-blue eyes boring into her. Ingrid, Peter, Corn, Anja and a nervous administrator fuss around her, confusing her even more. *Just be quiet*, she wants to say. *Let me think*.

'We'll walk you back to your hotel.'

Cornelius and Peter hoist her up. They take most of her weight as they follow the fretful, fussing public servant out of the building. Isabelle tenses in fear that they might pass through the silver-blue room on their way out, but the guide takes them another way, through discreet hallways and hidden offices.

Anja is borderline hysterical. 'When was the last time you ate, Isabelle? You should probably eat. Those pills on an empty stomach can really mess with you. Especially if you've had a few drinks. Shit. How many cocktails did you have?'

'Calm down, Anja,' Ingrid says commandingly. 'I'm sure it wasn't the pills.'

'Are you sure?' Anja looks frightened. 'Still, I think she should not have any more. Isabelle, you still have the spare ones I gave you, right? I think you should hand them back.' She holds her gloved hand out expectantly.

'Shut up, Anja,' Ingrid says flatly. 'It wasn't the pills, was it, Isabelle?'

'No.'

Ingrid marshals the group into some kind of order and they begin walking across the square towards Isabelle's hotel. They skirt the hordes pouring from theatres and clubs, Corn and Peter holding Isabelle firmly by an arm each. Cornelius murmurs something encouraging to her as they walk. Anja and Ingrid walk behind them, Anja still prattling on about the pills. In a few minutes they come to the entrance to Isabelle's hotel.

'I'll be okay from here,' she says.

'Are you sure? We can see you safely inside. You might faint again.'

'No. It's fine, really. Thank you.'

'Of course.'

Ingrid scrambles through her handbag for a scrap of paper and scrawls some numbers on it.

'This is my mobile. I want you to call me tomorrow when you wake up, okay? And if there's any problems – headache or dizziness or nausea – just phone me. We're in Prague for another two days. We can organise medical attention for you.'

Isabelle takes the paper. 'Thank you. Sorry to be such a bother.'

Cornelius gives her a warm hug. 'You take care of yourself, all right?'

Ingrid leans in, takes Isabelle's cheeks in her hands and kisses her full on the mouth. The others wave and then slip off into the night. Isabelle pushes the doors open into the low light of the lobby. Grigor doesn't look up until she is at the counter, waiting.

'Yes?' he says, blowing cigarette smoke in her direction.

'I'd like my key, please.'

Grunting, he leafs through the hanging wooden salt and pepper shakers for Isabelle's key.

'Thank you.'

He grunts again for answer and goes back to reading his newspaper. The hotel is very quiet, as it was the first night Isabelle arrived. The lift grinds and shudders to her floor. Her room has been made up and the radiator turned off. It is cold. Very cold. Isabelle closes and bolts the window, turns the heating up to its maximum setting, raids the cupboard for extra blankets and spreads them on the bed. She takes Anja's pills from her pocket and leaves them on the table. She strips and enters the shower tube, enclosing herself gratefully in the steaming chute. The hot water makes her feet hurt.

She closes her eyes against the water but Libussa's impossibly blue irises are immediately there before her. Again, the sense of déjà vu overwhelms her. She wipes the water from her face and opens her eyes. The darkened room is radiating a silver-blue light, as if an echo of Mucha has followed her home. She has the strange but persistent feeling that some force hovers nearby. Not The Black Place. Something else. It waits, benign but powerful, for some gesture from her, but what exactly she cannot determine. She feels slightly nauseous and unsteady, perhaps from the blow to her head. She examines her skull with her fingers, locating a tender half-egg behind her right ear.

Isabelle pulls on her pyjamas and climbs into bed, piling the blankets on top of her. She needs to reboot. To think. To moor herself in a calm, still place. She falls into sleep, down and down into opaline still water.

From: evan117@hotmail.com
To: IsabelleNorthwell@dppar.wa.gov.au

Are you freaked out that we had sex, Belle? Is that
what this is all about? Do you think you've stolen
something from me? From God?

If anything you've liberated me. I've never believed
in a micro-managing God who keeps tabs on what
bits people put where. I told you that night we
potted your plants that the no-sex thing isn't a moral
question for me. It was a sacrifice in thanks. For
whatever reason after Dad died and things were
so monumentally hard, God (or the universe or
karma or fate or chance) took pity on me. It's an
old-fashioned word but I'd received what I can only
call 'grace'. It's not the kind of thing you can write a
thank-you note for.

For me it was never an 'I'm a virgin till I marry'
deal. At some point I knew that God and I would
be square and the sacrifice on my part wouldn't be
necessary any more.

The problem with that kind of reasoning is you start
hedging your bets. The sex thing (or lack of) was
surprisingly hard to give up. Without realising it, I'd
been bargaining with God. *You keep managing my
grief and I'll keep it in my pants.* The flipside being, if
I take it out of my pants You might return me to
that place when I was ten. Back to the chaos and

the impotence and the fear. Back to being the kid
who has to get up in bedsheets and make laws to feel
safe again.

I'd locked myself into a fortress. Mind and body. My
own rooftop. In one of my emails before I said we're
all f*cked when we operate from fear. That we have
to stare it down. I really believe that. So I stared it
down. We made love. I told you I love you. I hold to
that. Whether you come back to me or whether you
don't, it was the right call.

Evan xoxo

NINETEEN

When Isabelle wakes it is still dark. She walks groggily to the bathroom and pours herself a glass of water. She has that strange mix of languor and clarity that comes when a fever has broken. She knows she is gathering strength. She slips back into sleep where her dreams are aquatic, velveteen and warm. Moonlight radiates through the water. By its dim fluorescence she pulls for the bottom but the water's buoyancy holds her tight to its surface like a toddler on reins. She duck dives for the sandy bed but is gently drawn back to float on the glassy crust.

When she wakes again it is full daylight and the Nice Lady is sitting on her bed.

'Hello,' she says.

'Hi.' Isabelle struggles to untangle herself from the bedclothes.

'I brought this for you.' The Nice Lady hands Isabelle a cup of black coffee.

'Thank you.' The coffee is muddy and weak. 'Thank you very much.'

'Are you feeling all right?'

'Yes. I think so. What time is it?'

The Nice Lady checks her watch. 'It is ten am. It is Wednesday.'

'Wednesday?' Isabelle backstrokes through her memory. 'Then I've been asleep for two days?'

She nods. 'Your friends came looking for you. They leave for you a note.' She hands Isabelle a thin piece of olive-green notepaper. It is from Ingrid.

Dear Isabelle,
I've been calling your hotel but they tell me you are unavailable.
We leave for Slovakia today. Please phone me or email me to let
me know that you are okay.
With love,
Ingrid

'I was worried. I hope you do not mind. I let myself in. Just to make checking you are all right.'

'No, that's fine. Thank you.'

'You are hungry?'

'Yes.' For the first time in weeks Isabelle has an appetite. 'I'll go and get something to eat soon. I wonder, could you help me with something first? I'd like to put a call through to Australia but I haven't been able to work the phone system.'

The Nice Lady nods. 'There is instruction card in drawer under the phone.' She moves from the bed and opens the drawer in search of the card.

'It's not there,' Isabelle says, 'I looked. I think Grigor takes them.'

'What? Who is Grigor?'

'Oh, it doesn't matter. Just my silly joke.'

The Nice Lady looks troubled. 'Is someone named Grigor taking the phone cards? Have you seen this Grigor?'

'No really. It's a dumb joke. There's no Grigor.'

'An Australian joke?'

'Yes. Yes exactly.'

'Okay,' she says, dubious. 'Do you have the number?'

Isabelle riffles through the bedside drawer and hands the Nice Lady the numbers she had written earlier.

'I'm Isabelle, by the way. I don't know your name.'

'I'm Marta.'

'Marta. That's pretty.'

Marta smiles then peruses the numbers, flicks her wrist and dials. She listens for the tone then hands the phone to Isabelle.

'This should work.'

Isabelle cradles the phone to her ear and mouths *Thank you*.

Marta stands up and waves goodbye. 'Come downstairs and have some breakfast soon, all right?'

Isabelle nods. She listens intently to the ring, trying to figure out what time it is in Perth. Each *brrrrinngg* trills her stomach with nerves.

'Hello?' Evan's voice is thick with sleep.

'Evan. It's Isabelle.'

'Is-A-Belle.' Each syllable is supercharged with relief. Isabelle can feel that relief tripping down the wire towards her, barrelling along the fibre-optic cables and flooding her little room.

'My God, Belle. Where are you?'

'I'm in Prague. In a little hotel in the new town,' and then, because everything she could say seems senseless anyway, 'near the Charles Bridge.'

'Are you all right? Did you get my emails?'

'I haven't checked my email since I arrived. Communications here aren't the best. And I've been... preoccupied.'

'But are you all right?'

'Honestly? I think so. I think I'm going to be. I've been through something. I'm still going through something. It's hard to explain.'

'I know, Belle. I know.'

His voice is soothing. There's a tangible sympathy in it that she can lean on. She starts to cry.

'Shhhhhhhhhhh, Belle, honey, don't cry. It's all right. It's all right. I'm right here. I'll stay on this line as long as you need me to. I'll get on a plane and come get you if you need me to.'

She curls herself around the certainty in his voice.

'I'm so sorry. I'm so very, very sorry.'

'It's okay. It's okay now that I know you're all right. You scared me, that's all.'

'I scare myself.'

'Why did you leave without telling me you were going?'

Great, hiccupping sobs ratchet her breath and keep her from speaking.

'Easy, Belle,' Evan croons. 'Let it out. It's all right. Breathe, Belle. Just breathe.'

'Just give me a minute.' She lets the tears pour out, making no attempt to stop them. Evan flicks on the radio. It's Dvořák, the Czech composer. He smiles at this, further proof of the tensile, invisible cord that connects him to Isabelle. After long minutes her sobs are spent.

'I didn't tell you I was going because I'm gutless. I didn't trust myself to be anywhere near you. I knew we'd end up in bed again. That I'd love you.'

'Yeah, that sounds pretty terrible.'

'I'm scared of us.'

'Why? What is so scary about me loving you?'

'That you might stop.'

They're both silent for a moment. Softly, not liking to speak his name even now, Evan says, 'I'm not Karl.'

'No. You're not.'

They listen to each other breathing down the line. They have the hesitation of weary generals who have brokered a fragile peace and are reluctant to overplay their hands.

Finally, Evan says, 'When are you coming home?'

'Saturday.'

'I'll pick you up, all right?'

'Thank you.'

'What will you do between now and then?'

'I don't know. Wander around Prague, I guess. Buy souvenirs for you.'

'Mmmm, presents. I endorse that plan.'

'Don't get your hopes up too high. The stock in trade here is shirts with bad puns. Tacky matrioshka dolls. Golem key rings.'

'Can you get me a Lenin puppet?'

'Why on earth would you want a Lenin puppet?'

'So I can boss you around when you get out of hand.'

She chuckles, feeling her way around this new banter of theirs, precursor to a love play for which they're not quite ready.

'There is one thing I'd like you to do for me, Belle,' his voice is serious.

'What's that?'

'If you can get to an internet cafe I'd like you to read the emails I've sent you. I think you need to see them.'

'I'll try. As I said, communications here aren't too flash.' She pauses. 'There's something I need to tell you, too.'

'Okay.'

'It's not easy to explain and it's probably not going to make much sense. I want you to promise me you won't laugh.'

'I promise.'

'Do you remember after the hospital you took me home and I asked you about hell? About what you thought hell was?'

'Yes. I said I didn't know, but that I did believe in a literal heaven.'

'Which I said means you must believe in hell. I know we don't talk about the hospital much, but something happened. Something…odd. I never meant to overdose. Suicide didn't really cross my mind, not in any conscious way. I wanted sleep. A reprieve. I was in a bad way after Karl left. I threw up everything I ate. I couldn't sleep. I'd seriously fucked-up at work and couldn't face going back. I fell into a really deep hole. And I was being —' she pauses, gathering her courage. 'Look, I'm going to tell you something and it's going to sound seriously weird.'

'I'm listening.'

'When we were up on the rooftop and I said what had hurt me wasn't human, I meant it.'

'Go on.'

'I get attacked by something. Something outside of me. My doctor would tell you it's called depression and anxiety and that's what all the leaflets and self-help manuals say. But it's bullshit. It's The Black Place and it's the most evil, horrible thing you can imagine. I didn't want to die, Evan, I just wanted to go into a kind of hyper-sleep because between The Black Place and Karl and work I couldn't cope. I guess I misjudged how much I'd taken. Or kept taking the pills robotically after I'd started to zone out.

'I vaguely remember you carrying me into the hospital and a doctor shining something into my eyes. Then nothing. When I came to they kept me pretty drugged-up. I'd be awake for a couple of hours and then I'd be sedated. During one of the waking times they sent a priest to talk to me. The hospital chaplain. I've always assumed you were behind that.'

'No. I had nothing to do with it. What did he say?'

'He wanted to talk about why I overdosed. I didn't want to talk about it. Anyway, I knew the drugs were about to kick in so I more or less ignored him. But then —'

'Then what?'

'I woke up. Except that I didn't. I was in this blue room. A kind of shimmering blue room, like the blue you see around glowing jellyfish in deep water. I couldn't move and I didn't know why but then I realised my hands were tied behind my back. My feet were getting hot and there was this pungent smell of smoke. I was tied to a stake. Burning. And all around me, in every direction were different versions of me. Hundreds of them. Old, senile Isabelles. Pregnant Isabelles. Triumphant Isabelles. Crying and broken ones. And they were all staring at me. All those blue eyes in the blue room locked on me.

'They were all the different possibilities of myself that I'd nearly killed off. And behind them, not seen but... but sort of sensed, were all the interactions they might have had. The little ripples that go out into the world with their little effects you don't see. I'm not explaining this very well.'

'No, I think I get it.'

'It was so vivid, Evan. So real. I felt my feet getting burnt from the fire and my lungs getting all clogged up with smoke. I haven't been able to stand the smell of smoke since. When I came out of it I was convinced my feet were burnt. The doctor had to hold my feet. She showed them to me. "Look," she said, "two textbook, perfectly normal feet." Even now when I think about it my feet get hot.'

'You think that was hell?'

'I don't know what to make of it. I can make sense of it on a metaphorical level. The brain gets starved of oxygen so you dream smoke and burning dreams the same way you dream of water when you need to go to the loo. Or maybe it was the chaplain. For all I know he sat there lecturing me about the sin of suicide and purgatory and my subconscious played it out. Maybe there really is some objective judgement that we all come to in the end. I don't know. Whatever caused it, it changed me. After you dropped me home I collected all my drugs, the ones you didn't find, and I threw them out. Every one. Not even in my own bin. I dropped them in a bin outside a house down the street so I couldn't retrieve them. I haven't filled a script since.'

'The drugs. They're for depression, I mean The Black Place, yeah?'

'Yes. Depression and anxiety. But they're words I almost never use. They're bullshit words. Made up words.'

'Is it safe? Going unmedicated, I mean. You're a psych, Isabelle. Do you think it's smart?'

'Of course it's not smart. From a clinical perspective it's manifestly dumb. But I made the call because it's the lesser of two evils.'

'Because you think you might overdose again?'

'No. No I don't. But I don't want it in my power. I don't want it there as an option. I'm so paranoid about it I even lock my bathroom cabinet where I keep my kitchen knives and my razors.' She pauses, but Evan doesn't say anything. 'Now you're thinking I'm completely loony tunes, right?'

'No. I get the grand gesture, I really do. It's not so different from my bargain with God. But you know as well as I do that some of the older TCAs are pretty safe. Something like desipramine. You're not going to be able to overdose on that.'

'Yeah, I know. It's something I'll think about when I come back. But like you said, I needed the grand gesture. The line in the sand. I'm telling you this because you need to know what you're getting. I'm never going to be what the world calls a success, what Karl wanted. But in my own way I'm tough, even disciplined in some ways. I can stick things out.'

'You think I don't know this about you?'

'I don't know. Sometimes I doubt it myself. The funny thing is, I was in a room at the Municipal House a few days ago – it's this gorgeous, gorgeous building, Evan. Amazing. And we came to this room that I'd seen before. It was exactly like what happened in the hospital. This silver blue that seemed to sheet down from the ceiling and these eyes boring into me demanding I explain myself. I might not have been dying but I was closing myself off again, shutting down all those other Isabelles.'

'Because you were afraid of us?'

'Yes.'

'But you're coming back?'

'Yes.'

Evan is quiet for a moment. Isabelle can hear the strains of Dvořák humming down the line. 'I'll be here.'

TWENTY

Isabelle climbs down the steps to the cafe that has become her second home in Prague. She is still a little unsteady on her feet, thanks partly to the half-egg that is blooming chartreuse, purple and sable under her hair. She descends from the swirl of cigarette smoke at the ceiling to find a table by herself at the back. She looks around for the pixie, catches his eye and gives him a wave. Immediately, he puts down the glass he is polishing, pours her a glass of green veltliner and brings it to her table.

'Would you like something to eat? Chef has made bean soup. It's good. I can bring you some.'

'That sounds perfect.'

Isabelle takes the papers from her bag, shuffles them into a tidy pile and sips her wine. They are Evan's emails, furtively printed out by Marta while Grigor wasn't looking and arranged in date order from the oldest to the most recent. Isabelle eyes them warily. She has promised Evan she will read them. She is determined to, but that doesn't mean she is unafraid. The pixie places her bean soup, white swirled with sour cream, with a thick wedge of crusty bread, on the table in front of her. The aroma makes her almost froth with appetite.

'God, this looks good. Thank you.'

She inhales the food and, so fortified, picks up the first email and begins to read.

When she looks up some time later, Socialist Man has silently taken up his post in front of her. He is dressed in his usual outfit of bumblebee jumper, black trousers and boots. She was so engrossed by Evan's words that even the pixie delivering his plate of bread and cheese and his stein of beer did not rouse her.

'I thought you go home,' Socialist Man says.

'No. I leave on Friday.'

'I not see you.'

'I've been touring. And then I wasn't well.'

'Where did you go?'

'Terezín.'

He grunts slightly and holds his hand up to catch the pixie's attention. With a barely perceptible flick of his finger he indicates that another beer and another wine are required, then he lights a cigarette.

'Why?'

'Excuse me?'

'Why did you go Terezín?'

Isabelle thinks about this for a moment. 'Do you remember I told you I went to the Jewish Museum?'

Socialist Man nods.

'The walls are covered in names,' Isabelle continues, 'eighty thousand names of the Jews that were rounded up from Prague. I hadn't meant to go there, really. I got trapped in a crowd. At first I didn't know what the names were. I thought it was old script and I was thinking that I needed to find a translation. When I realised that it was names and why the names were there it sort of struck me dumb. I was in front of all these names and a tourist, an American, said "Gee whiz". Do you know that expression?'

'Geewhiz?' Socialist Man tries it out, making it one word.

'Yes. It's like "Golly gosh" or "Goodness gracious" or...' Isabelle wonders how to explain. 'Imagine you're confronting the worst thing that human beings are capable of and in the middle of that someone says something silly.'

'You upset because American is silly?'

'Something like that.'

'Americans,' he says, and then shrugs philosophically.

'I think I went to Terezín because I wanted to stare the darkness down. I felt like I owed something to the people whose names were on the wall. Something more than "Gee whiz". I'm not explaining this very well. I went to do penance, I suppose.'

'Penance?'

'To say sorry. To weep. To remember. I know I sound holier-than-thou but I don't know any other way to explain it.'

They are silent for a while. Socialist Man drinks his beer. Isabelle plunders the last of her soup with her bread. Her body feels like a furnace she needs to pour food into. She wants fries, burgers, sundaes. Fatty, imperialist food, as Peter said. Socialist Man chain-smokes, lighting the next cigarette from the ember of the last.

'What was it like?'

'What was what like?'

'Terezín'

294

'You've never been there?'

'No.'

'God, what is it with you Czechs and your history?' Isabelle thinks of Ingrid. 'Your capacity for avoidance is truly impressive.'

Socialist Man is unperturbed, shrugging his shoulders slightly. 'So. What was it like?'

Isabelle thinks hard for a moment. 'Did you ever have nightmares when you were a child?'

He nods.

'Terrifying nightmares that made you afraid of the dark?'

He nods again.

'Imagine your nightmares made a bunker to shelter from the things *they* were afraid of. That's Terezín.'

Socialist Man eyes Isabelle closely, fixing his gaze on her. His eyes are slightly cloudy and shot through with veins. Isabelle wonders if he can see properly.

'Your diary?' he gestures towards the papers in front of Isabelle.

She shakes her head. 'No. Letters from a friend.'

'He misses you, I think, this friend.'

'Yes,' Isabelle says softly. 'Yes, he does.' To her mortification tears pool in her eyes and spill down her cheek. The cavalcade of emotions aroused by Evan's emails advance towards her from all directions. It is like being bombarded by equal forces on all sides so the net effect is to leave her still. Socialist Man eyes her dispassionately, then drains his beer. He returns his packet of cigarettes to his pocket, leaves some crowns on the table, and stands. He looks at Isabelle expectantly.

'Well. You are coming?'

'What? Where?'

'Barge.' He says, then waits for her to pack up her papers, wind her pashmina around her neck and follow him into the street.

The sky is sleety and low, pressing on their shoulders. They make for the river, Socialist Man surprisingly fleet of foot. He smokes the whole way, somehow contriving to keep his cigarette lit in the drizzle. It is a thirty-minute walk to where the barge is moored in a curve of the Vltava away from the jolly tourist boats with their window boxes and streamers.

Socialist Man turns to take Isabelle's hand along the sleek gangway towards the boat. Officials have made some effort to blend the boat in with its other, happier cousins. The wooden deck is oiled and tan-coloured and the name of the boat rendered in swirling calligraphic Czech along the bow. But immediately Isabelle dips her head into the cabin the meaner import of the vessel is clear. The woodwork is chafing, peeling in great flakes from the walls and the ceiling. Damp spots poke through some of the paintwork, turning a mouldy, oozing green. From somewhere beneath the cabin where they stand, Isabelle hears a low muttering of conversation and the tepid smell of Czech coffee.

Socialist Man gestures towards a padded bench and Isabelle sits down. He positions himself in front of an old-fashioned wooden steering wheel and begins manoeuvring gears. There is a thudding noise as some-one throws the ropes from the jetty onto the stern. The boat judders and chokes a little, coughing out diesel fuel, then eases away from the jetty and into the slick grey midline of the Vltava. Isabelle watches the dark water sliding by, Evan's letters lodged in the deepest cavern of her heart. The words stampede in her blood, demanding egress.

It is Karl who clarifies first from the swirl and tumult. She remembers the day he approached her in the tearoom at Civics and Arts. They had been working together for a couple of months and she had registered him as funny if a little tart, good-looking, and with a talent for making himself amenable to all and sundry. A diplomat, Evan had called him. She had pulled heated soup from the microwave and was tasting it to make sure it was warm enough when he approached her.

'Isabelle,' he had said.

'Hi, Karl.'

'Do you have a minute?'

'Of course.' She put down her spoon, expecting a query about the funding round she was coordinating.

'The thing is, I've got this almighty crush on you. I find you funny, charming. Gorgeous, of course, but I'm sure everyone tells you that. Can I take you to dinner on Saturday night?'

Far from working against him, the workaday surroundings of the tacky yellow chairs and chipped, ill-matched crockery in the tearoom had delivered her right to him. To someone whose horizons were in ever-present danger of dissolving, Karl was irresistible. His certainty didn't so much win her over as capture her, the way a larger planet will pull a smaller one along with it. She had loved him because it seemed inevitable that she would. She had given that love without reserve, her trust equalled by his certainty.

How misplaced that trust had been is sick-making. She sees it all projected onto the dove-coloured surface of the river. How he had withdrawn from her after her fall from grace at work. How he had activated the replacement he had been keeping in the wings almost from the moment he'd come home to find her, tear-stained and red with shame, after Jack had driven her home. And how, and this makes her so angry she has to pound her fist into the foam of the bench on which she sits, he had brought her and Cindy together so he could size them up side by side, deliberating.

She remembers being mildly surprised that Cindy had been not fat but plumpish, certainly not the sylph-like type Karl usually went for. With a flash of insight she knows that Cindy has now been starved down. With a couple of well-timed, seemingly innocuous comments and Isabelle's shapely ghost before her, Karl will have seen to Cindy's transformation. And Cindy will be utterly oblivious to the fact that it is Karl who has manoeuvred her into her omnipresent hunger.

He finally admitted his adultery on the day he left. Isabelle had suspected it within days of her spectacular failure at work. Something in the complex minutiae of their lives went askew shortly thereafter, a detail so fine-grained she couldn't isolate it and say, 'There, that's what's amiss.' On the surface, Karl was all sympathy and concern, coming home from work as soon as she told him what had happened. He had held her as she rocked backwards and forwards on the bed, reliving her shame

298

again and again. He brushed away her despair that The Black Place would always defeat her. Always win.

When she tried to verbalise the way her horizons felt unsteady, Karl would take her hand and hold it against his cheek in that way he had. As if the contact dissolved their skins and he attained a state beyond sympathy. He would ask calm, reasoned questions about her mental state. Had she been taking her medication correctly? Was she continuing with her sessions? Had she been disciplined with her meditation practice?

Isabelle stacked his patient sympathy against her snippets of evidence – unexplained absences, new tricks in bed, a linger of jasmine scent – and always come down on Karl's side. Karl was the first person, besides doctors, she had ever told about The Black Place. That he would turn this against her was inconceivable to her then.

It was a Saturday morning, the last morning they would spend together. They had made love as they usually did, languid and unhurried, basking in a day of little to do and time in which to do it. Isabelle had determined to go back to work on the Monday. She had gone to the kitchen for juice (cranberry, she remembers) and come back to find him tearing through their cupboards, stuffing clothes into a bag.

'Do you have a game?' she had asked, handing him a glass.

'No.' He ignored the juice. He was filling a bag with work shirts and ties. She felt her bowels ice over.

'What are you doing?'

'What does it look like?' he muttered. 'I'm leaving.'

She had stood there, naked and stunned, the cranberry juice growing warm in her hand as Karl collected up his clothes, his shoes and his cologne, cataloguing the myriad reasons she had made it impossible for him to stay.

'You're not going anywhere. You're not doing anything. You can't even get through a presentation at work without having a meltdown. Why? Because of a black place? What does that even mean?' He upturned a box of cufflinks then dropped the bag and waved his arms through the air. 'There's nothing there, Isabelle. Nothing. Look.' He challenged her to divine fairies in the clear air between them. 'You expect me to live with a child who's afraid of the dark? Christ. No wonder...'

'No wonder what?' she had whispered.

'No wonder I got involved with Cindy. The miracle is I've stuck it as long as I have.'

At the sound of her name, Isabelle buckled a little, spilling some juice onto the rug. The stain is still there.

'What?' he shouted. 'You're surprised? Outraged? What the fuck did you expect?' He started muttering to himself then, but Isabelle distinctly caught the words 'head case'. Wave after wave of accusation rolled through her, so powerful that even later, when the first shock had dissipated, she couldn't assemble a convincing defence for herself.

Isabelle had met Cindy a few times at soccer events and parties and been put off by her super-friendly, super-positive super-ness. Maybe Cindy had felt guilty about her involvement with Karl and was trying to compensate by fawning over Isabelle. 'Gosh, you're so tall,' she had gushed. 'So tall and fit-looking. I bet you work out, huh?' Or perhaps she had got a sexual charge out of their proximity. Isabelle remembers Kate leading Jack away from the kitchen for a post-lunch romp, high on competitive adrenalin. Or maybe Cindy just wanted to study the creature who had repelled Karl and sent him looking for an alternative.

'Fuck,' Isabelle says, to the river, the rolling green hills, the low sky. All the anger she has refused herself till now explodes, magnified by having no target. Karl, who should be the recipient of the rage she is pounding into the mildewing cushions, is long gone.

From below she hears the sound of footsteps and a man's head appears from the corridor behind her. He steps into the cabin and addresses himself to Socialist Man in Czech. He is a tall, wiry man of indeterminate age with a navy-blue beanie pulled low over his forehead.

'We have guest,' says Socialist Man, gesturing towards Isabelle seething on the bench. 'This is Isabelle. Isabelle, Jorg.'

Jorg removes his beanie and shakes Isabelle's hand. She tries not to stare at the silvery train tracks that run from his left temple to the base of his hairless skull.

'How do you do, Isabelle?'

'Very well, thank you.'

'Do you like our river, grey and cold as it is?'

'Yes. I love Prague. I love everything about Prague.'

'Everything?' he gives her a quizzical look. 'You've clearly not been here long.'

'Isabelle is Australian,' Socialist Man says, 'but she does not like beer.'

'No? Will they let you back into the country?' Jorg asks with mock seriousness.

'Perhaps not. Perhaps I will have to live out my days here helping you two drive the barge.'

'There are worse fates, I suppose,' Jorg says, though it sounds as if he is struggling to imagine one.

'Your English is awfully good, Jorg.'

'Thank you. It's the sign of a misspent youth.'

Socialist Man snorts.

'How long have you been driving the barge, Jorg?'

'I don't steer this ship, I'm merely a guest.'

'You live here?' Isabelle asks doubtfully.

Jorg nods and Isabelle blushes hot at her faux pas. To her intense embarrassment the tears commence their descent down her face again.

'Forgive me,' she says, mopping at her cheeks with the corner of her pashmina.

'There's nothing to forgive.' Jorg's blue eyes are crinkled with concern. 'Please don't distress yourself.'

'It's not just this. I'm…I'm having a difficult day.'

'I understand,' he says, in accents that suggest he really does.

'Excuse me.' Isabelle turns away to bring her emotions to heel, but it's pointless. The tears come and they come, alternately dredged up from inside her by anger, sorrow, regret and the internal bruising from all these emotions butting against each other in the shallow vessel of her body. Tactfully, Jorg turns away from her and addresses himself to Socialist Man in Czech.

They converse in low voices for some time, watching the prow slice through the dark water, which darkens further still as the slate clouds gather and drop. Despite the cold, Isabelle has a visceral urge to strip the layers of clothing from her body and dive into the river. She wants to be suspended in the water Libussa cupped in her white hand and drank from. To touch the slick, smooth stones on the riverbed and hide, frog-like, beneath the surface while the boats churn above her.

Confident that she has her emotions under control at last, she turns back towards her companions. Both stare straight ahead at the water and speak in short sentences. They have known each other for a long time, that much is clear, but they are not completely at ease in one another's company. Isabelle thinks of her brother, whom she rarely sees and to whom she struggles to find anything to say. Socialist Man takes a fresh packet of cigarettes from his pocket and hands it discreetly to Jorg, not looking at him. A wad of Czech crowns is also slipped across in the exchange. Jorg secretes cigarettes and money in his jeans without a word.

'Well, Isabelle,' Jorg says, stepping towards her, extending his hand, 'it was nice to meet you. I hope you enjoy the rest of your time in Prague.'

'Thank you. I'm sure I will. It was lovely to meet you. Sorry about before.'

Jorg says something in Latin that Isabelle doesn't understand, but from his tone she knows it is kindly meant. Jorg descends into the bowels of the boat.

'Jorg's English really is amazing,' Isabelle remarks to Socialist Man.

'Intellectual. All intellectual speak perfect English.'

'Intellectual?' Isabelle tries to reconcile Jorg with her idea of a tweedy, bespectacled academic writing papers in a university office. Socialist Man is silent for some time, concentrating on steering the boat now that the visibility has dropped. There is a crack and then lightning splits the sky. Rain sheets down, fat drops bouncing off the river. You can almost feel the relief as the clouds unclench.

'I was *apparatchik*,' Socialist Man says above the rain. 'You know this word?'

'Apparatchik? It's like "bureaucrat", isn't it?'

'Yes. But Communist Party member. You understand?'

Isabelle thinks for a moment, afraid of making another faux pas. 'I think so,' she says cautiously. She pictures the bathroom in her hotel room: white-tiled and easily wiped clean of the blood and faeces of dissidents. She looks askance at Socialist Man, wondering what his job had entailed.

'I was manager for factories outside Praha 5.' He stands up straighter, assuming a military bearing, and shouts, 'Expand even wider the socialist competition to raise productivity and the quality of work! Long live Soviet trade unions, the school of management, the school of economy, the school of communism!' he slumps back to his usual posture and voice. 'I have many luxuries. A car. I went to spa in Sochi once. Twice I holiday on Black Sea. My wife had washing machine. We shop in special shop where we buy real butter. Sweet cheese. Meat.' He pauses to light a cigarette, his hand trembling slightly. 'Jorg spend seven years in Soviet prison for industrial sabotage after the Spring.' Socialist Man trails his finger from his temple to his neck, indicating the scar on Jorg's skull. 'You understand me?'

'I think so,' Isabelle says softly.

'Now I drive barge. Every day. No charge.' Socialist Man taps the steering wheel with his large orange hands. 'Penance.'

'Fuck,' whispers Isabelle, because she cannot think of anything else to say. And then she is capsized by emotions that are too big for her. 'Fuck,' she says again, louder, her voice scarcely audible above the thunder rolling along the blue-green flanks of the Vltava.

Barely conscious that she is doing it she yells the word. She spits it at the red metronome marking time high above them in Letná Park. At Karl. At The Black Place.

'Faaaaaaaaaaaaark.' She screams herself hoarse with it, waving her arms around in a manic effort to shake the electricity from her body. She hurls the expletive at the wall of names, at Terezín, at her foolish reliance on signs. At Jack. At her fear of loving and being loved by Evan. And finally at herself, for the gross conflation of her personal sorrows with the ugliness of the twentieth century.

And every time she spits the expletive, Socialist Man, his eyes fixed on the barely visible prow, presses his lips together and nods, as if she is expressing some profound historical truth he's been groping towards for an age.

TWENTY-ONE

From: IsabelleNorthwell@dppar.wa.gov.au
To: evan117@hotmail.com

Dear Evan

Well, I've read all your emails. I keep reading them.
Keep thinking about them.

I'm sorry you had to get involved in this mess with
Jack. Frankly, it's embarrassing. You're right about
him. He is beige, though I feel like a complete b*tch
saying that now that he's gone and lost his job and
Kate's threatening to leave him. I hope they patch
things up. I really do.

It wasn't love. Wasn't anything but the fevered
product of my own imagination.

I do that. You could call it a side effect of The Black
Place. I don't have a lot of faith in my own instincts,
my own judgement. It's hard to trust yourself when
one minute you can feel completely fine and the

next – out of nowhere – you're drowning in panic and darkness. So I see portents and signs and follow those instead. I know it's stupid, like living your life by what your horoscope tells you or the shape of your tea-leaves.

I've never had a sign about you and that can only be a good thing. It means it's real. Imperfect and messy and real. Like me. But I'm starting to think I deserve this, deserve us. Like I said, in my own way, I'm tough. When I gave you my word after the hospital that I wouldn't do anything like that again I did more than just words. After you dropped me off I started packing up the house straight away. I found a lot of medications and scripts you'd missed. By the time I finished packing I had a good stash of alprazolam, Edronax, Seroquel, Temaze, Stilnox, clonazepam and Valium. I threw them into a plastic bag and into the bin.

When I was trying to get to sleep that night, I felt like I could hear the bag rustling, as if the pills were trying to climb out of the bin. Finally I got up, threw a shirt on over my nightie and took the garbage bag downstairs to where the wheelie bins for the complex are kept. I threw the drugs in there then went back upstairs. But there were still three days till the next garbage collection and I was scared I'd weaken and retrieve them.

So you know what I did?

I went back downstairs, took the drugs out of the
bin and set off down the street. You know that large
Federation house on the corner? The one with the
labrador that always growls at us when we walk past?
When I got to the house I slipped my thongs off and
walked across the lawn. It was about one in the morning
but I could see pretty well because there was a full moon.
I moved really slowly in case there was a sensor light. I
reached over the fence and groped for the latch. The gate
creaked a bit as I opened it. I was thinking, *My heart's
banging so loud it's going to wake up the whole household.*

On the other side of the gate I found myself in a sort
of bower that blocked out the moonlight. I remember
smelling lavender. I stood still for a moment waiting
for my eyes to get used to the darkness, then I saw
the bins clarify out of the black. I held the plastic
bag tight to my chest so it didn't rustle. I opened the
nearest bin but it was almost empty except for a few
branches at the bottom. The drop might create too
much noise so I eased the lid down and tried the
second bin, which was nearly full. I placed the bag as
softly as I could on top of the litter and closed the lid.

I stood there thinking I needed to say something.
Some pithy Latin motto or an ancient prayer of
wisdom. Something Libussa would have said. But
I couldn't think of anything so I toasted the bin with
an imaginary champagne glass (yes, really). Then
I turned around and headed back to the gate.

I was about a metre or so away from it when I sensed something behind me. I squeezed my eyes tight shut and then opened them again, willing myself to turn around. When I did a dog was standing there looking at me. You know how sometimes animals have expressions that you'd swear were human? The dog had his head cocked to one side and one paw up from the ground. If he'd had a speech bubble above his head the message couldn't have been any clearer: *Umm, excuse me, but what are you doing here?* I had the definite feeling that he recognised me as the woman who often passed his gate, wet-haired and reeking of chlorine, and that he was puzzling over why I was there, in his yard, at that hour, in my pyjamas.

I kept eye contact with the dog as I shuffled backwards. He let out a low, questioning growl and dropped his paw to the ground. When I bumped up against the fence I lifted my arm centimetre by centimetre to the latch. The dog took another careful step towards me.

'I was getting rid of my drugs,' I told him. 'I'm trying to start again. To be braver.'

He snorted, as if in disbelief, which made me a bit indignant. I pushed up the latch with my index finger and held it there for a moment. The dog took another step. When the latch was at maximum tension I wheeled on one foot, yanked the gate open and threw myself through it. The dog hurled himself at the gate, howling and gnashing. The household woke up behind me.

I sprinted across the lawn, scooped up my thongs and bolted back to my complex. All the lights came on behind me and then every other dog in the neighbourhood started barking and people came outside and started asking each other questions. Someone talked about calling the police. I didn't stop running until I reached my place. I crouched down on the floor and waited until my heart rate returned to normal and the alarm died down.

I felt a bit dizzy and a bit foolish but I also felt brave. I'd put suicide and accidental overdose out of my power. I was going to live, was going to give all those other Isabelles every chance.

What else can I tell you?

I'm glad you punched Karl. It's petty and mean of me but I'm glad you did. I hope it hurt.

Prague is beautiful. I want you to see it. We should save up and come back here together.

I want us to have Mrs Graham over for dinner. She knew you were mine before I did.

I couldn't find you a Lenin puppet. Instead I bought you a shirt that says, 'My girlfriend went to Prague and all I got was this lousy T-shirt.' If you're not at the airport on Saturday I'll understand. There are much more functional people you could get involved with. If you are there, I hope the shirt fits.

I love you,
Isabelle

The plane wheezes and pitches in search of a smooth corridor between the buffeting turbulence. With each crackle of lightning Isabelle feels as if she is being X-rayed by God. Between Prague and Singapore she has bitten her nails down to the blood line. She has not checked her emails since she sent off her letter to Evan. She careens between joyful certainty that he will be there to meet her and black conviction that he won't. Between these poles other thoughts assail her.

Work.

Oh, God.

Every time Isabelle thinks about returning to work she has to lean forward and bang her forehead on the window. She needs contact with something hard to give her relief from the hot, red shame that rolls over her. Internal investigations are supposed to be kept confidential but whispers always leak out and get magnified into rumours. People are going to know that she is the reason Jack left. Maybe they will blame her for it. Isabelle tries to appraise her own guilt. She chased down Jack with manic intensity and rode roughshod over his marriage. But make him commit fraud? Force him to misappropriate government funds? The hot wave of mortification dumps her again, starting with the curl of her toes and ending with the bang of her forehead against the window.

'Excuse me?' The slender, suited lady on the seat next to Isabelle taps her hesitantly on the shoulder, 'Are you all right?'

She is a pretty lady. Very poised. The tears come, hot and streaming, down Isabelle's face. Isabelle has cried so much over the last few days she is convinced a channel is being dredged through her cheeks. 'No,' she says. 'No, I'm not really okay.'

The lady cocks her head to one side and her sharp, pencilled brows contract. 'Can I do anything?'

'No. But thank you.'

'Would you like to talk about it?'

'No.'

The plane drops suddenly and pitches left. Isabelle's stomach splits neatly in two, half falling into her feet, the other half hitting the ceiling. The magazine that the lady next to her was reading slides from her tray table into Isabelle's lap. She hands it back.

'I'm going home to face the music,' Isabelle says, more to herself than to the lady sitting next to her. 'Big, ugly music. And I'm afraid.'

As the plane rights itself the halves of Isabelle's stomach knit together again.

'Is it as bad as all that?'

'I had an affair with someone I work with.'

'Oh.'

'He's married.'

'Oh.'

'He's my boss.'

'Oh.'

'He got fired.'

'Oh. Oh.'

With each 'oh' the lady's voice drops a register. Her impeccably kohled eyes grow wide.

'Do you love him?' the lady says gently, as if she is pressing on a raw wound.

'No. It would be some justification if I did, wouldn't it? I loved the idea of love. The feelings. He was almost... incidental.'

'Does his wife know?'

'Yes.'

'Are they still together?'

'I don't know.'

'Do you have to go back to your job?'

'Yes.' *At least for a while*, she thinks. *HR will probably write me a glowing reference just to get rid of me.*

The tears keep coming and coming. Hot, like they're pouring out of some molten core at her centre. The lady looks away, her eyes trained on the slim strip of aisle. She hails a hostess. She wants to be moved to another seat, Isabelle thinks wildly. I have disgusted her and now she wants to be seated elsewhere. Isabelle turns back to the window and shuts her eyes as if that might seal off the leak and force the tears back down.

'Here you go.' The lady hands her a plastic cup of ice and amber. 'Whisky. Neat.' She taps her own cup to Isabelle's and gives her a half-smile. 'It's the best I can do.'

'Thank you,' Isabelle says. And she really, profoundly means it. This simple gesture of sympathy has

313

immeasurably moved her. She turns back to the window, afraid that in her gratitude she will do something wholly inappropriate.

'I had an affair once,' the lady next to Isabelle says in a low voice. Isabelle turns towards her again. She is rolling the whisky around in her cup thoughtfully.

'Really?'

She looks too manicured, too together for anything so indecorous. Isabelle suspects her socks always match and she throws away her knickers before the elastic crumbles.

'Mmm hmm. It nearly cost me my marriage.' She downs her drink in one robust swallow. 'But you know, in a strange sort of way it turned out to be a really good thing. It made Rick and me – Rick is my husband – face up to a few things that otherwise we just would have left to fester indefinitely. And those things would have ended the marriage eventually anyway. Are you married?'

'No.'

'Attached?'

'Yes,' Isabelle says hopefully.

The lady hails the hostess again, who brings another two drinks. Isabelle doesn't really like whisky but she would drink vinegar if it came from her hand. 'All I'm saying is that, sometimes, the things that cause us the most pain and make us the most ashamed of ourselves can be the things that turn us around. Cheers.'

They clink cups again and then lapse into silence. Isabelle has thought of her life as an equation that balances to zero. On one side is the fact that she must

314

live, on the other the fact of The Black Place. How does love factor into the equation? With Karl, love had been an ally of The Black Place. It propelled her into hospital and near death. She pictures Evan's lithe, tanned body. The simple cross tattooed on his shoulder. The tight curve of his white flank. Can love be a bulwark against The Black Place? An extra arsenal?

A bit drunk now, Isabelle brings up the wide fields around Terezín on her inner screen. She pictures a farmhouse: whitewashed, flagstoned and humble. Evan and Isabelle will invite Mrs Graham to live with them and she will see out her days with a real garden. They will grow beans. Mrs Graham will sit on a reclining chair and direct Isabelle as she stakes the ground and ties string around the shoots to make them grow true. Socialist Man will visit and both he and Mrs Graham will pretend not to notice that Isabelle is making a match between them.

At night Evan and Isabelle will button their coats and walk into the town, hand in hand, for their night classes. They are learning Czech. Isabelle hopes to become so proficient that she can work as a guide, an accomplished custodian of history. As she becomes fluent her brain circuitry will reroute itself, flashing a different electronic signature. The Black Place will be confused and unable to locate her. But even if it does (and it will) its effacing hand will snag on the hooks love has made in her memory.

The plane makes a sharp turn and noses through the darkness, whining. Lights, few at first and then in greater and greater clusters, twinkle below. Isabelle watches the scurrying cars, praying that Evan is in one of them on his way to collect her. Suddenly the plane lurches, punched on the nose by a violent gust of air. The suited lady and Isabelle exchange nervous glances. As they descend the engines strain. The plane heaves from side to side.

Is this it? Isabelle thinks wildly. 'Maybe I won't have to face the music after all.'

The lady reaches over and clasps Isabelle's hand. 'Somehow I don't think you're going to get out of it that easily.' The whining pitches higher and she grasps Isabelle's hand tighter, laughing nervously. They are a couple of metres above the ground and still the plane is pitching so wildly that the wings seem about to skim the tarmac. Then…thud!

They are on the ground and Isabelle is home. She counts to thirteen and then the plane miraculously slows and crawls towards the terminal. The lady lets go of her hand.

'Told you.'

'Welcome to Perth Airport,' says the hostess. 'We trust you have enjoyed your flight.'

The seatbelt sign flickers off and people rise from their seats, arching their backs and yawning. They pull bags from the lockers overhead and they queue, waiting for the doors to open.

What if Evan isn't here to collect me?

Isabelle has about ten dollars in her purse, not enough for a taxi home. She spent the last of her money on some wildly overpriced Australian beer she found at an importers' for Socialist Man. She left it with the pixie at the cafe, along with cartons of cigarettes for Jorg and Socialist Man to share. She also left Socialist Man Samara's drawing. She pressed a fat tip onto Marta against her protests.

The passengers surge forward through the tube connecting them to the terminal, everyone but Isabelle eager to start for home or commence their holiday. *Right, then.* She shakes herself and files into line at Immigration.

'Good trip?' the man behind the counter asks her as he flicks through her passport.

'Yes, thank you.'

'The Czech Republic, huh? Never been there myself. Do you recommend it?'

'Yes.'

'Welcome home.' He vigorously stamps her passport and returns it.

Isabelle locates the baggage collection where, perversely, her suitcase is among the first to appear as the carousel chugs into life. She faces the arrival doors. They glide open and shut, open and shut as people walk through, pushing their trolleys laden with duty-free and luggage. At each glide she strains for a glimpse of Evan on the other side.

The sight of him gives her a little start. It is his beauty that is startling. The memory she has carried in her head is accurate as to his features but lacks the shock, that something like pain that comes with real beauty. His summer-browned hands are curled around the barrier, his knuckles white. Isabelle recognises the tension in his hands. She has gripped the railing like that up there on the rooftop. Clinging to life and denying The Black

Place. No doubt she will do so again. The door opens and Evan sees her. He smiles and begins to raise his hand in greeting as the door moves shut again.

Well, this is it. A deep breath. And another.

And she walks through.

ACKNOWLEDGEMENTS

Writing a novel is like setting out on a journey by night with only a small lantern to guide your way. You have a vague idea of your destination but the maps you navigate by are sketchy and unreliable. Sometimes, the lantern burns so low you can barely make out your feet beneath you.

Many people helped me along the way. I am indebted to the Marlborough Street Book Club for reading and commenting on an early version of the manuscript. The Advanced Year of the Novel course members at the Wheeler Centre helped me find a new direction when I became hopelessly lost. Special thanks must go to Andrea Goldsmith, Jenny Ackland, Erina Reddan and Christina Stripp for their patient reading and insightful comments. Jasmina Brankovich, Jane Gleeson-White, Andrew Nicoll, Bec Starford, Amanda Curtin, Robyn Mundy, Annabel Smith and Fiona O'Doherty read all or part of the manuscript. I thank them for their fearless critique. Dr Karen McKenna and Dr Rachel Taylor generously provided advice and guidance on the medical aspects of this book.

To Terri-ann White and everyone at UWA Publishing who felt this book deserved an audience, thank you.

As ever, my family and friends served as literary pit crew. My sister Bec accompanied me to the Czech Republic, braving the wrath of tour guides and curators by taking furtive photographs for my reference. Hazel, Steve, Nina and Donna shared an unwavering faith in my ability to get there in the end. My husband Jason, to whom this book is dedicated, was endlessly patient and supportive. In between appropriating my computer for her own ends, my daughter Tessa gave me many a sustaining cuddle.

Finally, I would like to acknowledge a longstanding debt to two extraordinary history teachers: Mandy Connor and Professor Rob Stuart. Both encouraged and nurtured my passion for modern European history, particularly the Cold War period with which this book concerns itself.